Massacre

at
Shirakawa

An Akitada Novel

I. J. Parker

I•J•P
2020

Published 2020 by I.J.Parker and I·J·P Books
3229 Morningside Drive, Chesapeake VA 23321
http://www.ijparker.com
Cover design by I. J. Parker.
Cover image by Misuno Toshikata
Back cover image by Toyohara Chikanobu
Publisher's Note: This is a work of fiction. Names, characters, places, and incidents are a product of the author's imagination.

Massacre at Shirakawa, 1ˢᵗ edition, 2020
ISBN 9798664376968

Praise for I. J. Parker and the Akitada Series

"Elegant and entertaining . . . Parker has created a wonderful protagonist in Akitada. . . . She puts us at ease in a Japan of one thousand years ago." *The Boston Globe*

"You couldn't ask for a more gracious introduction to the exotic world of Imperial Japan than the stately historical novels of I. J. Parker." *The New York Times*

"Akitada is as rich a character as Robert Van Gulik's intriguing detective, Judge Dee." *The Dallas Morning News*

"Readers will be enchanted by Akitada." *Publishers Weekly* Starred Review

"Terrifically imaginative" *The Wall Street Journal*

"A brisk and well-plotted mystery with a cast of regulars who become more fully developed with every episode." *Kirkus*

"More than just a mystery novel, (*THE CONVICT'S SWORD*) is a superb piece of literature set against the backdrop of 11th-cntury Kyoto." *The Japan Times*

"Parker's research is extensive and she makes great use of the complex manners and relationships of feudal Japan." *Globe and Mail*

"The fast-moving, surprising plot and colorful writing will enthrall even those unfamiliar with the exotic setting." *Publishers Weekly,* Starred Review

". . .the author possesses both intimate knowledge of the time period and a fertile imagination as well. Combine that with an intriguing mystery and a fast-moving plot, and you've got a historical crime novel that anyone can love." *Chicago Sun-Times*

"Parker's series deserves a wide readership." *Historical Novel Society*

"The historical research is impressive, the prose crisp, and Parker's ability to universalize the human condition makes for a satisfying tale." *Booklist*

"Parker masterfully blends action and detection while making the attitudes and customs of the period accessible." *Publishers Weekly* (starred review)

"Readers looking for historical mystery with a twist will find what they're after in Parker's latest Sugawara Akitada mystery . . . An intriguing glimpse into an ancient culture." *Booklist*

Characters

Japanese family names precede proper names

Main characters:

Sugawara Akitada	nobleman, official
Sadako	his wife
Akiko	his sister
Tora, Genba, Saburo	his retainers
Fujiwara Kosehira	his friend
Arihito	Kosehira's son
Nakatoshi	another friend
Kobe	police superintendent ret.
Dr. Sugito	coroner

(also: the prime minister, policemen, servants, and soldiers)

Characters associated with the Shirakawa affair:

Fujiwara Yorimune	brother of prime minister
Lady Motoko	his senior wife
Hireko	their daughter
Lieutenant Hakeda	investigating police officer
Kanemori	a veteran warrior
Hiraga	another veteran
Jocho	a sword smith
Fujiwara Munesuke	governor Sanuki Province
Yamada Yasuhito	impoverished nobleman

Characters associated with the case of the schoolmaster's wife:

Tanizaki	a schoolmaster
Tomoko	his second wife
Nariko	her sister, a prostitute
Miyagi-san	brothel owner
Yasumasa	her son
Yoichi	a homeless boy

(also: a sergeant, a tailor, an old crone, a maid, and the staff and students of a college.

1

The Betrothal

The killer approached cautiously. He knew he might have to wait till dark. The sun already slanted through the tall cryptomerias, but the open meadow below the rustic buildings was still in bright sunlight. A colorful group had assembled there, their clothes glowing in the setting sun like exotic flowers growing in a green field.

The killer stopped his horse and watched for a long time. The celebrants sat here and there on new *tatami* mats, their edges bound in white and black silk. They had not bothered with curtain screens for the women. It was, after all, a family affair.

A young woman in peony pink silk sat bent over a *koto,* deftly touching the strings to produce a familiar tune. Nearby sat a handsome young man in a blue silk gown over white silk trousers. He held the second young woman's hand and leaned toward her, gazing into her face. She turned her head shyly, to look out over the river at the forests and hills to where the great city lay below. Her elaborate costume was of pale green silk shading to gold. She wore a richly embroidered Chinese jacket of a deep rose color over it. A sprig of flowers was pinned to her long glossy hair.

Two middle-aged ladies watched them, smiling, whispering to each other. Their robes in deeper jewel colors were no less festive. With them knelt a maid in a short blue overdress and white trousers.

Behind, some distance away and close to the house, five or six male servants in undyed cotton with blue sashes busied themselves hanging colorful paper lanterns on the veranda and readying torches to light the scene after sunset.

The killer ignored their presence. The time was now, not later. His eyes fixed longest on another group of five males. They sat in a circle around a large earthenware bowl. Two of the men wore recognizable rank colors, marking them as belonging to the *kuge*, the highest court rank. The other three were younger. One wore the brilliant red uniform of the imperial guard. They talked and occasionally filled their wine cups from the large bowl and toasted each other. One of the older males, a jolly, plump man, laughed aloud now and then and waved his hands about as he talked. The other sat more stiffly reserved but smiled frequently. The young men chatted with each other familiarly and were obviously friends.

The killer knew that the occasion of this gathering was the signing of a marriage contract between two great noble houses. He had paused some fifty yards from the group to prepare himself for what he had to do.

He was fully armed as if for battle. Blood-red silk laced his armor. His battle robe was of black silk with a design of white cranes. He wore both a helmet and a black-lacquered iron face mask One arm and one hand were bare.

After a moment, he sighed deeply and took up the great bow bound with red-lacquered rattan. He reached over his shoulder for the first of the black and white feathered arrows, then gave his big horse the signal. The animal obeyed and he rode slowly into the clearing, the sounds of his approach muffled by the thick grass, the *koto,* and male voices and laughter.

He covered half the distance before they noticed him and pointed. They seemed pleasantly startled. One of the men cried, "Another surprise!" and clapped his hands.

The warrior raised his bow and placed the long arrow.

The girl stopped playing the *koto* and stared.

The young man in blue prepared to rise to his feet.

The killer released the arrow. It pierced the neck of one of the older men. Blood spurted briefly and he toppled on his side without a sound.

The killer reached for another arrow and urged his horse to canter around the group. The second arrow was meant for the young man in blue who had started for the armed man. It missed its target and struck the young woman behind him in the chest. Her gown turned red and she sagged to the ground. One of the older women was next.

3

Finally someone screamed. The servants shouted and scrambled about. The young man turned back to his stricken companion.

And the killer moved on.

His next arrow struck the second older man and was followed instantly by another that hit a young man in the waist. The young man in blue was again trying to catch up with the killer.

The mounted warrior ignored him and urged his horse into a gallop as he circled and aimed at his victims one by one, loosing arrows, wheeling, and aiming again.

In such a manner young warriors practiced their battle skills, circling around a dog tied to a post in the center.

He was skillful. His arrows found the *koto* player, who collapsed over her instrument, then the other older woman who screamed briefly. Those who remained started to run for the house. Most fell to his arrows before they reached it.

The killer then turned his attention to the young man in blue, who still attempted to stop him, even though he was bare-handed and hampered by his full silk trousers. The killer reached for another arrow and found his quiver empty. With a muttered curse, he wheeled away and galloped off into the forest.

2

Tanabata

The seventh day of the seventh month.

Akitada held his wife's hand. They were sitting on their veranda overlooking the garden. He pointed at the starry sky, "The milky way," he said. "I suppose the star lovers are already together, making love."

Sadako squeezed his hand and sighed. She was still recovering from the loss of her first child.

He smiled at her. "Never mind. I shall be as patient as they."

Alarmed, she asked, "You will wait a full year?"

He pulled her close. "I almost lost you. I can wait forever rather than risk another pregnancy."

She pushed him away gently. "Nonsense," she said. "I wanted this child. And I want to try again. I'm no longer young, but I proved that I can still bear children."

His heart twisted. She was thirty-six; he was forty-six. They were both too old to be parents again. He shuddered at the thought. His daughter would soon be married and have children of her own. His son was a student at the university and would, in due time, take up a career in the government like his father and grandfather before him. He, too, would take a wife, or several. Grandchildren were quite all right with Akitada. He looked forward to them, but he did not want another child of his own.

She looked at him searchingly. "Akitada?"

He said, "I love you. I think I have never loved anyone as much. I want nothing else in my life."

Her eyes filled with tears and she crept into his arms. "Then I shall be content," she whispered. "Oh, my heart is so full."

They would have sat longer, and then they would have gone to bed to lie in each other's arms like the star lovers in the Tanabata legend, and Akitada would have put desire from his mind and settled for tenderness. But this was not to be.

Noise from beyond the garden wall had been growing steadily until it seemed unlike anything that might be explained by drunken revelry on a festival night. Then rapid footsteps sounded from the corridor and Tora called out, "Sir?"

"Something must have happened," Akitada said to his wife and got to his feet. "Come in, Tora."

Tora was still fully dressed. It crossed Akitada's mind that a younger Tora would have been in the city at this time, celebrating with friends. They were getting old.

But Tora looked excited and seemed suddenly years younger. He smiled at Sadako, who had come to join her husband, and said, "Sorry, Lady Sadako . . . and sir."

Akitada frowned. "Never mind. Is something wrong?"

"Yes, sir. Something must have happened. Horses have passed from the direction of the palace. They were going fast. People are saying they've gone to meet the enemy."

"What enemy? Are those damned monks at it again?"

"I don't know, sir. It must be them."

They stood staring at each other, remembering, when heavier footsteps approached and Genba walked in. He looked embarrassed and also started, "Sorry sir, my lady—"

Akitada cut him off. "What is it, Genba?"

"A messenger from Lord Kosehira's house, sir. It sounds serious."

Akitada touched his wife's shoulder. "Don't wait for me, Sadako. Go to bed."

She looked nervous but nodded, and he went to talk to the messenger.

He found Kosehira's old retainer, Hirono. The white-haired man was accompanied by one of the Fujiwara servants. Both looked upset. The old man said quickly, "The second lady sent us, sir. Something's happened. In the mountains, sir. It can't be good. Ah, may Amida have mercy!":

"Calm down, Hirono. Is there any danger to Lord Kosehira's family?"

The old man wrung his hands. "Yes sir, yes sir. His lordship and the young lord and the first lady went to a party there. At Lord Yorimune's villa." He paused, then added, "In the mountains, sir. In Rakuto. It's by the Shirakawa River."

Akitada nodded. "I know it." He was still dumbfounded. Rakuto was the name for the north-eastern area of the foothills east of the Kamo River. It was a place where retired emperors and high-ranking nobles had built summer palaces, villas, or modest homes. It was cooler there than in the stifling summer heat that hung over the capital.

It was not the location of the trouble that puzzled him, though Rakuto was fairly unlikely for an attack by hostile armed monks. It was the fact that Kosehira had taken his first lady there. Women stayed home, as a rule.

Hirono had fallen silent and was looking at him pleadingly. Akitada asked, "Er, he went to see Lord Yorimune?"

"Yes, sir, to sign the contracts." When Akitada still looked blank, Hirono added, "For the marriage between our young lord and Lord Yorimune's daughter."

"Oh." Akitada was appalled. Had they drifted so far apart that Kosehira had not even told him of this? He searched his memory. "So Arihito's taking a wife?"

Hirono and the servant nodded.

"I didn't know. But what happened?"

"We don't know. The second lady heard there was an attack and that people are dead. She wants you to go find out what's wrong."

Akitada tried to interpret these details. An attack? By the monks? But why attack a family gathering, even if it involved one of the great ministers? It must be something else. A band of robbers perhaps. Though

8

they were rarely this violent and brazen. In any case, it was not a request he could ignore. He said, "Thank you, Hirono. Tora and I will leave immediately. Tell Lady, um, tell the second lady not to worry. It may be a false alarm."

Hirono bowed and left with his companion.

Tora asked quickly, "Full armor, sir?"

"No. Light. I cannot quite believe they're fighting a battle. I'll meet you outside."

He returned to their room and told Sadako what he knew while he flung open his clothing trunk and rummaged for his half armor. This alarmed her.

"You won't be fighting?" she cried. "You must be careful. Please, Akitada, do not get hurt. I couldn't bear it."

It was not the time to lecture his wife on her husband's duties. He put on the half armor over his hunting jacket and the narrow trousers and smiled at her. "I shall be careful, my love. Don't worry. It may be nothing." He patted the armor. "This is being careful. And I shall take my sword."

She murmured, "Oh, Akitada!"

He put on his boots, then went to kiss her. "I must hurry."

Tora was holding the two horses. Genba, with a torch, stood beside him. He looked shocked. "Take good care, sir," he said. "Both of you. We'll be waiting."

Akitada did not bother to reassure Genba, who knew about battle and also knew that they had no choice but to fight if it became necessary.

It was fully dark, but the moon lit the way. The sounds of celebration still came from behind tall walls. It was the night of the Tanabata festival, the night when the Celestial lovers met.

9

They took Nijo Avenue and then Nijo Bridge over the Kamo River. After that, they followed the Tokaido for a few miles before turning off into the foothills at the Shirakawa River. There had been little traffic in the city and on the highway. Now there was none. Their journey and its purpose seemed unreal.

The night grew quiet as the city fell back behind them. Fields gave way to forest, and the air became cooler. Neither Akitada nor Tora had spoken since they left the house. They had maintained a gallop as long as they could. When the road began to climb, they allowed the horses to slow to a canter.

Eventually Tora asked, "Do you know the place, sir?"

"Yes." Yorimune's villa was not far from the house his friend Nakatoshi had built for himself and his family, though the Fujiwara property was several times larger and overlooked the river.

Akitada began to doubt the tale of a violent attack, but suddenly a red-coated policeman appeared around a bend in the road. He came trotting toward them, clearly in a hurry. Akitada stopped him.

The constable was breathless. "No time, sir. Official business."

"I know, Constable. I'm on my way there. What happened?"

"Don't know, sir, but they're all dead." And with this he trotted off, probably to get reinforcements.

Akitada looked after him, shocked to the core.

Kosehira dead? And his first lady? Akitada remembered her kindness and the warmth she had shown him when he had stayed with them. During all the subsequent troubles with Yukiko, she had treated him in the kindest manner when he had expected her to take her daughter's side. And Arihito? That nice young man who had shown so much promise and who was Kosehira's heir. It was all beyond belief.

It could not be true. It must not be true.

Not Kosehira!

Akitada felt the tears come to his eyes. He traced their history in his mind: the long friendship since their university years together. Kosehira, always full of laughter and affection. Kosehira always supportive when everybody had turned against him.

It had been that long friendship which had caused Kosehira to promote the marriage between Akitada, recently widowed and grieving, to his young daughter Yukiko. Yukiko was barely nineteen and had fallen into a case of hero worship of him because her father had filled her head with stories of Akitada's past. Little did she know that the much older Akitada was a mere staid government official. And to his shame, he had allowed himself to be seduced by so much young beauty and adoration.

The ugly break-up of their marriage had also distanced him from Kosehira. And now? Now it was too late. Far too late. Akitada wiped his eyes with his sleeve.

Tora said, "Sir? Shouldn't we go see what's happened?"

3

Shirakawa

They heard the river before they heard human voices. A smaller road branched away from the one that led on to Shirakawa village. It took them through dense woods to an open area and Fujiwara Yorimune's villa.

The moon lit the scene with a pale light. They saw several torches moving about, and the veranda of the house was strung with colorful lanterns. The lights and colors belied the horror of what must have happened here. Akitada reined in his horse.

In the open area below the house a number of *tatami* mats lay scattered, and among the *tatami* lay unmoving bodies covered with pieces of clothing. Red-coated men with torches moved among the dead.

"This was no battle," Akitada said after a moment's shock. "This was a murderous attack on a family celebration."

Tora nodded. "Yes. The soldiers would have been here if there'd been fighting."

"Given the rank of the dead, I think they'll be here soon. Come, let's find out what happened."

They rode to where the bodies lay among the mats and dismounted. A policeman hurried to meet them. He was middle-aged, a lieutenant by his insignia, and he shouted, "Who are you? What do you want?" He gripped his sword, and several constables ran to join him.

"We're friends," Akitada said. "I'm Sugawara. First secretary in the Ministry of Justice." A pity that Kobe was gone. These days the police no longer knew him, or Tora. "My companion is my retainer, Lieutenant Sashima."

The police officer suddenly grinned. "You must be Tora," he said to Tora, who nodded. Sobering, he turned back to Akitada. "Lieutenant Hakeda. Bad business this, sir! Six dead and five wounded. A fine marksman, but he missed a few."

Police work tended to consider the practical side of crimes.

"He? Who did this?" Akitada asked.

"We don't know, sir. We're still talking to the survivors, but they say his helmet hid his face and they didn't recognize his armor. It was still light then, but the sun was setting and he came from the west. They were blinded at first. Later they were too busy trying to get away."

Akitada nodded. He went to look at the dead.

The first body belonged to the Great Minister of the Left, Fujiwara Yorimune. The silk robe that covered the body, the body itself, and the mat it lay on were soaked in blood. He lay on his back, and the

14

blood was black in the uncertain light and glistened only faintly. Akitada gagged slightly at the smell.

A constable came to light the area with his smoking torch. Akitada wished he had not. The sight was horrible enough in the dim light of the moon. A long, black and white feathered arrow stuck up from Yorimune's throat. It had passed all the way through and caused the dead man to lie there with his head raised. As his eyes were open and stared and his mouth gaped, he looked horribly alive.

Fujiwara Yorimune was the prime minister's brother, and the second most powerful man in the nation. Kosehira had chosen wisely in the matter of his oldest son's marriage.

Ashamed, Akitada banished the thought of Fujiwara marriage politics and turned his back on Yorimune to look around. Where was Kosehira?

The next two bodies were young men. Akitada did not recognize them. The arrows had struck efficiently enough. Both were shot in the chest and had collapsed where they had been sitting.

One mat was empty, though heavily stained with blood. Had Kosehira fled the attack? Better not hope too soon. Akitada went quickly to the other covered bodies.

He found two young women. One still had flowers in her hair. Perhaps she was the bride-to-be. The other had fallen on her *koto*. Both lay face down. Their clothes showed them to be of equal rank. A little fearfully, Akitada lifted the *koto* player's hair. No, it was not Yukiko, nor, as far as he could tell, one of her sisters.

He next found an older woman, perhaps the bride's mother. There was no sign of Kosehira's first lady. Akitada allowed himself to hope.

And where was Arihito?

Two more dead lay closer to the house. Both were servants.

The police lieutenant had followed Akitada around silently. He now asked, "What do you think, sir?"

Akitada looked at him bleakly. "I don't know. What about the wounded? What did they say?" He hoped his friend and his family had escaped unhurt or were only wounded. The first reports had suggested that Kosehira was dead, but that constable on the road could have made a mistake and so could the messenger who had reported the event to Kosehira's second lady. He wondered belatedly about Kosehira's other sons. If they had not attended the event, they should have rushed here at the news.

The lieutenant said helpfully, "The wounded are in the house. They haven't been much help. There's one witness who's unhurt, but he hasn't said much."

Akitada nodded and turned for Tora, who came, leading both horses and looking uncharacteristically subdued. Akitada said, "Let's go inside." Tora just sighed, tied up the horses, and followed him

They walked to the stairs. A man in a blue robe sat hunched over on the top step, his head in his hands. Akitada wondered if this was the witness. When the man heard their steps, he looked up.

"Arihito!"

Kosehira's son looked unhurt. His clothes were bloodstained, but he did not seem to be wounded.

"Akitada? You here?" Arihito looked dazed. His eyes were red from weeping.

"Your father? Where is he? And your mother?"

"Inside. The physician's removing the arrows. He sent me out here." He turned to look back at the doorway behind him. "Amida! Father's very bad."

"But they're both alive?"

Arihito sank back down and hung his head. "Last I saw, Father was barely alive. And Mother was in so much pain."

Akitada climbed the steps and sat down beside Arihito. He put an arm around his shoulder. "I'm so very sorry. But we must hope."

Tora joined them. "I wish Seimei were here," he muttered. "This physician? Is he any good? I can ride back and bring another man."

Arihito shook his head. "I don't know, Tora. I don't think there's time."

Opportunely, a white-haired man in a brown monk's robe came out of the house. He was wiping his bloody hands on some paper and said, "Well, they're out, young man. Your mother will do very well, I think, but your father . . . it's in the hands of the Buddha now."

Arihito and Akitada stood. Arihito said, "When can I take them home?"

"Your mother can travel, but she will not leave your father, and he must stay. If he lives through the night, you can ask me again." With that he turned on his heel and disappeared into the house again.

Akitada, full of questions, grumbled, "He has no manners, that old man."

Arihito said, "He has other wounded to see to."

"Yes, of course. That was thoughtless of me. Shall we go see your parents?"

Arihito nodded and they went into the villa. It was filled with subdued sounds after the deadly silence outside. The soft chanting of monks mixed with moaning and cries of pain. The wounded had been brought into the reception room of the villa and were lying here. Monks sat praying along the walls. Some of the Fujiwara servants moved about to assist the physician.

Arihito made for two figures lying side by side in one corner. Kosehira was unconscious and deathly pale. His wife, Lady Hatsuko, lay beside him, holding his hand and watching his face. Both wore bloody clothing. Akitada saw that she had aged since he had last spoken to her, but Kosehira's appearance shocked him deeply. Not only was his skin bloodless, but his features were slack.

Arihito said, "Mother? Akitada has come. And Tora, too."

She turned her head and blinked at them. "How kind," she said softly, and started to weep.

A young woman, probably Lady Hatsuko's maid, rose to make room for Arihito beside his mother.

Akitada went to kneel beside Kosehira. His clothing had been cut open to reveal his shoulder and part of his upper body. He had put on weight. A huge pad of moss had been placed over a wound just below his left shoulder. Akitada lifted it and took a look. The opening was large and ragged. It started to bleed again and he quickly replaced the pad. The physician had done a creditable job, removing the arrow and treating the wound. Akitada hoped it was not too deep, but his memory of the arrows in the dead people outside was not reassuring. At least, he thought, it had not been a barbed arrow.

Lady Hatsuko asked in a breaking voice, "Is it very bad, Akitada? Please tell me."

He managed a smile. "It looks clean and should heal." No sense in worrying her any more. "Where are you wounded?"

"My thigh. It's nothing. The physician bandaged it. But my husband . . . such wounds are often fatal. He said so."

Mentally cursing the physician, Akitada said, "He's a lay monk only. And I doubt he's seen many arrow wounds."

She looked relieved. "Oh. Yes. Of course. You and Tora would know more about that. Thank you for coming." She closed her eyes and seemed to doze off.

Akitada glanced across at Arihito and motioned with his head toward the door. Arihito nodded and they both rose to go back outside. As they walked out of the room, one of the wounded who was surrounded by servants complained bitterly. "Who is that?" Akitada asked.

Arihito looked. "Suenaka," he said. "Sumitoma's full brother. And Hiroko's."

"Is he seriously wounded?"

"No. Sumitoma got an arrow in the buttock as he was running. He'll live."

"Who is Hiroko?" Akitada asked.

"She was to be my wife. She's dead." Arihito's voice was bitter.

Akitada murmured, "I'm sorry. It's a terrible thing."

Suenaka's querulous voice called loudly for the physician, who was busy binding up a wound on one of the servants. Grimacing, Akitada escaped outside. Tora followed them.

Here they were confronted again by the sight of the covered bodies in the field. The constables huddled together, listening to instructions from the lieutenant. Akitada said to Tora. "Go and see if you can learn anything from the family servants." Tora nodded, looking relieved.

"Now tell me what happened," Akitada said to Arihito.

"How much do you know?"

"I know nothing. The second lady sent a message that your father had been attacked and possibly killed here. Tora and I left immediately."

Arihito sighed. "I sent our servant. We brought only one and Mother's maid. I don't know where he went and what he said. I don't remember what I told him. He was inside during the attack." He frowned. "I would have thought more people would have shown up by now."

He was right. It seemed strange that the prime minister and Yorimune's other relatives had not taken immediate action. But Akitada said nothing about that, repeating merely, "Tell me!"

"We had signed the papers and . . ." Arihito paused. "You knew I was to take Yorimune's daughter to wife?"

Akitada nodded.

"Well, we had signed the papers. About the dowry and so forth, and then we had a meal. Father suggested that since it was Tanabata and Tanabata was all about uniting lovers, we—Hiroko and me— should be allowed some privacy to talk to each other and get to know each other better. Yorimune didn't like it, but they moved outside to drink and watch the sunset and they let us sit together while they talked." He hung his head. "Oh, Akitada, she was so pretty and really nice—not like her brothers. I liked her." He paused again. "You know, Akitada, I think I could have fallen in love with Hiroko."

Akitada reached for the young man's arm and squeezed it. "I'm sorry, Hito," he said again.

Arihito straightened his back. "Well, this warrior suddenly appeared. He came from over there." Arihito pointed to the forest between the road and the field. "We were surprised. I thought Yorimune had arranged for an entertainment. Anyway, nobody did anything. We sat and watched him come. Then he raised his bow and placed an arrow." The young man shuddered. "We sat and waited. And he shot Yorimune through the neck. Blood spurted into the air and I jumped up and started to run toward him—the man on the horse, I mean—but he released another arrow and I heard Hiroko cry out and turned back." The words came pouring out now.

"She was standing by then. The arrow hit the middle of her chest. Her clothes turned red and she . . . just crumpled. I ran to her, but I could see it was already too late. So I chased after him again. He was riding around in a circle, killing people. I couldn't catch him. These trousers . . . .." He covered his face. "I'm ashamed, Akitada. I'm the only one who doesn't have a scratch on him. I can never look people in the face again. Oh, and Father! What if he dies? It's as if I'd killed him."

Akitada snapped, "That's utter nonsense! Stop this talk now. It is not your fault. And you seem to have been the only one who tried to stop the killer."

Arihito lowered his hands. His face looked ravaged with grief. "I wish he'd killed me, too. He tried to, but then he rode off. Out of arrows. Oh, gods!" And he fell sobbing into Akitada's arms.

Akitada held him, patting his back awkwardly. His eyes fell on the road. Armed men on horses were coming toward the villa. For a horrible moment, he thought the killer had returned with reinforcements, then he realized that finally the soldiers had arrived from the capital. "Arihito," he warned. "We have company."

4

Secrets

Arihito brushed a sleeve over his face, and looked.

Mounted soldiers slowly poured from the road toward the house. Their leader wore a captain's insignia. He and his officers were fully armed and riding fine horses. More armed foot soldiers followed and spread out along the road.

"Dear gods," muttered Arihito. "What do they want?"

"An attack on a grand minister is seen as an attack on the nation," Akitada said.

"But what good will it do?"

"Not much, but they must make the gesture."

"And here are more people."

Several other mounted men arrived, these in hunting outfits and carrying only swords, much like Akitada and Tora.

"Ah, the family members are arriving," Akitada said.

The captain had reached the scene of the massacre. The police lieutenant hurried over and saluted, then bowed deeply. The police were semi-military but ceded precedence to soldiers. Besides, a captain outranked a lieutenant.

Arihito said, "That must be one of the prime minister's sons. I think two of them are captains in the guard. It's hard to keep track. They keep getting promoted and assigned to important posts."

Akitada said, "I know. He's getting off his horse. I suppose he means to look at the victims."

They stood side by side and watched, glad for the distraction. The captain walked over to where Yorimune lay. The police officer hurried to lift the robe that covered the corpse, and the captain looked. Having looked, he turned away and vomited.

Meanwhile, the other newcomers had also dismounted and were going to inspect the site. The captain now seemed to be berating the police officer who stood humbly bowed before the other man's anger.

Akitada sighed. "My guess is the captain is outraged that Yorimune was not carried into his house. The policeman was quite properly preserving the scene of a murder. I doubt this will be pleasant, Arihito. Be thankful that your father is unconscious."

"They wouldn't dare speak that way to my father."

"Hmm. Perhaps not, but then there are still the two of us to take the brunt of their attempt to blame someone."

"Oh. I don't really care. I only care about my parents. And Hiroko."

24

"Yes, but be prepared."

Below, the captain had looked around and now saw them on the veranda of the house. He pointed and asked the police officer something. Having received an answer, he strode toward them purposefully.

Akitada sighed and touched Arihito's arm. "Try not to be offended. It will serve nothing."

The captain arrived. He was still in his twenties, a well-grown young man with a round face and a little mustache. He glowered. Climbing the steps, he demanded, "What are you doing here, Sugawara? You have no business here. You will leave!"

Arihito tried to speak up, but Akitada touched his arm again. "I was called in by Lord Kosehira's family, sir," he said, bowing. This young Fujiwara outranked him by several degrees.

"This has nothing to do with Kosehira. Get out! And keep your mouth shut or I'll see to it that you end your life in Kyushu like your ancestor."

It was an outrageous threat. Akitada felt a surge of white-hot anger. He was no longer used to being spoken to in this manner. And in the distant past, the men who had addressed him thus had been much older. With an effort he controlled himself. This arrogant young man, regardless of his birth and rank, was too stupid to waste his energy on.

But Arihito burst out, "Mind your words! Sugawara is a family friend."

The captain stared at him. "You look familiar."

"Fujiwara Arihito," snapped Arihito.

The young captain grinned suddenly, then looked embarrassed. "Oh, right. You and cousin Hiroko! Sorry, Arihito." He looked past them at the door. "Where's your bride?"

Arihito, white with rage or grief, pointed. "Down there. Dead!"

The captain's face fell. He flushed. "Oh. Yes. I didn't realize. Horrible. Did you see what happened?"

Arihito turned his back on him and went inside the villa.

The captain glanced at Akitada. "Hmm," he said. "Did you see it?"

Akitada looked back gravely. "No. I came afterward."

The captain frowned. "Well, who saw it?"

"Those who were here. But some of them are dead, some wounded, and some were inside the house."

The young man thought this over. "I'll speak to the wounded," he decided and started up the stairs.

"Not Kosehira. He's unconscious. And not his wife."

The captain paused. "Oh. That's too bad. No, not his wife. Women cannot be trusted to get things right." He thought again.. "Wait! Arihito. Wasn't he present?"

"Yes, but I doubt he'll have the patience to talk to you just now."

"He must. My father wants to know what happened and why. Did Arihito tell you?"

"He told me some of it."

"So, what happened?"

That had been the question from the start. Akitada was sure he did not know the answer even now. But what he had learned he tried to convey to this brash and unintelligent young man and hoped he would not garble the account too badly when he related it to his father, the prime minister.

26

The captain's only comment was, "You don't know any more than that policeman."

Akitada said nothing and the captain shook his head and walked inside.

Down below, the new arrivals had made their way to the villa. They were all Fujiwara family members of high ranks and powerful positions. All looked very serious and most merely glanced at Akitada, who stood to the side, bowing to each man as he reached the veranda and went inside.

One stopped and looked at him closely. "Sugawara?"

"Yes, sir."

"Good. Anything you can tell us?"

"Not much, sir. Nobody got a good look at the killer. He wore a helmet with a face mask."

The other man nodded. "Well, do your best," he said and walked inside.

Akitada sighed and went down to the open area where constables and monks were busy gathering the dead to take them to the house. Lieutenant Hakeda, his face grim, supervised. To Akitada's relief he was making sure that the location of each body was marked. A flaming torch was pushed into the ground where the victim's head had lain.

The torches seemed less bright, and Akitada looked up at the sky to see that the light was changing. In the east, the sky was turning red and overhead a pale gray obscured the Milky Way. The star lovers had parted. A new day was beginning here on earth, and some would never see it.

Shouts alerted him to more arrivals. On the road appeared a line of outriders and then a sedan chair carried by four strong bearers and followed by another line of mounted men. The banners announced an important visitor.

As they came closer, the lieutenant beside him cried, "Down on your knees! The Prime Minister!"

The constables fell down with bowed heads. Akitada merely bowed very deeply. To his dismay the sedan chair halted before him, and the prime minister peered out. "Sugawara?"

"Yes, Excellency!" The lined face of the great man seemed more forbidding than ever.

"What do you know?"

Akitada summed up the events as he knew them. The prime minister asked, "Did anybody recognize the murderer?"

"No, Excellency. He was masked." He hesitated and then asked, "Did your brother have an enemy?"

The prime minister's expression froze. He glared and snapped, "Are you saying that my brother did something that caused him to be killed? How dare you? You will leave this to the authorities!" He told his bearers to move on.

Akitada stood looking after him. He had offended the most powerful man in the country.

His question had seemed natural enough to him, if perhaps a little abrupt. The prime minister's violent reaction suggested that they had something to hide. Akitada was becoming convinced that this massacre had happened because of Yorimune. That must be where he would find answers.

However, he was expressly forbidden to pursue the investigation.

And it would be dangerous to do so.

A dilemma.

Akitada would have turned his back on Yorimune and his family, but Kosehira was a victim who lay in the villa, possibly dying and perhaps already dead. How could he abandon this case?

At the villa, the prime minister stepped from his sedan chair and climbed the steps to the veranda. Was he grieving as a brother and uncle? Yorimune had been his full brother. Did he fear an attack on his family? On Fujiwara power? On the emperor and the nation?

Yes, they had personal enemies, even if His Excellency did not want to admit it. And there were also many who wished to remove them from power. This strangely dramatic and semi-public attack by an elaborately armed but anonymous warrior must have been meant to send a powerful message.

But what message? And who was behind this shocking act?

Akitada detested power politics and had closed his ears to rumors and gossip for years. Now he wished he had listened though he dreaded the knowledge.

He sighed, wondering what was happening inside the villa, hoping that Kosehira was still alive, and that Arihito would keep his temper.

It was almost fully light by now. Akitada looked at the site of the massacre where the constables were leaving. The monks were carrying away the last body. The police lieutenant, having witnessed the prime minister's anger at Akitada, had drifted away.

Soon only the torches remained, marking the places where people had died. Akitada wished they had also marked where the wounded had been. He wanted to walk around the area, picturing the scene as it must have been: The men sitting together by the wine bowl, the place where the *koto* player had been, and where Arihito had sat with Hiroko, their mothers nearby, the servants at a distance.

He noted the hoof marks of the killer's horse as it had circled the group and he found the tracks leading from this circle to the woods.

He walked along the tracks. Just inside the outer line of trees was a place where the rider had waited for a time. The horse had been restless and had moved about while its master had looked down at the people he would kill.

Akitada wished he knew what had been in the man's mind. Had he hated them all or had he intended to kill only one or two and then decided to cover up this intention by killing others? Either way, it was a brutal mentality that had done this, killing men and women, masters and servants.

It occurred to Akitada that the killer might be insane, someone who enjoyed killing for the sake of killing. Someone who gloried in his power to take away what people held dearer than any other thing, their lives. Notwithstanding the Buddha's teaching, people clung to their lives and the lives of their loved ones.

He shuddered and returned to the villa.

5

Witnesses

Akitada found Tora in the kitchen behind the villa. This was a small building next to the stables. Its doors stood wide open and the room was filled with the usual implements. There was a rice cooker, large tubs, buckets, and piles of firewood. There was also a fire where a cook was stirring a suspended pot.

Tora sat on a raised platform, busy slurping a bowl of gruel while listening to the cook's chatter. Trust Tora to locate his morning meal while making friends and gathering information.

His retainer casually waved his bowl in Akitada's direction and told the cook, "Don't worry. It's just my master."

Akitada frowned at this impropriety, but the cook, a fat man, grinned, bowed, and murmured, "An honor!"

Akitada nodded in return. "Good morning, Cook. It's a terrible day. I hope Tora hasn't bothered you."

The cook said with a chuckle, "No, sir. Not at all. We know each other from way back."

Akitada sat down beside Tora. "Is that so?"

Tora said, "It's a long time ago. We fell in with some bad characters. Why not have some gruel? It's excellent. Keiji's a great cook."

Keiji beamed and filled a bowl. Akitada gave Tora a searching look. The only bad company he could recall Tora having was the gang of bandits he had rescued him from. Tora winked.

Akitada, whose stomach had been rumbling for a while, accepted the food. The gruel was indeed delicious, being mixed with chopped nuts and dried plums. He said, "You're an artist, Keiji."

Keiji grinned. "My master likes it this way. It's very filling and good. It also has some honey in it. The master has a sweet tooth." He paused. "I mean, he *had* a sweet tooth." He shook his head mournfully. "It won't be the same now. I may be out of a job."

Akitada, who had already decided that this cook had little love for his master, said, "It does you credit that you mourn your master."

The cook pursed his lips. "Well," he said, judiciously, "There'll be changes for us. Different problems."

Tora handed back his bowl. "Change is a good thing. It'll keep you on your toes."

"Never you mind, Tora. I've been kept on my toes so much, I've none left."

"Was your master hard to please?" Akitada asked.

"Terribly hard. I'd been worrying that he'd have me whipped for letting the octopus balls stand too long. They were cold when we served the dinner." He looked glum.

"Well, cheer up! You escaped a whipping," Tora pointed out.

But the cook had fallen into gloom. "They're all alike, that family," he muttered, then looked over his shoulder when the door opened and a servant slipped in. Keiji put a finger to his lips and asked the servant, "What do you want? I'm busy with these gentlemen."

Akitada said quickly, "Don't mind us. We just had a bite to eat. Come in and have your gruel. You've had a long night and more work waiting."

The servant's eyes grew round with astonishment. He slunk in with a bow. "Thank you, sir, but I can eat later. Sorry, Keiji."

Keiji sighed. "Here. They're not going to want it." He handed the man a full bowl. "Sit down over there. What's happening in the house?"

The servant took a large sip, chewed, and said, "This is good! They brought the bodies inside. Then His Excellency came and a bunch of other nobles and they sent us outside. I thought I'd grab a bite before they start putting us to work." He buried his head in the bowl again.

Akitada asked, "Did either of you see what happened earlier?"

The cook shook his head. "I was here. Washing the dinner dishes. I heard some screaming, but it wasn't very loud and I thought they were just having fun. Some fun! Did you see it, sir?"

"No, Tora and I came much later. They say the killer wore armor and a helmet. Who could do such a thing?"

They both looked blank and shook their heads. The servant, after a moment, volunteered, "Fuhito saw it, but he just looked at the horse."

The cook guffawed. "Not very bright, our Fuhito. He's besotted with horses."

Tora asked, "What did he say about the horse?"

The servant grinned. "Who knows? Fuhito's crazy. All those nobles killed by that warrior, and he looks at the horse."

"Where is Fuhito?" Akitada asked.

The servant finished his gruel and the cook refused to refill the bowl. The man got up. "He's inside, with the bodies, and the wounded. The young master keeps us running. Got to go back." He turned to leave. "Thanks, Keiji. That was good."

When the door closed behind him, Akitada said thoughtfully, "Sometimes people like this Fuhito have very good memories."

The cook laughed again. "Yes, we wish he didn't. He chatters on and on."

"I'd like to talk to him."

"I'll tell him when I see him, sir."

There was nothing else to be done. Akitada worried about Kosehira's condition, but he did not want to run into the prime minister again. In the end, he walked outside and peered around the corner. No sign of the prime minister, but Arihito stood on the veranda, searching the surroundings. Akitada stepped out and waved, and Arihito ran down the steps to join him.

"I'm avoiding the prime minister," Akitada said, pulling him back around the corner. Seeing the young man's glum face, he asked, "Your father?"

Arihito sighed. "The same. I'm angry at the prime minister. He has no respect for my mother. How dare he trouble her with his questions when she's in pain and upset?"

"He wants to know what happened. I hope you behaved yourself?"

"Barely. I came outside when he turned his attention to that useless nephew of his. Why are you hiding?"

"I'm forbidden to continue the investigation."

"What? But why?"

"I asked him if his brother had enemies."

Arihito frowned. "You're not giving up, are you?"

"No, but I have to be careful and hanging about here is not a good idea."

"Any progress?"

"Very little. The servants didn't like their master much. One of them is said to be a rather acute observer of horses. He saw the attacker."

"His name?"

"Fuhito."

"I'll find him."

"No, Arihito. Not while the prime minister is about."

"He'll leave soon. As for the other matter . . ." Arihito hesitated. "I didn't know Yorimune well. My father got along with him. I never heard anything against him."

Akitada nodded. "I doubt very much that any serious offenses would've been acknowledged or discussed in that family."

Arihito flushed. "Father would not have covered up any crimes."

"I know, Arihito. He probably didn't know. It's really the prime minister's reaction to my question that made me think there must be something serious enough to provoke revenge."

Arihito relaxed a little. "Yes. It seems strange. It's a natural question to ask. But he was very upset. You cannot really trust what a man says under the circumstances."

Akitada nodded again. "You're right. I'll keep it in mind."

A brief silence fell.

Tora strolled out of the kitchen and joined them. "How's your honorable father, sir?" he asked Arihito.

"Still unconscious. What do you think, Tora?"

"I'd like to talk to the servants who were outside. They may have seen something. And then there's some halfwit called Fuhito who looks only at horses."

"A halfwit? Much good that will do."

Akitada said, "Tora exaggerates. I rather think the man is a little bit awkward and has this obsession with horses, so they make fun of him."

"I can go back in and send the servants out."

"Surely that would attract attention."

"I'll think of something."

But just then they heard some shouted commands and Arihito peered around the corner. "He's leaving. He's getting into his sedan chair. You and Tora stay here. I'll check on Father and Mother and then send the servants out to the kitchen for their morning meal."

Akitada nodded. "Thank you, Arihito."

Looking after him, Tora said, "Does him credit to think of the poor bastards' stomachs."

They returned to the kitchen and, true to his word, Arihito did send the servants from the main house. They trickled in one by one, looking tired, worried, and hungry. Seeing Akitada and Tora there threw them into a panic, and the cook had to reassure them as he filled their bowls.

Eventually they separated those who had been outside during the attack and invited them to discuss the event. The men were reluctant at first but slowly they spoke.

"I saw him coming. He was huge. A giant."

Another nodded. "With fiery eyes."

A third murmured, "He wasn't human! He was sent to punish evildoers."

Akitada fixed on this comment. "Did he kill only evil doers?"

That gave them pause. They seemed to agree that maybe some of the dead had not been so very evil. Their knowledge of the dead servants was better than what they knew of the sins of their masters, and the argument of divine retribution faltered somewhat. But while it was impossible to pin them down to voicing any charges against their master and his sons, they also refrained from exonerating them. They could not add anything about the appearance of the killer beyond what Arihito had already described.

One of the men, the youngest, a thin man with hair that stood up in two large tufts like strange ears, had remained quiet. Akitada finally asked him what he thought.

The other servants laughed. "Fuhito's not very bright. He only sees horses," one explained.

The slight young man colored and hung his head. Akitada smiled to encourage the shy youngster. "Well then, Fuhito, tell us about the horse."

Fuhito looked at the others. He clenched his hands and opened his mouth. For a moment, no sound came out. Then he gasped, "I-it was b-b-brown . . . it h-had a b-black m-mane and t-t-t . . . ." He broke off to a chorus of mocking laughter from the servants.

"Ah," said Akitada and nodded. "A black mane and tail. Anything else you recall?"

Fuhito took a deep breath. "I-it was b-big, like the man. B-but it moved well. Very well f-for carrying such a b-big man. And it had one b-black sock." He saw Akitada's astonished look and pointed to his ankle. "On his foreleg. It made me th-think it had l-lost all its socks b-but one." He chuckled at his joke, and Akitada saw that he had buck teeth that made him look like a rabbit. In fact, the whole man struck him as rabbit-like in his nervous timidness.

He said, "Yes, very funny. It would look like that. Excellent. Thank you, Fuhito. We may find this horse before we find the man."

Fuhito blushed with pleasure.

"Did you notice if the animal was lathered?" Tora asked.

"N-not lathered. B-but it needed to b-be rubbed d-down."

"Then it was tired?"

Fuhito thought. "N-no. It was a very good horse. I-it ran well and it obeyed well."

This was all they could gain from Fuhito. They let the servants go back to their duties. Akitada said, "So we know what the horse looked like and that it had traveled a moderate distance that afternoon."

Tora was glum. "Looking for a horse is crazy. This is a big area."

"It's something. And there are not that many horses in these hills. Speaking of horses, please check on ours. It's time we returned."

6

Aftermath

In spite of his words to Tora, Akitada was not very
hopeful either. Looking for a horse was certainly
not something he and Tora could undertake. However, now that the prime minister and his entourage had
departed, he could check on Kosehira again.

He found the room nearly empty of people.
Most of the wounded had been taken to their rooms or
to other areas. But Kosehira and his wife were still
there.

To Akitada's relief, his friend was conscious, if
in considerable pain. Lady Hatsuko was sitting up and
Arihito knelt on his other side. Lady Hatsuko still held
her husband's hand.

"Akitada!" Kosehira attempted his usual light-
hearted greeting but failed to raise his voice above a
whisper.

Akitada went to kneel beside Arihito. "How are you, my old friend?" he asked, searching Kosehira's face.

"A little uncomfortable. Did I really have to get nearly killed to see my friend again?"

Akitada flushed. "I'm sorry. Forgive me."

"No, no. I didn't mean it. Pay no attention. I'm very grumpy when I hurt." He turned his head. "Let go of my hand, love," he said to his wife. "I need it to gesture."

She obeyed with a weak giggle.

"Best not gesture," Akitada warned. "You had an arrow in that side of your chest."

Kosehira peered at the bandage. "Arihito says it's out." He wiggled his fingers and grimaced. "This is horrible. Yorimune's dead, and so are his daughters. And his first lady and two friends. Find out who did this, Akitada."

Arihito said, "Remember, Father, what the prime minister said."

Kosehira frowned. "He didn't know what he was saying. He'll change his mind."

Akitada was encouraged that Kosehira sounded rational and said, "It may be that Yorimune was the real target. In that case it may be a matter of revenge. What did Yorimune do to bring this upon himself and his family?"

Kosehira blinked. "I don't know."

"There has to be something. The prime minister doesn't want me to find out what's going on."

After some thought, Kosehira shook his head. "I don't know, Akitada. I stay out of things as much as possible. You know me." He glanced at Arihito. "If I'd

42

known of anything very bad, Son, we wouldn't have been here."

"I know, Father. I'm sorry that Hiroko had to die. I liked her."

They heard a small sob from Lady Hatsuko. Kosehira unwisely sought for her hand and groaned with pain. He gasped, "Your mother liked Hiroko. She said she was a very nice girl."

Lady Hatsuko, who had taken her husband's hand again, now wept openly. "So sad," she sobbed. "That sweet young woman!"

Kosehira looked at Akitada. "We're going home. This place is filled with poison."

"The physician said you couldn't be moved for a few days," Akitada pointed out.

Kosehira glared and repeated quite fiercely, "We're going home. Arihito's seeing to it."

Arihito nodded. "The lay monk was very pleased that father is conscious. We'll risk it. They are coming with a carriage and two steady oxen."

Kosehira said, "Come with us, Akitada. You and Tora. Then all will be well."

Akitada agreed. The note of desperation in his friend's voice alarmed him. Kosehira was clearly badly shaken by what had happened.

While they waited for transport, Akitada sought out Lieutenant Hakeda. He found him dispatching messengers to his headquarters in the capital.

Akitada said, "We'll be taking Lord Kosehira and his family back soon. Have you found out anything in the meantime?"

The Lieutenant said quickly, "Can I speak to Lord Kosehira? Or his lady?"

"Not yet. He is barely conscious and must conserve his strength for the journey. I have asked him what he saw and he had nothing to add to what we know. One of the servants described the killer's horse as brown with a black mane and tail and one black foot. Lord Kosehira confirms that the horse was dark, possibly brown. He saw the helmet with its face mask and, when urged, recalled that the armor was threaded with red silk. That's all he saw before the arrow struck him."

"You mean one of the horse's legs was darker?"

"Yes. Just above the hoof."

"Hmm. What does the servant say about the man?"

"Nothing. It appears he only notices horses."

The lieutenant stared, then he smiled. "It's been my experience that people notice the most extraordinary things, all absolutely useless."

"Perhaps this one may not be. Find the horse, and you'll find the man."

Hakeda looked appalled. "But where would one start?"

"I don't know, but many witnesses may in the end produce a full picture."

"I would be grateful if you would share whatever else you may learn, sir."

"I promise to keep you informed, and you do the same."

The smile appeared again. Hakeda bowed a little. "Honored, sir."

The meeting encouraged Akitada a little. He liked Hakeda and reflected that he might yet again be able to work comfortably with the capital police, even though Kobe was no longer there.

The ox-drawn carriage arrived eventually, carefully lined with bedding, and accompanied by Kosehira's servants and his trusted ox driver. The transfer of the wounded was accomplished, painfully for Kosehira and anxiously for Lady Hatsuko, and they set off on the journey homeward.

Kosehira not only survived the ordeal but was in a much better humor when settled in his own luxurious quarters with servants running, fetching, and carrying away food, drink, pillows, books, and large bowls of icy water to chase out the summer heat. Kosehira's family regularly imported ice from the mountains to cool its rooms in the summer.

Lady Hatsuko was similarly cosseted by her maids. Their personal physician had awaited their arrival and had approved their treatment by the lay monk.

Akitada finally returned home as the sun set again. It surprised him that so much time had passed without his notice, and then he was equally astonished that so much had happened in the span of less than a day and a night.

Sadako and the others had been anxious. Some news had finally reached them and at least reassured them that no battles were being fought. But Akitada's wife ran to him and searched his face when he trudged up the stairs to the veranda.

Those stairs seemed steeper and longer than he recalled. His body felt alien, like that of an old man. When he heard her call out his name, he pulled himself together, put a smile on his face and made an effort to climb more easily. He did not fool her.

"Oh," she said, when he finally stood before her, "it was very bad, wasn't it? How are Kosehira and his wife?"

Sadako could always read him. He sighed and told the truth. "It was very bloody. Six people dead, four of them young and at the beginning of their lives. Kosehira was barely alive, but by a miracle a good physician removed an arrow from his chest without killing him. Lady Hatsuko got an arrow in her thigh. They are home now and we must hope Kosehira will heal."

She wrapped her arms around him. "My poor dear," she murmured. "How terrible to see so much death. But it might have been Kosehira. Or his wife or son. Don't look so beaten. You need food and rest. Tomorrow will be a better day."

And, as usual, she was right.

He slept, but there were dreams, terrible dreams. When he woke in the morning, daylight filtered through the blinds and he was drenched in sweat. He lay still, bringing himself back from the nightmare of dismembered bodies and seas of blood. He had seen many terrible things in his youth, and murder scenes had never been pleasant in the intervening years, so he tried to understand why he was so shaken this time. He used to shrug this sort of thing off. The dead were at peace, so why should he relive their deaths? That was for his waking hours, for his work, not for the nights when unseen spirits twisted the events in order to create an evil world of endless dying that tried to swallow him up.

To chase away the false reality of the dream, he thought back to the scene in Shirakawa and tried to imagine the arrival of the killer. He had been a complete surprise to the members of the party. Arihito had said that they had waited for some sort of performance. But what of Yorimune? He must have known that this was no part of any entertainment he had planned. What had he thought? Did he suspect he was about to die?

At this point, Akitada looked for Sadako. She had already left the bed. No doubt, she had done it silently so as not to disturb him. Of such small things, her consideration and his appreciation of it, love was made. The thought brought a smile to his face and he got up.

In a hot bath he washed off the sweat of his troubled night and the smell of blood he imagined his body still held from Shirakawa. Then he went to his room, dressed, and drank the tea and ate the gruel left for him by the maid.

Or more likely by his wife. He smiled again.

But there was nothing to smile about in the matter at hand. He must find out what had happened at Shirakawa and why. Unless he did this, he could not be certain that the killer would not finish what he had started with Kosehira's family.

He went in search of Tora or Genba and found both on the front veranda.

"I was just coming," Tora said. "They sent a servant from Lord Kosehira's house to say that he had rested well and was feeling a bit better. But the doctor is coming and they think the prime minister may also show up. Maybe we should go a bit later."

"Thanks, Tora. Good news, I think. Yes, we'll visit this afternoon."

Genba said, "What can have caused a man to attack such powerful people? He must be mad."

Akitada had wondered about this also. He said, "I have a hard time understanding it myself."

Genba eyed him. "You'd best be careful, sir. Madmen don't care who they kill. Tora said this one

47

killed two young girls and their mother. Who does something like that?"

"We may find out soon. Thank you both for your concern."

In the end, Akitada went to see Nakatoshi. Nakatoshi was another close friend who supervised the Ministry of Ceremonial, a function that involved even more tedious paperwork than Akitada's position at the Ministry of Justice. The difference was that Nakatoshi loved his work, while Akitada was frequently bored and deserted the fine print and the endless quibbles over ancient laws by men maneuvering for positions and land leases. His dabbling in "low crime" brought him regularly to the attention of his superiors and not always in a good way. Even his assignments to governorships had invariably been on the order of reward mixed with punishment. Nakatoshi meanwhile had prospered in the capital and knew nearly everything worth knowing about people in the government.

He was a slender man Akitada's age and received him expectantly. "I knew you'd come. I bet you went to Shirakawa. A terrible affair, but I'm glad as always to see you, my friend."

They embraced. Theirs was a friendship unalloyed by unwise marriages or arguments. Nakatoshi's temperament was too even for such upheavals. In addition he was the most loyal man Akitada knew.

Nakatoshi's office in the *shiki-busho* was, like Akitada's, in a separate enclosure within the *daidairi*, and like Akitada's, it held a desk, some cushions, and shelving for documents. Nakatoshi also kept wine for visitors. Akitada rarely had visitors and only worked in his own office. They sat down, Nakatoshi poured, they drank, and then they smiled at each other.

"I thought of your place as I rode up to Shirakawa," Akitada told him. "It had always seemed peaceful, a little like living in another, better world."

"Unlike Yorimune, I'm a humble man," said Nakatoshi. "And mine is a humble life and a humble abode. I cannot recommend it enough, my dear Akitada."

"I've been tempted, but at the moment I shudder at the thought. Now monsters may appear from those green forests and I have no defenses."

Nakatoshi nodded. "I can understand that, but such monsters aren't interested in people like us."

"I may be unimportant, but I've made enemies. I don't know, maybe that's a distinction of sorts."

His friend chuckled. "Not at all unimportant. You're a famous man while nobody knows me. But you came to ask me questions."

"I'm sorry. It must seem as though I'm only visiting when I want something. Forgive me."

Another chuckle. "No, no. I know better and I enjoy your interests quite as much as you do."

"Well," said Akitada, "I need to know what evil deeds Yorimune has done in his past."

7

The Evil Men Do

Nakatoshi raised his brows. "You think this was some sort of revenge directed at Yorimune? But if so, why kill all the others. And nearly kill your friend Kosehira?"

"I don't know what it was, but I intend to find out. Yorimune doesn't have a good reputation. I assume there are reasons for it."

Nakatoshi nodded, scratched his head, pursed his lips, stared into the distance, and finally said, "There were some things. Minor as such things go among the good people. He ordered his servants to beat another man's servants; he wounded a man in a sword fight over a woman; he ruined a merchant because the merchant had cheated his *betto*—or he claimed the man had cheated. Nothing to cause such an elaborate attack."

"I don't know. Some people will react violently to what may seem like minor offenses to us. What about that fight over a woman?"

"A slight wound. The prime minister covered up the matter by assigning the man to a lucrative post somewhere."

Akitada made a face. "I take it the rival was a Fujiwara. Lucrative posts do not go to other families."

"You are wrong about that. But as it happens, it was a cousin and they were both young."

"What about the merchant?"

"Nothing is known about him. He left the capital to go east. But there may be much better reasons elsewhere. In his youth, Yorimune held several governorships. He enriched himself grossly and is said to have mistreated the local people. The problem is that the distance makes it impossible to get details."

"Oh." Akitada thought this over, then asked, "What provinces?"

"Tamba and Tosa."

"Not close enough. I had hoped they'd kept him near the capital."

"He was young and I suspect the appointments were a form of punishment. A sort of exile. The court feels that when the young misbehave, the best thing is to remove them from temptation."

"The misbehavior involved women?"

"I don't know, Akitada. I'm not privy to the sins of my betters." Nakatoshi paused. His lip twitched. "Usually."

"You can find out?"

"What? The crimes that sent him to those places, or what he may have done there?"

"Both." Akitada sighed. "Clearly, Yorimune has done enough to justify the attack."

"Yes. Probably. I never liked the man, though he's been courteous enough. Why did Kosehira choose Yorimune's daughter for his eldest?"

"It's a puzzle. He told me that his first lady, Arihito's mother, met the girl and liked her very much."

Nakatoshi said drily, "Surely not his only reason."

"No. The connection was politically advantageous." Akitada felt a pang of shame for Kosehira, but who was he to criticize another man for striving to assure his children's success? The entire Fujiwara clan kept their power within the family. It was all the more puzzling that Kosehira had bestowed his favorite daughter on a mere Sugawara.

They sat in silence, thinking about the situation. After some hesitation, Nakatoshi asked, "What is Kosehira's explanation?"

"He has been too ill to question closely. Besides there were always people around him. He may not have an explanation. He may not know much about Yorimune."

Nakatoshi grimaced. "Unlikely, I'd say. He must have thought about him before arranging the marriage of their children."

And this was also true, though Kosehira was naïve and trusting to a fault when it came to people.

Akitada sighed again and rose, "Please see what you can learn. I'm actually worried about him. He may have been the target along with Yorimune. And that means he remains in danger."

Nakatoshi nodded and walked with him to the door.

Akitada made his way next to the Ministry of Popular Affairs where he asked to see records from Tamba and Tosa provinces. The archivist did not question his authority, bowing quite deeply to Akitada's rank colors. Akitada had reached the junior fifth rank, upper grade, and knew that there would be no more promotions. The ranks above him were reserved for the decision makers, and they were almost exclusively imperial family members and Fujiwaras.

He sorted out quickly the entries for the years of Yorimune's governorships in both provinces. In Tamba, Yorimune had been a mere twenty-three years old. Akitada noted the year when the young courtier had been sent there: it had been in 998. Tamba was an unimportant province, but it was quite close to the capital. Whatever Yorimune had done to be sent away, his family had seen to it that it did not entail too many hardships and they could keep an eye on him. The documentation revealed nothing out of the ordinary during Yorimune's four years as governor. Toward the end of his stewardship there were some complaints about unfair taxation, but no personal misdeeds were noted. Of course, the proximity to the capital meant that he had paid frequent visits home.

The appointment to Tosa Province was another matter altogether. Tosa was quite large but it was a great distance from the capital and could only be reached via the Inland Sea. It was part of Shikoku and only slightly closer than Kyushu, the exile province of choice in the far West. The year of his appointment was 1020. Not too much time had passed after Yorimune's return home from Tamba before he had apparently offended again, and this time his punish-

ment was Tosa. Again the documents offered no reasons for this or mentioned his behavior while in Tosa.
Here, however, a number of riots had broken out
against provincial tax collectors, and Yorimune seemed
to have judged these harshly.

All of this was a long time ago. Almost 40 years
had passed since the first appointment. After Tosa,
Yorimune had apparently behaved acceptably. Akitada
briefly considered that Michinaga, the great Fujiwara
prime minister and grandfather of several emperors,
had died in 1028. Michinaga had probably been behind
Yorimune's punitive removals from the capital.

It was not much, but his research had given
Akitada two dates: 998 and 1020. In those years or the
years immediately before, since governorships were
generally announced at the beginning of a year,
Yorimune had been involved in something sufficiently
shocking that it had been thought wise to send him
away.

But would a victim wait this long to enact his
revenge?

No point in trying to find answers until he had
all the facts. He walked to his own ministry, where he
grabbed a youngster, who was loitering in the corridor,
and told him to pull information about offenses committed in the capital in the years 997-998 and 1019-
1020. The boy's face fell, and since Akitada recalled his
own miserable years in the ministry when he was this
youngster's age, he relented.

"You may ask someone to help you," he said
and left.

It was midday by now and Akitada wanted to
see Kosehira. As his friend's house was in no condition
to feed visitors, so he stopped for a bowl of noodles on

the street. He found them surprisingly good and re-called with some nostalgia his days as a student when he had always been starved and practically lived on noo-dles.

Kosehira's household had the appearance of nervous normalcy. The mood established perfectly the condition of its master and mistress. Both were well enough to issue orders, though these were not always reassuring. Lady Hatsuko had sent urgently for ice to cool her husband's room. "Fever?" the servants mut-tered to each other.

Akitada found his friend alert but flushed and restless. He was also in pain.

"There you are," Kosehira said, looking irrita-ble. "They're driving me mad with visitors and doctors and food."

"Oh," said Akitada, "should I leave again and let you rest?"

"Nonsense! I meant the others. Come sit be-side me and tell me what you've learned."

Akitada sat and looked at his friend. He was not only flushed, but his eyes looked feverish. "Allow me?" he said and touched Kosehira's forehead. It was quite hot. Kosehira pushed his hand away.

"I'm all right," he snapped. "So much fussing!"

"You're feverish and you're in quite a lot of pain," Akitada informed him.

"What? Are you turning into a physician now?"

"I recall times when I was hurt and you sat be-side me and worried."

Kosehira looked away and blinked. "Not the same," he muttered.

"Perhaps not. You're more seriously wounded. That arrow went all the way through you."

Kosehira moved his shoulder and grimaced. "No need to tell me."

"What does your doctor think?"

"Oh, you know those doctors of medicine. Half their skills have more to do with chasing away evil spirits and painting magic signs on paper."

Akitada chuckled. "I did think your man was a bit more practical."

There was a brief silence, then Kosehira said, "I asked you what you've found out."

"Not much. I've been proceeding on the assumption that this was meant for Yorimune."

"Well, it couldn't have been me. But why Yorimune? And his wife? And the two girls?"

"Yorimune used to have a bad reputation. Maybe someone from his past wanted revenge."

Kosehira was silent for a moment. "It's possible. What did he do exactly?"

"I'd hoped you'd know."

"No. You and I were still students when he went away to his first post. And later I was governor myself. Besides, you know I never had much to do with the court."

Akitada bit his lip. He had not expected this. Surely, Kosehira would know something about family secrets, even if only vaguely. Worse, he was not sure if Kosehira was covering for Yorimune. He said, "You were closely related. And you decided to link your two families even more closely with Arihito's marriage."

Kosehira moved irritably and gasped with pain. Through clenched teeth, he said, "I would hardly have chosen Yorimune for Arihito's father-in-law if I'd known of some terrible deed in his past."

"No, of course not. Forgive me. And now is not the time to talk about this. You're in pain. Is the doctor in your house?

Kosehira closed his eyes. "I don't know and I don't care. I'm very tired all of a sudden. Forgive me."

Akitada touched his hand and left quietly.

8

The Schoolmaster

He went home and fretted the rest of the day about Kosehira, though it was his condition that was foremost in his mind. The fact that his friend had not been forthcoming with information about Yorimune he put to the back of his mind. Late in the day he sent for news, and was told that Kosehira rested. The following morning, he sent again. Kosehira was apparently much the same, and Akitada fretted again.

He intended to go see for himself, taking Sadako with him for a visit with Lady Hatsuko, when Tora came to tell him he had a visitor. It turned out to be an old acquaintance: his son's former tutor. Tora said the man was agitated and had clearly come for help of some sort. Akitada went to speak to his wife who was getting dressed to go out.

Seeing her bent over her mirror to apply small touches of color to her face brought a smile to his own. "Come, my love," he said, "You're much too beautiful already. Do you want to make poor Lady Hatsuko feel even worse? I'm sure she'll be in no condition to dress for your visit."

Sadako looked guilty. "Oh. I hadn't thought. Maybe a plainer gown? Do you think she'll care?"

He chuckled. "No, she'll be happy to see you, but you must go alone. Yoshi's tutor has come to speak to me. I'll follow as soon as I can."

"Yoshi's tutor? You mean Tanizaki? But Yoshi doesn't have a tutor any longer. Or is something wrong?"

"Not with Yoshi— I hope. No, I think it's a personal problem."

The tutor was waiting in Akitada's study. He had aged; his hair was nearly gray and so was his small beard. When Akitada entered, he bowed instantly, and it was the gray hair that Akitada noted first.

"Good morning, Tanizaki," Akitada said. "It's been a while, but I'm very glad to see you again."

The tutor straightened. He was pale and agitated, and he gasped a little as he said, "Thank you, sir. I could wish . . . it were under better circumstances . . . I trust Yoshitada is well and . . . em . . . making good progress at the university."

"Yes, thanks to your efforts he's doing well. Is something wrong?"

"Yes, sir. I need help." To Akitada's dismay the elderly man began to weep; choking tears and sobs shook his body.

"Please be seated, Tanizaki. Allow me to send for some warm wine. Or perhaps some tea?"

The tutor sat and tried to stop weeping. "No, n-nothing, sir. Very kind, but I couldn't. My wife. I found her. Dead. I can't believe it." He sobbed again.

Akitada felt slightly sick. Not more death! He said, "That's terrible. When was that?"

The tutor wiped his face with his sleeve, sniffed, and tried to control his tears. "This morning. When I went to her room, there she was. And there was blood everywhere." He gulped. "I went closer to see what was wrong and she'd been stabbed." He gulped again. "Stabbed many times. And she was dead." His head sank and he took a shuddering breath. "What shall I do? Dear gods, what shall I do?"

Akitada waited a moment, then he asked gently. "What do you think happened?"

The older man looked up. "I don't know. There wasn't anyone there. Her maid went to visit her family. There was no one in the house but my wife and I."

"Do you lock your house at night?"

"Yes, yes. Always. The neighborhood's got so bad. It's my parents' house. I always lock up when we go to bed."

"You didn't sleep with your wife?"

The other man flushed painfully. "Not that night," he mumbled.

Akitada waited, hoping for more, but nothing else of substance came. Tanizaki moaned and pleaded,

"I need your help, sir. The police will arrest me for murdering her. Please!"

Akitada sighed inwardly. Tanizaki had picked the worst day to ask for help. He had no time for the tutor's dilemma. Apparently the man was afraid he would be accused of the murder because he had been alone in the house with the victim, though Akitada suspected there was something else that might implicate him. He felt guilty brushing the man off so quickly, then had an idea. "Perhaps you had better show me. We'll take Tora along. He's been very useful to me in the past."

The tutor burst into grateful speech and bowed so deeply that his head touched the floor.

Tora came quickly, all interest, and Akitada filled him in as they followed Tanizaki. The tutor headed across the city to the western side. Akitada knew it well. His first wife's father had had his house here. There were still a number of fine old houses standing in overgrown gardens, abandoned by their noble owners for more fashionable quarters in the eastern half of the city and even in the eastern mountains.

Tanizaki lived in one of the old houses, somewhat to Akitada's surprise, because he had not thought the tutor could afford a house of this size, even in the unfashionable part of town. But Tanizaki had been right: all around the substantial property were abandoned ruins, leaning shacks, a few dilapidated row houses for multiple families, and other ramshackle shelters built by the poor. Most likely, the inhabitants included a number of criminals.

When Tanizaki unlatched the gate, Akitada said, "What an impressive property. Your family must have been wealthy."

Tanizaki stopped. He seemed to welcome a chance to talk. "We are descended from a branch of the Ki family," he said proudly. "My ancestors served in the government like you, sir." This embarrassed Akitada who had always treated Tanizaki as an upper servant. Tanizaki added a little sadly, "I'm afraid we've come down in the world. When I finished my studies, the only work I could find was tutoring or being a city clerk. I liked tutoring better. Now, of course, I'm a schoolmaster, which is a step up."

"You've done well then." Akitada realized too late the inappropriateness of the remark and cleared his throat.

Tanizaki had not noticed. Her stared at the house with a look of panic. He muttered, "Thank you, sir. I teach at the Tachibana school. I teach Chinese history. But I'm afraid the house is not in very good shape."

Tora, who had said little so far, now said impatiently, "How about going in and taking a look, Tanizaki?"

"Oh! Yes. Oh, dear!" The schoolmaster swayed a little.

Akitada said firmly, "Come, let's get it over with. You must pull yourself together. You can grieve later."

This seemed to do the trick, for Tanizaki now hurried along the path and used his key on the door to the house. They stepped into semi-darkness. The house was large, the space divided by many walls. It was unnaturally silent. Tanizaki had stopped in a hallway that led into even deeper darkness. He started shaking again.

Akitada said, "Please tell us the way. You needn't come yourself."

Tanizaki pointed. "The last door on the right."

They walked down the long hallway. Near the last door, Akitada caught the familiar, sickening smell of blood. The door, a sliding one, stood half open. Inside, a feeble lamp had almost used up its oil. By its light, they could make out the figure on the floor and approached it. She lay on her back in her undergown with her hair tumbled about her. Her bedding was unrolled near her. The white undergown was so soaked in blood it almost looked black in the feeble light.

To Akitada's surprise, she was a young, pretty woman, her hair glossy and her face strangely peaceful for someone who had died from such violence. There was a lot of blood and it was still somewhat fresh and wet. Akitada felt her neck. The skin was already cold and clammy.

"Dead?" Tora asked, peering over his shoulder.

"Oh, yes." Akitada stood and looked around. "That lamp is about to go out. Let's find more light."

Tanizaki had crept a little closer in the corridor. "Is she . . .?"

"Your wife is dead," Akitada said. He had expected her to be someone Tanizaki's age. As it was, the dead woman might have been his daughter. It was not his place to judge the man, given his own foolish marriage to Yukiko, his beautiful, but adulterous ex-wife, but his own history raised a host of new possibilities in his mind. For a schoolmaster, having a beautiful young wife seemed unnecessarily self-indulgent and possibly foolish. Was there another, older wife? He asked, "You live here alone with your wife?"

"Yes, yes. I told you." Tanizaki wrung his hands. "This is horrible. Who could have killed Tomoko?"

"And you have no children?"

"No children." Tanizaki looked sick and gulped as if he might vomit.

Akitada asked, "Where can we find lamps and candles?"

Tanizaki turned. "This way. In the kitchen."

The kitchen was not outside but part of the house. It was in the back and a step lower than the rest of the floors. It had probably been added at a later time, when the outbuildings had been lost. Like everything else it was large but worn and plain. A rice cooker was built into the stone floor and bins, casks, and large baskets stood along its walls. Wooden chests and shelves held small utensils, and pots hung suspended from the rafters. A set of narrow steps led to a loft that was probably used for storage. It all seemed much too large for two people. There was no fire under the rice cooker. Tora went to check the door that led outside and found it solidly barred from the inside.

They carried candles and oil lamps back to the room, then lit and distributed them about the dead woman. Tanizaki hovered just outside the door. He asked anxiously, "Should I have sent for a doctor?"

Akitada was busy studying the wounds, while Tora prowled around. There seemed to be seven stab wounds, mostly to her upper body, though the weapon had sliced open a palm and another slash had cut her upper arm.

The wounds to her hand and arm indicated that she must have defended herself, but her killer had made short work of her. The chest wounds were all deep. Akitada asked Tanizaki, "Did you remove a knife?"

Tanizaki's voice rose in horror. "No. I didn't see one."

"Did you see a knife anywhere, Tora?"

"No, sir. No knife. No bloody clothes."

Akitada nodded. He had checked Tanizaki's black robe already and, while he could not be completely certain, it looked clean. He stood up and looked around him. This was a woman's room. There were clothing trunks for the four seasons, a small silver mirror, two clothes racks covered with robes and sashes, several combs on a small bamboo table, and an open lacquer box containing assorted paints and tooth blackening containers, as well as ribbons and hair oil. Akitada was familiar with such things, having had three wives. One, Yukiko, had been particularly lavish with face paints and other methods to make herself beautiful in the eyes of the court. Akitada preferred his wives to cover up their natural appearance as little as possible. Tanizaki's wife had clearly been used to painting her face during the daytime. Had she been pleasing her elderly husband?

Tanizaki still shuffled nervously outside the door. To be quite sure, Akitada asked him, "Did you sleep at home last night?"

The schoolmaster jumped. "Yes, er, yes. I always sleep here."

"But not in this room?"

"No. Well, not last night. Tomoko said she had a headache and wanted to go to bed early."

"Where exactly did you sleep?"

"In my study. I sleep in my study when I . . . when I'm by myself."

"Show me!"

Tanizaki hurried down the corridor with Akitada on his heels. He opened a door, saying, "Here."

This room was also spacious. It had shutters that were closed and barred. Akitada went to open them. He looked into a small graveled garden with a lantern, a pine tree, and some mossy stones: a scholar's garden. It was surrounded by tall fencing.

The room itself, now that he could see it better, was also a scholar's domain. There was a desk, a bamboo rack holding quite a number of books, a writing box, and an armrest. Tanizaki's bedding still lay spread out on the floor. Tora poked around in corners and inspected the contents of trunks.

"You have only the one servant?" Akitada asked. "The maid who is absent?"

"A man comes sometimes to look after the garden and to do the heavy work. But my wife and I, we do most things for ourselves."

Tanizaki had calmed down considerably. Perhaps it was because he no longer needed to face his murdered wife. He had wept before, but Akitada could not be sure if it had been out of fear for himself or because of grief for his loss. He stood staring at the schoolmaster, pulling his earlobe as he pondered the situation.

Tanizaki blinked and moved nervously. "Wh-what do you think, sir?"

"I wonder that you didn't hear your wife screaming. I'm sure she must have been screaming. She received a number of wounds before she died."

Tanizaki paled. "I'm a very deep sleeper," he said. "It must have been one of the thugs who live in this part of town."

"But you said the house was locked up."

"I don't know. He must have crept in some-place. Maybe he came through the roof."

They looked up. These old houses had steep roofs and used to have smoke holes above open fire-places, but Tanizaki's home no longer had an open fireplace. Still it might be possible to enter through the roof. Both Akitada and Tora knew thieves who made a practice of it.

"Do you keep a lot of money here?"

"No. I'm a poor man, but we've always kept to ourselves and people may have thought we were wealthy."

The items Akitada had seen in the two rooms were of some value, but they were not new. He frowned. "And you said you were here all night?"

Tanizaki was twisting his hands again. "I slept here, in this room, as I said. What will happen to me?"

Akitada sighed. "I expect the police will arrest you."

Tanizaki paled and staggered. "No, oh, no! You must save me!"

9

Tora Takes Over

"Look, Tanizaki," Akitada said a little impatiently, "you came to me for advice. That's all I can give you. You should have gone to the police immediately."

Tora joined them. He said, "I've looked around, sir. No sign of a knife in the other rooms. But there were knives in the kitchen, of course. Clean. And I haven't searched this room."

Tanizaki cried, "You cannot suspect me! She was my wife. Why would I kill my wife? Oh, gods in heaven and on earth, if *you* think I did it, I'm truly lost." He sank to his knees and started to weep again.

Akitada said coldly, "Go ahead and search, Tora."

Silence fell, while Tora systematically probed all the trunks, boxes, and containers, shook out the bedding, and felt along any beams that he could reach. No knife turned up. Tanizaki watched, heaving a sob now and then and beginning to look more cheerful. When Tora was done, he said, "See! I told you. I'm innocent."

Tora shook his head. "Doesn't prove anything. You could've tossed the knife into a canal on your way to see us."

Tanizaki wailed. "No, no! I didn't. Why do you do this to me?"

Akitada sighed. "We had to check. The police will do the same. It doesn't mean much if the killer came from the outside."

Tanizaki got to his feet. "Oh, yes. Of course. Yes, he must have done so. You will take it on then, sir? You'll find Tomoko's killer?"

"I regret I cannot. I shall be working on the murder of Minister Yorimune and his family. But Tora will see what can be done. You can speak to him. But first you must go and report the murder to the police. And mind you, tell the truth and don't leave anything out!" He said the last with particular firmness and a stern look.

Tanizaki looked offended. "Of course I shall do that." Then he glanced at Tora and was cast back into misery.

Akitada turned to leave, waving to Tora to come along. Back on the street outside the house, he stopped and said, "I think he's hiding something. I'd like you to chat with his neighbors." He gestured at the run-down and disreputable habitations, smiled, and added, "This should be perfect for your special skills. Keep me informed."

Tora grinned. "So you think he's been lying? But why? Unless he did it."

"I don't know why, Tora. That's for you to find out."

Tora glanced at the shacks and leaning buildings. "They aren't really neighbors, sir. Tanizaki locked his doors against them. They won't know anything about him and his wife. Unless one of them did it."

"It's been my impression that the poor people who live among us and who rarely ever come to our notice watch us with the greatest attention. I expect you'll learn a lot about the schoolmaster."

Tora watched his master walk away with mixed feelings. In a way, he was enormously pleased to be given this case, a serious murder case involving a respected man of learning, and in another, he regretted that it now prevented him from working side by side with his master on the massacre in Shirakawa.

With a sigh, he turned toward the nearest dwelling.

This happened to be a one-room shed put together from remnants of old buildings. There was not much of it, but the size of the salvaged timbers gave it a certain magnificence. It had a wide and high doorway with a door which stood open. Tora walked in. The roof was lopsided, but it rested on heavy columns. Patched *tatami* of assorted sizes covered a floor made from assorted boards. The back of the shed was open, and Tora saw a kitchen with a fire pit under a slanting roof of boards held up by two more massive columns.

The place belonged to a tailor and his wife. They were actually both tailors, though Tora knew well enough that it would be the husband who handled the

business, such as it was. He judged from the clothing he
saw hanging from nails and piled in corners that the
clientele was poor and the clothes were adaptations
from robes and trousers that had belonged to more
successful people. A tailor of second-hand clothing.

Both tailors were home and both wielded needles and thread. Tora had entered politely, with a small
bow and a, "Good morning to you, friends."

They were middle-aged, or had aged prema-
turely from their labors and their habitual postures of
sitting bent over their work. But they had sharp eyes
that gauged Tora's clothing and deduced his background and likelihood of spending any money. And
that meant they lost interest quickly. They did not reply,
but nodded.

"I'm Tora," Tora informed them, sitting down
uninvited. "I'm here because something happened in
the house over there." He pointed over his shoulder.
"Where the schoolmaster lives."

This sparked interest in their eyes. The woman
asked, "What happened?"

"The schoolmaster's wife is dead."

They looked at each other. Then the woman
asked, "Did he kill her?"

Tora raised his brows. "What makes you think
that?"

She grinned, showing bad teeth. "He's old.
She's young and pretty. That's never good."

Tora considered this. "He says he didn't do it.
He says someone came into the house at night and
killed her."

The woman chuckled. "There! I knew it. He
murdered her!"

Her husband gave her a look. "Stop grinning like a cat, woman! Someone's been killed." He turned to Tora. "There's been killings in the mountains. This have anything to do with that?"

Tora was surprised that the news of Shirakawa had reached this slum. "No, of course not. Why would you think so?"

The tailor looked at a small family altar with a roughly carved Buddha figure and bowed to it. "When the nobles start killing each other, they upset the gods, and all sorts of evil spirits come out. One evil begets another evil. We'll none of us be safe in the capital."

Tora suppressed a shudder. The idea of evil spirits roaming the city struck a chord with him and for a moment he considered the possibility. But better sense prevailed and he said quite firmly—as his master would have—"Nonsense!"

They both looked at him doubtfully. The wife said, "Then what's been going on over there? They lock the place up tight all day and night. Who could get in unless he wasn't human?"

Tora felt his scalp prickle. The schoolmaster had said himself that he always locked the house. Locking up a house did not, of course, stop spirits. But his extensive experience with riffraff told him that there were people who could enter even the most tightly locked up houses. Perhaps a thief had crept in and been surprised by the wife, so he had had to kill her.

He asked, "What sort of man is this Tanizaki?"

They looked at each other again. The tailor grunted. His wife smirked and said, "He went out a lot at night."

Tora was astonished. "At night? What for?"

73

"Probably getting a well-deserved cup of wine," the tailor said, giving his wife a look. "A man works all day, his throat gets dry. Why shouldn't he go and have a cup or two?"

She glared back. "Schoolmasters don't drink," she announced. "And neither should tailors. It's a waste of money and you know you can't work the next day."

"Shut up, woman!" he snarled. "Always bitching. Never satisfied. Maybe the schoolmaster got tired of his wife's bad humor." He flung the garment he was working on across the room and stomped out.

"Go on then, Fool!" the wife screeched after him. "See if I cook your rice tonight."

Tora decided he had outstayed his welcome and took his leave.

He spent the next few hours knocking on other doors, or rather, shouting his arrival through a variety of tattered door curtains or across small vegetable patches surrounding leaning sheds. He gained little for his troubles. Most of the people who answered said they knew nothing of the murder and little about Tanizaki's household. The knowledge that he kept his doors locked was widespread and resented. They did take a great interest in the incident, however, asking many questions about the nature of the crime and what the body looked like. Tora fended these off the best he knew how.

Only one minor piece of news surfaced. A very old woman sitting under a shade tree mumbled something about children in the schoolmaster's house. Since she was quite aged and given to mumbling to herself, Tora was not sure if she was in her right mind, but filed the fact away for later.

10

An Unpleasant Encounter

Having passed the former tutor's problem on to Tora, Akitada went to see how Kosehira was doing.

The Fujiwara compound, on a city block the same size as his own residence, was immeasurably more luxurious inside and out. Servants in matching clothing moved about busily, horses were being exercised, a boy was sweeping up leaves under a stand of trees, and on old man was raking the gravel. The activity was reassuring. Akitada climbed the stairs to the main house and was met by Kosehira's majordomo.

"My Lord. Welcome!" The elderly man bowed, then smiled at Akitada. "His lordship will be glad to see you, sir."

Akitada smiled back. "He's better then?"

"We hope so. He's very demanding and shouts quite a bit."

Akitada chuckled. "Both are good signs."

The majordomo nodded. "We think so, sir. Come along."

As he followed the man inside, Akitada asked, "And her ladyship?"

"She is resting, sir."

Kosehira was sitting up, leaning on an armrest and frowning. His face cleared when he saw Akitada. "There you finally are!" he growled. "What took you so long? This infernal wound is keeping me from seeing to things." His face gleamed with perspiration.

Akitada sat down beside him. "You are feverish. What are you doing up? You should be lying still. This is bound to be painful and may set the wound to bleeding again."

"People die lying down. I'm not about to make it that easy."

"I've seen people die standing up. You're being stubborn and silly."

For a moment it looked as though Kosehira would burst into resentful speech, but then his features smoothed and he smiled. "Yes, elder brother," he said meekly. "Forgive me. As always you know best. Help me lie down again, but then let's talk."

This effort was clearly painful and brought more sweat to Kosehira's face. He cursed softly under his breath, but eventually relaxed, his head resting on a wooden pillow. Akitada saw a small pile of tissues and used some to dab his friend's face. Seeing him in such pain and still so feverish made him fearful again.

"Did your physician leave some pain medicine for you?"

"It makes me feel like vomiting. Better this way." Kosehira caught Akitada's hand. "You know I love you like a brother? No, better than my brothers. You are the brother I found for myself. I love you, Akitada."

Akitada squeezed the hand and blinked away tears. "I'm honored, younger brother. You are in my heart also."

"Silly trouble over Yukiko! Have you forgiven me?"

Akitada's fears increased. Was Kosehira preparing for the long farewell? He said, "There was nothing to forgive, but I'm sorry I offended you. Sorry I brought you pain. I did not mean to."

"No, no. My fault entirely. Silly girl! I love her too much, you know."

"One cannot love a child too much."

Kosehira's hand relaxed. "Perhaps not. She turned away from me and I was very angry with her, but she brought me her child to raise. Another little girl, quite as perfect as her mother was. I'm loving this child as much as I loved and still love her mother."

The child was a sore point for Akitada. The little girl was the result of a torrid love affair between his young wife Yukiko and a court noble while Akitada was far away, serving as governor in Mikawa Province. Akitada, confronted with her unfaithfulness by Yukiko, had offered to raise the child as his own to avoid the scandal if the matter became known. But Yukiko had refused to leave her position at court and her lover, and Akitada had finally divorced her. That was what lay between them now.

These memories made him sigh, and Kosehira released his hand. "I'm sorry, Akitada," he murmured.

"It was none of your doing. You merely wished the best for both of us. Alas, our karma did not permit us to find the happiness you hoped for. How is your little granddaughter?"

His friend's face brightened. "Very well. She's walking and talking. She's a very bright child." He paused than added, "But she is my daughter. I adopted her."

"Yes. I remember." It had been a good solution to a bad affair. Yukiko had not married her lover.

"And what about you? Any hope of more children?"

"Sadako lost a child, a little boy, recently. I'm afraid another pregnancy will kill her."

Kosehira patted his hand. "I'm sorry, my friend. Fortune and misfortune are a tightly woven rope."

A brief silence fell as they contemplated their past and current lives.

Akitada said, "Have you thought at all about Yorimune?"

"Oh, that. Nothing in my memory, but one of my cousins happened to reminisce about Yorimune. He didn't mean to blame the man, who was young then anyway, but he mentioned an incident that upset the previous emperor. It was during the First Fruits Festival. You know how the court clings to those old Shinto observances. Well, it's an excuse to have a big party. The banquet always serves lots of *sake* made from that year's rice and a grand fish dinner. There are entertainments and everybody gets drunk. The dance rehearsals take days and the emperor himself rewards the young men and women who are performing with a special serving of wine. A lot of boys from the temples are involved. Well, Yorimune and his friends, who must have been about twenty-one or –two, got drunk and amorous.

There were no women around, so they turned their attention to some very pretty novices." Kosehira sighed.

Appalled, Akitada asked, "What happened?"

"My cousin says one of the novices got raped. Repeatedly."

"By Yorimune?"

"By him and some of the other young men."

"Horrible. If Yorimune was twenty-two, this would explain why he was sent off to Tamba."

Kosehira sighed again. "Maybe. The emperor found out and was very angry. And Michinaga was head of the family then."

"Who was the novice?"

"No idea."

"From a good family?"

"Oh, yes."

"It's certainly serious enough for an act of revenge."

"It was too long ago. Why wait so long?"

This had been the problem all along. Akitada felt that Yorimune must have done something far more recently to bring about the extraordinary revenge by the armed warrior.

He took his leave soon after and was walking out through the large, ornate reception room, when a door opened and a woman slipped in with a rustle of rich silks.

They saw each other simultaneously and both stopped.

"You!" she said.

"Good morning, Yukiko." He kept his voice mild.

"What are you doing here?"

"Your father is my friend."

"You have never been a good friend to him. Why don't you stay out of our lives?"

There was perhaps some truth in the first remark. The second, uncalled for though it was, also made him feel guilty. It showed how much he had hurt her. She had married him, thinking to find the dashing hero she had thought him from her father's tales, which had surely been exaggerated. And she had found instead a staid bureaucrat who spent all his time on paperwork. Then, when a killer attacked her, he had failed to defend her. He bore a great responsibility for the hurt he had given her. The fact that she was still angry enough to lash out at him proved how great that hurt must have been. The massacre and Kosehira's injury reminded him forcibly that life was fragile and one had a duty to deal in a kindly manner with others.

He said, "You look well. More beautiful even than when I first saw you."

Yukiko had indeed grown more beautiful. Maturity had given her a classic look when it had taken away the girlish softness. She snapped, "Nonsense. I trust your new wife pleases you better than I did."

He smiled. "You're two very different women. I hope you also are happier now."

She came a little closer and he saw that her gowns were spectacular in their combination of colors and layers. Her hair, too, shimmered like silk. Yukiko wore court make-up: her face was lightly covered with white paste, her eyebrows plucked and painted, her lips a sensuous shade of crimson. It was not a style he greatly admired, but she looked very well indeed.

She studied him also. "Your hair is turning gray."

He nodded. "How are you, Yukiko? Are you still serving Her Majesty?"

She made an impatient gesture with her hand. "I'm well. I'm to be made director of the wardrobe office."

The wardrobe office was traditionally staffed by high-ranking women of the court. It carried with it a court rank and a generous income. Yukiko would gain the same rank as his own. The irony of this did not escape him. He said, "My congratulations. Are you married?"

"No. I see you haven't been discussing me with Father."

He did not comment on that. "My visit had more to do with his condition and the attack. I'm trying to find out why he and your mother were hurt. Do you happen to have any information? Perhaps Her Majesty's ladies may have mentioned something in passing?"

"You think we spend our time in idle gossip, don't you? In fact, Her Majesty regularly receives news and discusses events with her noble brothers and cousins."

"Indeed. And what news are you privy to?"

She drew herself up. "I do not discuss court matters with outsiders."

He sighed. "I'm working on your father's behalf."

"You're inventing scandals to blacken the Fujiwara reputation. Be very careful, or your pleasant existence with the charming and accommodating Sadako will come to a very unpleasant end. I came to warn Father about you."

Anger finally rose inside him. Clearly the prime minister's reaction had been passed on to all and sundry, even to Her Majesty and perhaps the emperor. She was right: these people had the power to stop him, and they did not care how they did it. He bowed, said, "I must go," and walked past her out the door.

11

The Police Investigates

After a satisfying midday meal in the market, Tora returned to the schoolmaster's house. He hoped to take another look at the premises. Surely if an intruder had murdered the man's wife, then there must be signs of his entrance.

As it turned out, he was foiled in this effort. He found the place occupied by police. They had brought the schoolmaster with them. He knelt in chains in his front garden, watched by two burly guards. He was still weeping, though his tears seemed to be for himself.

Tora, grown cynical through the years, felt that the man had been far more upset with his own situation than with his wife's murder. Tanizaki had feared being arrested. The forces of law and order might occasionally be slack in the capital, what with periodic releases of criminals in efforts to appease the gods and Buddhas and avert some calamity, but while a man was under arrest, he belonged to the constables and they specialized in dealing out the punishment they felt the miscreant deserved.

In any case, Tanizaki greeted Tora's arrival with hopeful entreaties: Tora was to explain that he was innocent of the crime, that he was a bereaved husband, that he was a law-abiding resident of the capital, that he was a schoolmaster who had never done anything illegal in his entire life, that his was a good family, an old family, that this should not be happening to people like him.

Tora promised to do what he could. He went into the house to look for whoever was in charge of the constables. To his dismay, it turned out to be a young sergeant who did not know Tora, had never heard of Lord Sugawara or Superintendent Kobe, and who seemed to believe that Tanizaki had done the deed.

"The house is empty," he said. "There's only the dead woman. Her husband says he kept the house locked up tight. His story makes no sense." He paused a moment, then added, "And you have no business here. Get out before I arrest you, too. You might be an accomplice."

Tora gaped at him. Then he frowned. "You need to learn some manners, young man. I can guess that you've come fresh from the country, because you know nothing about police work in the capital."

The sergeant whistled and two constables ran up. "Arrest this man," he commanded. "He's a suspect."

One of the constables, an older man, took a closer look at Tora. "Sergeant, that's Tora," he said.

"So? What of it? He walked in here, snooping, trying to get his friend off. He admitted he knows him. Mark my word, he's up to no good. They probably killed her together."

Tora laughed.

The sergeant turned purple with rage and slapped him. Tora roared and attacked. He pushed the sergeant back and bashed his head against the wall several times. "You son of a fox and a snake," he snarled. "How dare you strike your betters? I'll see you dismissed for this. I'll have you know I'm Lieutenant Sashima, formerly of the provincial guard of Kyushu."

The two constables stood by, watching this with interest. The sergeant grew still and rather pale. After a moment, Tora released him and stepped back. It had occurred to him that his master would not thank him for this little fracas.

He said, "You're lucky I'm not in uniform. What's your name?"

The sergeant did not answer. He was speechless.

The older constable said, "His name is Saeki, Tora. Are you really a lieutenant?"

Tora frowned at him. "Yes, I am, though I haven't been using the rank. Where did they find this Saeki. I'd have thought they'd send someone senior on this case."

"They're all busy with the murder of the grand minister and those other people. Are you and your master investigating this, Tora?"

"The master was here earlier. He told Tanizaki to report his wife's murder to the police and he told me to ask the neighbors if they'd seen anything. I came back to have another look at the house."

The sergeant had followed this conversation. He looked utterly confused. Tora glanced at him, and said, "Sorry, Sergeant, but you had no business hitting me. I guess it's because you're new. Most of them know me."

The sergeant said through gritted teeth, "I may be new here, but I know that outsiders have no business on a crime scene. My superiors wouldn't like it at all if I just let you wander around here."

Tora grinned. "You've got a point. Anyway, no hard feelings?"

Silence fell. The two constables waited to see what would happen next.

Eventually, the sergeant nodded. "No hard feelings. Did you find out anything from talking to people?"

Tora liked the fact that Saeki was more concerned with his investigation than with his dignity. He said, "They confirmed that Tanizaki kept his house locked up tight."

The sergeant said dryly, "You might wonder how they knew that."

That got him some chuckles. Tora grinned and went on, "They did think both he and his wife were snooty people but honest. I didn't catch much resentment. There was some suggestion that Tanizaki went out drinking at night."

The sergeant said, "He claims he was home all night. That's why I put him under arrest. He was lying. If he'd been there, he should have heard her screaming."

"My thought exactly."

"Then you also think he did it?"

"Not necessarily. But he did lie, I think. So where was he?"

86

Before Saeki could respond, an elderly short, fat man emerged from the room where the body was. He saw Tora and cried, "Not you again, Tora? Is Lord Sugawara investigating this one?"

Tora grinned at him. "Glad to see you on the job, Coroner. No, the master's busy with the Shirakawa business. He had me take a look. Tanizaki used to work for us. Why aren't you at Shirakawa?"

The fat man chuckled. "The great people do their own investigating. They sent back Lieutenant Hakeda. The palace guard is in charge and they use their own doctors."

"So what's your verdict, doctor?" interrupted Saeki.

The coroner looked at him. "She's dead."

Saeki bit his lip.

Tora said quickly, "Come, Doctor, let's have a bit more. When did she die? She seemed pretty stiff to me this morning."

The coroner cocked his head. "What, have you studied medicine now, Tora? Setting up in practice yourself because you're getting too old for fighting?"

Tora laughed uneasily. "I've seen a few dead people."

The coroner nodded. "So you have. Well, she died late last night—."

"When?" interrupted the sergeant. "Before or after the hour of the rat?"

The coroner answered testily. "Give me time, Saeki. Before. That's all I can tell you now. Have your constables bring her to my morgue and I'll do a more thorough investigation, but it should've been pretty obvious she was stabbed and bled to death."

They said nothing, and the coroner nodded and walked out of the house. The sergeant shook his head. Turning to the two constables, he said, "Take the schoolmaster back to the jail, and tell the others to take the body."

When they were alone, Tora asked, "Did you or your men find the weapon?"

"No. But there are plenty of long knives in the kitchen."

Tora nodded. He had already seen them. "Let's go take a look," he suggested.

They went to the small kitchen and examined the knives closely. They were of several sizes, eight of them. At least two looked murderous enough and were the right length for killing. However, all the knives were clean, a testimony to the housekeeping of the dead woman. And possibly the care of the murderer.

Tora poked around a bit, looking into bins and baskets and feeling around on high shelves. The sergeant said impatiently, "My men have done all that."

Tora nodded. "I only trust my own eyes." He peered at the narrow, tall steps that led to the storage area above the kitchen.

The sergeant said, "There's nothing up there. No way to get in. They've checked the entire roof."

"Right," said Tora and climbed the stairs. It was a laborious undertaking and reminded him that he was not only out of shape, but heavier and bigger than in his youth—or than the slender, small woman who had lived here.

The storage area was not large. It held supplies of rice, beans, and millet, as well as some turnips and large radishes. Piles of old bedding and straw mats lay under the eaves. But it was very clean and had a small window that let in light. The window's shutter stood open. Tora went to peer out. Below was the back garden. He had hoped for a lean-to shed, a ladder, or a pile of firewood that could have been used to climb up, but there was nothing, just the sheer wall. It was unlikely that anyone could have come into the house this way. With a sigh, he turned away.

Hearing voices in the kitchen below, he went back down. The sergeant had left. Tora took this as an invitation to explore the other rooms. They were empty and had not been used for a long time. None had doors to the outside. That left only the schoolmaster's study. If he had slept there, nobody could have come in that way either.

He found the sergeant in front of the house. Tanizaki was gone. The sergeant and two of his men stood around a frightened old man who trembled as they shot questions at him. Tora joined them.

"Who's this?" he asked the sergeant.

"His name's Osamu. He says he tends the garden and splits wood. He's not allowed in the house, but you know what that is worth. He's *hinin*. Their village is about a mile from here."

The old man wore rags so faded and dirty you could not distinguish any colors. He was bent and bare legged and bare armed, his skin darkened by the sun, his hair and beard white as snow. He was also frightened out of his wits. The constables kept asking him when he had last been in the house and telling him he was lying when he answered.

Tora said, "Maybe it's the truth."

The sergeant stared at him. "Look at him. He's worked here for the past five years and has never been inside that house? With the schoolmaster gone all day and his young wife alone inside?"

"He's an old man, and she wasn't raped."

One of the constables said, "He may be old, but I bet he tried and when she fought him, he stabbed her."

The sergeant told the constables, "Search him!"

The old man panicked. He turned and started to hobble away as fast as his legs could carry him. The younger constable was on him in a moment and kicked his legs out from under him. The old man fell hard and cried out. The constable put his foot on his back.

The sergeant said again, "Search him."

They balked. "He's *eta*. He's dirty."

Tora said, "Let him get up. If you treat him better, he may answer."

The sergeant growled something. The constable removed his foot and told the old man to get up. When he stood, the constable tore off his shirt and flung it aside in disgust. It fell with a thump. They all looked at the shirt which appeared to be blood-stained. The other constable stepped over and picked it up with two fingers. Several pieces of lacquered wood fell from a sleeve.

The old man whimpered. "You broke it!" He clutched his chest. Blood trickled from between his fingers.

The sergeant looked at the pieces. "It's some sort of stand. Carved. Looks expensive." He turned back to the old man and said in a threatening tone, "I thought you said you never went into the house. I think you stole this."

The old one wailed, "I didn't. She gave it to me. To mend. And now it's broken into many pieces. What will I tell the lady?"

One of the constables laughed. "That's the least of your worries, scum."

Tora looked at the object also. "I think it's a mirror stand. Lady Sugawara has one just like it."

"Where would a schoolmaster's wife get such a thing?" the sergeant asked. "He must've stolen it some place."

The old man protested. The bleeding had stopped, but it was clear now that he had cut his chest when he fell on the object.

Tora said, "It looks like someone had already glued one of the legs. I think he told the truth."

The sergeant frowned. The constable who had tripped up the old man said, "I bet he's been inside. Even if his story about mending that thing is true, he lied about being inside. I bet he came back after dark and she caught him."

"She would have had to let him in while her husband was in the house," Tora pointed out.

The sergeant sighed. "Give him back his shirt and let him go. We can always find him again."

The old man got up and put on the torn shirt. He glanced at the broken stand in Tora's hands. "Who's going to pay me?" he asked. The constable raised a threatening hand, and the old man hobbled away, muttering to himself.

They watched him. The sergeant said to Tora, "Well, we're done here. We'll take the body back to the coroner. Be seeing you."

It had all been very discouraging.

12

The Sister

Tora left the sergeant and his men with a wave of his hand and headed off after the old *eta* man. He caught up quickly and called out, "Hey, Osamu? Wait."

The old man turned. The frightened look was back on his face.

"I'm sorry you lost your earnings," Tora said. "Let me make it up to you." He took a piece of silver from his belt and extended it to the old man who looked at it blankly. "Go ahead and take it. All work should be paid for. Those constables behaved badly."

The old man looked up at him. "You're not with them?"

"No. I work for Lord Sugawara. They treated you roughly because the schoolmaster's wife has been murdered. Murder upsets the police and they tend to take out their anger on anyone."

"Murder?" Osamu started shaking. "She's dead? I didn't do it."

"No. That's why they let you go. Here, take the coin."

The old man nodded and took it. "This is too much."

"Well, it's to make up for the bad treatment."

Osamu was not completely convinced of Tora's good intentions. "What do you want?"

Tora gave him a smile. "Nothing. Or maybe just a chat. Did you like the schoolmaster?"

"He paid me for my work."

"You don't happen to know if he was home the night she was killed?"

Osamu shook his head. "I didn't go there that day. I'm never there at night."

"Did you like his wife?"

Panic made the old man step away from him. "I didn't touch her."

"I believe you. I meant was she friendly when you worked there? Kind?"

Osamu thought about this. "She was like him. Only more so."

"What do you mean?"

"I'm *eta*. And he was one of the good people. You expect them to turn their heads when they see us. She used to be *hinin* herself, but he made her his wife and now she's better than us. She never let me forget it."

It was clear that the wife's manner had rankled. For a moment, Tora wondered if perhaps this old man might have become angry enough to kill the young

94

woman. But it was not likely, given his age, though he must be fairly strong and used to hard work. He asked, "How do you know she was *hinin*?"

"I have a daughter in the quarter. She knows all about her. The schoolmaster's wife used to work in her place. The schoolmaster was crazy for her, so she took all his money and when he had nothing left, she made him marry her."

Tora was so overjoyed by this information that he reached into his sash and gave Osamu another silver coin. "Where does your daughter work?"

The old man was flabbergasted by such generosity. He tucked this coin away also and grinned. "You want to know about the quarter? I can tell you all about that. I can take you and show you."

"Not necessary. I know my way around the willow world. Married a dancer from there. So, your daughter works there?"

The old man nodded proudly. "Hanishi was a choja and saved her money. She bought the *hananoya*. Now she owns several houses. Nariko still works for her."

"Nariko?"

"She's Tanizaki's wife's sister."

"Really?" Tora could not believe his luck. He refrained from reaching for another piece of silver, however, and instead thanked the old man for his information. They parted on excellent terms, with Osamu offering to supply more information as it might be needed.

Tora knew the willow quarter well. He had spent much of his youth there before marrying Hanae. Hanae used to be a talented dancer and much in demand at the sort of parties attended by the "good" people. She had not yet moved into the world of prostitution and as he forbade her continuing to work in that world, she equally firmly forbade her husband's casual excursions in that direction.

Since then he had lived many years of marital bliss, and the willow quarter, like all things in life, had undergone changes. Beautiful young women came and went. Many fell into abject poverty, some married, others invested their earnings wisely in the business. It was a very lucrative business for its stars.

The *hananoya* was a large building heavily decorated with lacquer and gilt. Many-colored paper lanterns hung about it, and lovely young faces peered from windows covered with carved grilles. He walked in, feeling a strange rush of memories accompanied by a surge of excitement. He was no longer young, but here, perhaps, it was possible to relive that intoxicating time for a short while.

His excitement faded a little when he saw that the *hananoya*'s clientele were mostly middle-aged and old men. The reception area held these hopeful customers and several young women, some of whom looked younger than Tora's son. He reminded himself that it had always been thus. The old men had the money and they wanted to buy themselves some youth, to spend a few hours forgetting their age, believing themselves to be attractive to these pretty young women.

Tora banished his gloom with the thought that he was here to investigate a murder. Not for him all this frivolous activity. When the auntie approached him with many bows and invitations to meet some lovely young women who had been pining for such a handsome man, he eyed her sharply and said, "You must be Hanishi. Your father told me about you."

Her face fell and she became nervous, looking around to see if anyone had heard. "I don't use my former name anymore," she said. "I am Miyagi-san here. Please come to my office. It's too noisy here."

He grinned and followed her into a tiny room, just large enough for two people, a small desk with paperwork and a sizable money chest heavily reinforced with metal bands and locks.

She gestured to a cushion. "Please sit down. What does my father want?"

"Nothing. He mentioned to me that you employ a woman called Nariko."

She heaved a sigh of relief and gave him a smile. "Ah, and you wish to meet her? She's such a talented girl. You'll enjoy your evening."

"I just want to talk to her. Has she been told about her sister?"

"What about her sister?"

"She was murdered last night."

Her hand went to her mouth. "No, not Tomoko?"

"Yes, Tomoko. I understand she also used to work here?"

"That is so. Amida! Poor Tomoko. What happened?"

"Nobody knows for certain but the police have arrested her husband."

She stared at him in horror. "Oh, no! And him such a fine man. Such a fine family. An old family! Tomoko was so lucky."

Tora thought this a ridiculous comment under the circumstances. The auntie caught it belatedly. She said, "I didn't mean that. It's just so shocking. At the time, we all thought how lucky she was. Her sister was so jealous. But how terrible that he should have killed her! Why? What did she do?"

That, too, was revealing. Miyagi-san assumed immediately that the victim must have been to blame. And then there was the sister's jealousy. All sorts of undercurrents swirled in the atmosphere of courtesans and entertainers.

But there was the matter of the money. Tanizaki was not a rich man. Tora asked, "He bought her out?"

"No. Tomoko had already paid back her purchase price. She could have made a good deal of money still, but she wanted to be respectable." The auntie shook her head. It was not clear if this was because Tomoko had foolishly preferred a respectable, but penniless schoolmaster or because she had had her respectable life snatched away from her.

"Was she happy about her decision? What did she tell you about her marriage?"

The auntie waved a hand and snorted. "That one? Come back here to the quarter? Never! She didn't want to remind her fine new husband and his family of where she came from."

Tora was surprised. "But he married her after finding her here."

"And then he was ashamed of her. It didn't stop him from coming to the quarter himself."

"What? Even after he married Tomoko?"

"Not here to the *hananoya*. I heard he visited elsewhere." The auntie snorted again. "Some men are like that. They come to the women in the quarter at night, thinking they are wallowing in mud, and the next day they pretend it never happened." She smirked suddenly. "Mind you, they pay for it. We women have feelings, too."

Tora chuckled. "Good for you."

Miyagi-san smiled, then grew serious. "I guess you came to tell her sister about it. She'll be upset. They were close, those two." She got up, saying, "Wait here!"

Tora waited and wondered about the sisters. They had been close, but there had also been jealousy. Then he wondered about the schoolmaster. He thought the man had nothing to be so proud of. He was a poor man by most standards. It now appeared that he had spent what he had on women. This schoolmaster, for all his respectability, had a taste for the floating life, and apparently the dead Tomoko had been unable to break him from his bad habits. Such a man might well have been tempted to kill an inconvenient wife.

The door opened and a splendidly dressed female with a heavily made-up face tripped in, bowing repeatedly. "I'm Nariko," she announced in a high, girlish voice. "I'm honored to serve the gentleman."

The auntie clearly had not told Nariko why he was here. He said, "Please sit down."

His manner puzzled her. She crept close to him, knelt and touched his knee. The scent of her hair oil was almost overpowering. "Why so unhappy?" she whispered. "Will you let little Nariko put a smile on your face?"

Tora did not know how to start.

She leaned even closer and murmured into his ear. Her words were frank to the point of obscenity and she followed them up by touching his groin.

"Stop that!" Tora roared, pushing her questing hand away.

She recoiled, and he felt sorry. This was no way to tell this woman of her sister's murder. He silently cursed the auntie.

He said, "Forgive me, Nariko, but I'm not here as a customer. I bring bad news."

The shock on her face changed to fear. "What? What's happened?"

He was blunt, not knowing how to soften the blow. "Your sister Tomoko is dead."

Her eyes widened, her mouth opened, and she cried out, "No! No! It's not true. You're lying."

Miyagi-san and two other women looked into the room. Tora waved them back out. "I'm sorry, but it's true. I saw her myself."

Nariko stared at him, then covered her face and whispered, "What happened?"

"She was found murdered in her house."

Her hands dropped into her lap. "He killed her!" she said in a normal tone of voice and with utter conviction. "The bastard killed her. Did the constables arrest him?"

"If you mean her husband, then yes, they arrested him. But he says he didn't do it."

"The bastard lied. He's always lied. From the start. I told her not to marry him."

"Did she love him?"

She gave a harsh laugh. "Love him? Are you mad? An old stick like that?"

Tora cringed inwardly. This was how these women looked at the men who came to them for comfort and a little pleasure, and he had become one of them. He said more harshly, "I expect the police will talk to you. You can tell them what you know. But remember, she married him. Why did she do that?"

Nariko was too shocked and angry to think how her words might sound to Tora. She said, "The stupid bitch wanted out of this life. She wanted to be a respectable housewife and mother. Can you imagine? And the bastard didn't have two coppers to rub together. He sold her expensive gowns and made her wear rough cotton and hemp. He wanted to sell her hair. He said she didn't need it, keeping house for him and it made her look like a slut. She was so stupid!"

All of this was news to Tora and did not fit at all well with his effort to clear the schoolmaster. And what would his master say to this story? Probably he would refuse to believe Nariko's tale. He had little respect for the life in the willow quarter.

"You went to see her?"

"Yes. She said he didn't want me to come." She started to weep. "The stupid bitch!" she mumbled through her tears. "Oh, the stupid bitch."

He knew it was grief and loss that made her talk like that. "You were close?"

She wiped her tears and looked at the black paint on her hand. "Yes," she said. "There was no one else. Our mother sold us and then she died. We had no brothers or sisters. We had nobody but each other. Oh!"

The "Oh!" was heartbreaking. She looked a fine mess by now and didn't seem to care. He reached out and put an arm around her shoulders. "I'm sorry, Nariko," he said. "Sorry it was me to bring the news. Sorry for you and sorry for her."

She choked a little, looked at him from smudged, watery eyes, and nodded. "Thank you." And after a moment: "You're kind. Would you like to come back? Some other time?" She smiled through tears and touched her face. "When I look better than this."

He smiled and patted her hand. "You look fine, and you'll do well! Courage!" And with another hug, he departed.

13

A Surprise Witness

Akitada had gone home after his meeting with Yukiko. He was sorry he had told her he was trying to find out who had hurt her parents. She would return to court and warn the prime minister that Akitada had disobeyed his order.

He worried about what would happen next but did not share his concerns with Sadako. Instead he told her about the schoolmaster's dilemma and reported on Kosehira's condition.

She was philosophical about the schoolmaster. "A terrible thing, but Tora will manage very well. Tora has a good heart."

He looked at her in surprise. It was true, of course, but he had never thought of this quality as helpful in a criminal case. His wife was a constant surprise

and delight. Greatly cheered, he spent a peaceful evening with her and an even better night. He took precau-
tions against another pregnancy, but their lovemaking
was altogether satisfying, and they fell asleep in each
other's arms.

When he woke the next morning, he knew that
he could not abandon the case of the Shirakawa assassin, regardless of the danger to himself. He decided that
he must speak to Lieutenant Hakeda again.

After hurried morning ablutions and a bowl of
rice gruel in the kitchen, he set out for police headquarters. There were two of these, one for the western half
of the city and one for the eastern. The western version
would most likely be working on the murder of the
schoolmaster's wife by now. He had almost forgotten
about that but he put the thought comfortably aside,
knowing that Tora would be dealing with it. The eastern
police headquarters were only a few blocks from his
house. In the past he would have sought out Kobe
there. The police superintendent, appointed by the
government, was usually a ranking nobleman. Kobe had
been an exception, a talented man who had been appointed due to outstanding military service and a good
university education. But Kobe had retired to a small
farm and the post now belonged to another high-
ranking official who spent little time there, and whom
Akitada did not know.

Thus, he asked for Lieutenant Hakeda and was
directed to a wing of the building, where, to his surprise,
he found Hakeda in intense conversation with Arihito.

Both stood when he entered. Neither smiled,
though Hakeda bowed.

"Lieutenant," Akitada acknowledged, and then, "Arihito? You here? Is your father . . .?" He paused, silenced by sudden fear.

Arihito nodded. "We worry about the fever," he said, "but we must be patient. It was a very bad wound."

Somewhat relieved, Akitada sat on an offered cushion, a rather threadbare item since lieutenants apparently did not deserve better. He hesitated how to start the conversation, since his rebellion against the prime minister and his family struck him as a matter for secrecy, but the lieutenant spoke first.

"I'm glad you happened to come, sir. We have some news. Well, Lord Arihito here has brought some very interesting information. We were about to look into it."

Akitada sat up a little and looked from one to the other. "News? About the killings? Please tell me. I'm vitally interested."

Arihito said, "I would have shared, sir, but there was the prime minister's interdiction . . . so I came here. I had to tell someone, and I . . . it seemed wiser not to contact anyone official." He flushed a bit. "I mean, I thought we should make sure of our facts first."

So Arihito distrusted the prime minister's people, and the lieutenant, like Akitada, had been warned off. Akitada nodded. "Very wise, but please tell me."

"There was a witness. I found him."

Akitada frowned. They had talked to all the servants and surely none of the wounded were likely to talk with Arihito. Still, it might have happened.

The lieutenant said, "It was a young wood gatherer. He was at his work in the woods and saw the armed man."

"Ah! But that is excellent. Where is he?"

"Still in his village," said Arihito. "I thought it best to leave him there."

Surprised, Akitada asked, "*You* found him? How did that happen?"

Arihito looked embarrassed. "Well, I knew both you and the lieutenant had been warned off. His Excellency did not dare speak to me in those terms, so I returned to Shirakawa. I wasn't sure I'd find anything, but I rode from village to village, asking questions. I learned nothing until I met this man on the road. I stopped, not expecting anything and asked him if he'd seen anything."

Akitada glanced at the lieutenant who smiled grimly and nodded. "Wait till you hear," he said.

Arihito flushed with excitement. "It was a lucky accident. He had heard about the massacre. They all had heard. Such news travels fast. And he said, 'I saw him!'"

Impatiently, Akitada urged, "Go on! What did he see? Did he recognize the killer?"

"He saw an armed man on a brown horse. The man was headed toward Shirakawa, toward Yorimune's villa. The time was right. It must have been the same man."

Disappointed, Akitada shook his head. "No doubt, but it doesn't help us."

The lieutenant said, "Wait, there's more."

Arihito smiled a little. "He recognized the horse, sir."

106

"Not another horse fancier, I hope!" Akitada said, recalling the stuttering servant.

"No, sir. Just an ordinary woodsman. But the horse belongs to a man in his village. He knows it because he delivers wood there."

The lieutenant clapped his hands. "There you have it, sir! We were about to go meet this man. Would you care to join us?"

Akitada felt a jolt of excitement running through his body. "Yes!" he cried. "Of course! What excellent news! Well done, both of you! Where's this village?"

"It's called Shikino. It's on the road to Shirakawa."

"I know it. I'll meet you there or catch up with you on the road."

Akitada ran out without waiting for comment and hurried home, where he got his sword, commandeered a horse, and set out for the eastern hills.

As it happened, he did catch up with Arihito and the lieutenant. As soon as he had joined them, they increased their speed, eager to confront the man in Shikino village.

This turned out to be a rather small group of farm houses, all but one no larger than one room each. The buildings huddled together in an opening in the forest where fertile soil had made possible the cultivation of a few rice fields. In addition, people had a cow or two, some chickens, and vegetable plots. There was a general air of poverty and hard work about the houses, but there was also peace and harmony. The only more substantial house stood by itself above the others near the tree line.

The lieutenant said, "I'd like to speak to that woodsman first."

Arihito nodded. "I doubt you can learn more, but he lives in the third house on the road. I'm not sure he'll be home, though."

He was home. He was beside the small house sorting twigs and branches and tying them into bundles for sale in the city market. An old man sat on a tree stump nearby blinking at them from rheumy eyes.

The woodsman was quite young by comparison. Akitada thought him to be in his twenties. He was well-grown and quite handsome, though his hair was long and loose and his beard unkempt. When he looked up from his work, he smiled. At that moment, he reminded Akitada quite strongly of the young Tora, the way he was when he had first laid eyes on him, a fugitive from the law.

Arihito addressed the young man first. "Greetings, Haseo. I'm back. I brought the lieutenant, as you see. And my friend, Lord Sugawara. They want to hear your story."

Haseo stood, bowed three times, and eyed Akitada dubiously. When he made motions to kneel, Akitada said, "Please don't bother with the courtesies. We are in your debt."

The old man blinked and asked in a quavery voice, "Who's that? Who are they? I've paid my taxes fair and square." He started to get up laboriously, leaning on a stick, but Haseo said quickly, "No, Grandfather. They are here to talk to me."

The old man subsided. "Good, then. But don't waste time. You need to take all that wood to the market."

Haseo said apologetically, "Grandfather doesn't see or hear very well. We can talk here."

The lieutenant said, "Lord Arihito reported that you saw the killer."

"I saw a man in armor on a horse," Haseo corrected.

"Yes, yes. But you recognized the horse. We think he's the man who killed all the people in Shirakawa."

Haseo nodded. "I hope you're wrong."

Surprised, the lieutenant asked, "Why do you hope so?"

"I think the man is Master Kanemori. He's a very nice man. I sell my wood to him. He lives in the big house up there."

All three turned to look up at the house near the trees.

Akitada asked, "Who is this Master Kanemori?"

Haseo scratched his head. "Don't know. He came last year. He bought the house from the tax collector."

"You called him 'Master'."

"On account of his teaching archery."

Arihito whistled and the lieutenant asked, "What? Archery?"

Haseo looked from one to the other and back at Akitada. "He's very good. He's got a target behind his house."

"Who are the people he teaches?" Akitada asked.

"Oh, I don't know. Some are in the capital. Soldiers. Some are from the good people. Young men and boys. He earns good money."

109

The lieutenant, who had been frowning, asked, "Does he live alone?"

"Yes. He does everything for himself. Except I bring the wood and stack it."

Akitada asked, "Do you think he's home now?"

"Maybe. I haven't seen him go out."

"Would you mind very much coming with us?"

The lieutenant said quickly, "What are you going to do, sir? The man is dangerous. Let's go back and get some armed constables."

Arihito also frowned. "If he sees you coming, he'll escape."

Akitada nodded. "I don't think he'd shoot arrows at us, but he may get frightened. Haseo, I think it would help if you took some of your wood to him." He saw Haseo looking at the pile of bundles and added quickly, "I'll buy all your wood. Even what you meant to take to the market." He smiled a little. "That should satisfy your grandfather."

Haseo flashed brilliant white teeth at him. "I don't mind, sir. And I'm not afraid of Master Kanemori. He won't harm us."

"Very well, but you may lose your sales by coming with me. How much are those bundles worth?"

Haseo counted the bundles, named a price, and Akitada paid.

The lieutenant said, "I think we should all go."

"That will surely frighten him. No. You and Arihito can follow and wait somewhere out of sight of the house. Only Haseo and I will visit."

They looked unhappy, but Akitada outranked them and was also older, so they submitted.

14

The Archer

They rode up the hill with Haseo walking alongside. In a grove of trees they stopped and
Akitada dismounted. Arihito and Lieutenant
Hakeda waited on horseback. The big house was just
beyond the trees.

Akitada and Haseo approached the house on
foot. It looked well kept, but all was silent and empty. A
short fence surrounded it and a small garden with a
healthy crop of vegetables. Birds twittered in the large
trees shading the house, a large wooden structure with a
roof of cedar planks held down by rocks. The roof and
walls had darkened with age until they were almost
black. A few steps led to a porch. Toward one side
stood a small shed.

Haseo called out, "Master Kanemori? It's me,
Haseo."

There was no answer.

111

The birds had fallen silent as if they, too, were listening for an answer. After a moment they started chirping again.

"Perhaps he's not home," Akitada said. "Let's go see." He walked up the steps and pounded on the door. "Anyone home?"

Another silence.

Haseo said, "I'll walk round back. Maybe he's practicing his archery." He hurried off.

Akitada thought that a very bad idea, given that they might have to confront a killer who was armed with bow and arrows, but he saw no alternative and followed Haseo. The vegetables gave way to fruit trees and azaleas. He turned the last corner and saw a great open area stretching uphill before him. In the distance, a target had been fixed to a tree. He looked quickly for Kanemori, but saw no one but Haseo who was shouting again, "Master Kanemori?"

Akitada turned to look at the house behind them. There was a veranda here, perhaps the place where Kanemori stood to aim at the target. If he hoped to hit it at that distance, he must be very good indeed. And he must have very strong arms. The doors to the inside stood wide open.

Haseo came and said, "He can't be far. The house is open."

For some reason this reminded Akitada of the schoolmaster and his carefully locked house. He asked, "Does he always leave the doors open when he goes out?"

"I don't know. Maybe, if he doesn't go far."

Akitada frowned, then walked quickly to the house. He did not know what he would encounter, but fear was not an option. He was on the veranda in two steps, and inside the house in another three.

Coming in from the bright sunlight outside, he was momentarily blinded, but he recognized the smell instantly. And then there were the flies.

Death.

Again!

The house was one of the old farm houses with the open hearth in the center. Beyond it, the floor was raised. There were the living quarters. Kanemori had made them comfortable with thick *tatami* and handsome chests and other furnishings. The walls held bows of different sizes, swords, and quivers with arrows. An elaborate set of armor resided on a wooden stand. This was the home of a warrior.

Its owner seemed almost insignificant among his possessions. He sat on a sheet of unbleached hemp, his body folded forward so that his head rested on the floor. It was an uncomfortable and unnatural position, but Kanemori was past caring.

Haseo had come in behind Akitada. He gasped. "He's killed himself."

It certainly looked like it. Akitada stepped up to the body. More flies rose. The large sheet of hemp was soaked in blood beneath the body, and Kanemori's hands were underneath him. Akitada had seen such a posture only once before. It had been many years ago, and then it had been a warrior who had committed *jigai* in shame over having lost a battle. He had ended in just such a position after letting himself fall forward on his short sword. It had been a painful death. Belly wounds were not immediately fatal. It had taken great will power not to scream and thrash about.

Akitada touched the clammy skin of the dead man's neck and the pooled blood. He had not been dead long.

Well, if they had found their killer, he had saved them the trouble of arresting him and trying him for the murders. His deed had been shocking enough to make it unlikely he would have been sent into exile, even the harshest kind, like the gold mine where Akitada had once suffered.

He turned to Haseo and said, "You'd better bring the others. Lord Arihito and the lieutenant."

Haseo nodded. The shock must have made him silent. Akitada watched as he ran from the house and disappeared. Then he bent down to the sheet of hemp and picked up a small piece of paper. It had been almost under the dead man's face and was slightly stained with his blood. There was some writing on it. A poem:

> *Praying to the gods of heaven and earth,*
> *I thrust my hunting arrows in my quiver.*
> *Now to the Far Isles—*
> *I depart—.*

Akitada let it fall beside the body, and looked at the gray head, the neatly trimmed beard, the body that even in death looked powerful and strong.

Had the poem been a last gesture before he had ended his life? Indicating that now his work was done?

Perhaps, and it would be a relief. At least no one else would die. There had been far too much dying already.

But there remained questions: Who was this Kanemori? And why had he killed people so mercilessly?

Footsteps sounded and Arihito and the lieutenant ran into the room.

"*Jigai!*" said the lieutenant immediately.

Akitada looked at him. "Why do you think this was suicide?"

The lieutenant stepped closer. He picked up the poem, read, nodded, then lifted the body rather gently. Arihito gasped again, and Akitada's stomach turned. A short sword, the kind warriors call *tanto* was buried to its hilt in the man's abdomen. Blood had soaked into his clothes and dyed them a deep red. The lieutenant nodded again. "That's the way it was done up north when we lost a battle. Only there a comrade would stand by to lop off your head so you wouldn't have to bear the pain too long. This Kanemori was a brave man."

"He killed five people," Akitada protested.

"Yes. But still he was brave."

Haseo said, "Kanemori was a warrior. A great one!"

These sentiments troubled Akitada who hated violence and death. Perhaps that was why their native religion warned men that death would contaminate them with its corruption. He had not been able to shed bouts of nausea ever since Shirakawa. He suddenly felt helpless.

It was as well that the lieutenant became all business. "Lord Arihito," he said, "ride back to the capital. Tell them at police headquarters what's happened and to send out constables and the coroner. Say that we found the killer and that he's dead. They'll know what to do."

Arihito ran out, leaving the others with the body. A heavy silence hung over the room. Akitada said inconsequentially, "You served in the northern army, Lieutenant?"

Hakeda nodded. "Three years. I was wounded and sent home."

Akitada sighed. "It certainly looks like a warrior's suicide. I saw it myself when I was governor of Echigo Province."

"No doubt about it, in my opinion. Yesterday I think. He even left the customary poem."

Haseo said, "He was always writing poems. He was a great man."

Another silence fell.

The lieutenant looked around the room. "Yes. He must have been a fine man. He taught martial arts?"

Haseo nodded. "There's a school near the capital. He taught mostly how to use the bow, but he also knew how to use a sword. The good people pay to have their boys taught by men like Kanemori." He added sadly, "I begged him to teach me so I could be a brave soldier like him, but he wouldn't do it."

Akitada himself had been trained this way, and his son Yoshi was still taking lessons—and hoping to prove himself in battle some day. He suppressed another wave of nausea. "Let's go outside. I want a look at the shed."

The fresh air, filled with the scent of pines, revived him a little. They walked back to the shed and found inside, as he had expected, a horse that was dark brown and had one black foreleg.

Akitada pointed, "That's the horse the servant saw."

Hakeda nodded. He turned to Haseo. "Did he have any family?"

116

Haseo looked blank. "I don't think so. He was always alone."

They sat down on the porch steps to wait for the lieutenant's people. From here on, the authorities would deal with Kanemori and with what he had done. A great man and a killer of the innocent. How could they coexist in one body?

It was over, but Akitada's world had darkened. He had seen a great deal of violence when he was young. He had accepted it then, but now that he was older, it seemed that life had become far more precious. The dead of Shirakawa, the schoolmaster's wife, and now this aging warrior. Even a man like Yorimune must be missed by someone. And his wife and daughters? The two young men? What had they done to deserve death? This Kanemori had become their executioner, and yet even he was mourned in his own death. Again there was this strong sense that he was surrounded by death, that it was like rising water, threatening to swallow him up.

He stood suddenly, unable to bear this place any longer. "Will you need me, Lieutenant? I have other matters to attend to."

Hakeda, who had also been sunk in thought, said quickly, "No, not at all. Thank you for coming. I suppose this closes the investigation."

"Yes. It looks that way." Akitada nodded to the lieutenant and Haseo and walked back to his horse.

As soon as he had left Shikino village behind, he spurred his horse to a gallop. In an irrational panic, he fled death. He felt a desperate need for his wife and family.

15
A Marriage

The morning after his visit to the willow quarter, Tora went to speak to his master. He had spent the previous evening and part of the night turning the schoolmaster's case over in his mind without finding a solution. The idea was to exonerate Tanizaki. But nothing he had learned so far had suggested a way for another killer to have entered the house. Or even the possibility that there might be another killer. Was it truly likely that Tanizaki had heard nothing when his wife was being attacked and brutally murdered a few rooms away? Tora had hoped that the dead woman's sister might know of someone who had hated her enough to kill her. Instead, she had immediately accused the husband.

He found the master in his study, sitting behind his desk and looking glum.

A cheerful "Morning, sir," produced a smile, a greeting and, "What progress on Tanizaki?"

"Well, not much, sir. The neighbors knew of nothing. They thought the Tanizakis were very respectable, quiet people. The murder surprised them."

"Hmm. So you've come for advice?"

Tora bit his lip. "Just a consultation. Things aren't making sense. I thought if we talked about them, I might find a new way of looking at the facts."

A nod. "It's as well. The killer in the Shirakawa case has been found. I shall have time now for Tanizaki's problem. Report!"

Tora's heart fell with a painful thump. It was no longer his case. He had wasted his time worrying it back and forth all night, and now it was over before he had properly begun. He sat down with an audible sigh.

"What's the matter? You look disappointed."

"I am. I was going to solve this murder." The injustice of it had momentarily blotted out what his master had said about the massacre. Tora's eyes widened. "You already found the killer in the Shirakawa massacre?"

"Not I. Arihito found a witness. The witness led us to the killer."

Tora's amazement bordered on disbelief. "All in one day? Yesterday? Genba said you'd come for your sword and a horse and gone off again. And it was that easy?"

The corner of his master's mouth quirked at Tora's tone. "Yes. It seems unbelievable."

"So the man was arrested? Who is it?"

"His name was Kanemori. And he's dead."

"You killed him?"

"No. He committed *jigai.*"

For a moment, Tora was puzzled, then he understood. "Suicide? Why? Because he wanted to escape torture and a trial? Or because it was more honorable than being cut down by you and the constables?"

"I don't know why, Tora. Finding him was not a good experience. Nothing this week has been good. First the massacre, then the schoolmaster's wife, and finally Kanemori."

Tora recognized the look on his master's face and suddenly saw his way. "There's no need for you to bother with Tanizaki, sir," he said quickly. "I have the matter in hand. I know you're worried about Lord Kosehira. The living are more important than the dead. Let me work on the other case."

This got him a very searching look. But finally the master nodded. "Very well. Thank you for understanding, Tora."

Tora hurried from the house before his lordship could change his mind. Not having a better idea, he went to see Sergeant Saeki at the police station.

Saeki received him in the friendliest manner. "Lieutenant Tora! How happy I am to see you. What are you up to?"

Tora returned the greeting but narrowed his eyes a little at such exuberance. "Still looking into the Tanizaki case," he said. "What have you learned?"

"We let him go. There's no proof. And his reputation is excellent. We're not in the business of terrorizing respectable citizens."

"Really? You surprise me." Tora let the note of disbelief linger so that Saeki could puzzle over his meaning. Did the comment apply to Tanizaki's innocence or the good behavior of the police?

Saeki flushed. "You don't have a case, Tora. Let it go. We'll eventually get the hoodlum who did it. The poor man lost his wife. Let him mourn and arrange her funeral."

"So you have nothing!"

"I have nothing that points to him."

Tora found himself with a dilemma. He had the information from the victim's sister, but if he shared it, Saeki might well arrest Tanizaki again. And that was surely not what the master expected him to achieve.

In the end, he nodded and went to call on Tanizaki.

He could hear the sounds of altercation when he turned the corner of the street where Tanizaki lived. A small group of people had gathered outside. They were listening with apparent enjoyment to the noise.

Tora made out that the argument was between a man and a woman. Moreover, the woman seemed to be the aggressor, for the man occasionally cried out in pain and his words sounded conciliatory while the woman's were mostly shouted insults and threats.

The audience sniggered, chuckled, and called out occasional encouragement.

Tora skirted them and ran into the house.

He found the combatants in the kitchen. Tanizaki, arms raised to protect his head, dodged blows from a wooden mallet swung by Nariko, his sister-in-law, who was yelling, "I'll kill you, you bastard!" and other dire promises.

Tora stepped behind her and wrapped his arms around her before she could land another blow on the cowering Tanizaki.

Surprised, she dropped the mallet and twisted around to dig her nails into Tora's face. He released her and stepped back. "Now look here, girl," he said with a grin. "That's no way for a lady to act."

"She was trying to kill me. She's a devil," screeched Tanizaki.

Tora saw that the schoolmaster's face was bruised and bleeding and one eye was swelling shut.

Nariko suddenly sagged and staggered to a barrel to sit down. She started to cry.

"I ought to call the police," said Tanizaki. "She attacked me." He wiped a sleeve across his nose, saw the blood and muttered, "Dear gods!"

"I have a notion, " said Tora, "that you don't want Nariko to talk to the police. They'll just arrest you again."

Tanizaki moaned, "What am I going to do? You're no help at all. May the devils take this woman. She's a liar and a slut. She hates me because I chose her sister over her."

Nariko rose from her seat, claws outstretched. "You filthy turd! You piece of rancid shit! You monkey's asshole!"

Tora stepped between them. "Sit down, Nariko. This isn't getting us anywhere. There's a crowd outside and the constables may be here any moment."

Nariko sat. "What he said is a filthy lie. I knew he was no good. I warned her. But she wanted to be respectable. Now see where it got her: she's dead!" Her voice rose as she turned to Tanizaki, "She's   dead, you monster, and you killed her!"

The sound of applause came from outside, and Tanizaki put his head in his hands. "Oh, the shame of it. How will I ever hold up my head again?"

Nariko cursed under her breath, then got up and walked out. Tora could hear her shout, "Go home! There's nothing for you here. Tend to your children so they don't grow up in the streets and get killed by rich old men."

Tora said, "She's left."

"Good riddance! The woman's a low slut, one of the *fusedama*. For all I know she's an *eta*. They're all trash." Tanizaki laughed mirthlessly. "They thought I was rich. I'm not. I'm poor. That's the trouble. This would never have happened if I were rich."

"What do you mean?"

Tanizaki flushed. "I don't know. They would have had more respect. Wealth is all they think of."

"You mean your neighbors?"

"Them and the women."

Tora frowned. His own wife had been a dancer, though never a prostitute. He said, "Your wife worked in the willow quarter, just like her sister, but you married her anyway. I would've thought a man who cared that much about respect would look elsewhere for a wife."

The schoolmaster nodded. "And you would be right. I should not have done it. I should never have gone to the quarter for a night with a woman, but I had been a widower for years. I was all alone and I worked every day teaching young people. After a while you feel as though you're not really alive. The ancients taught that a man needs a woman regularly to stay in good health. I was beginning to have all sorts of small ailments. My eyes were failing. My hearing, too. And there were days when every bone in my body hurt. I was afraid I would die soon if I did not have a woman."

Tora was familiar with such ancient precepts. He began to see the logic of Tanizaki's actions.

Almost.

"But you didn't have to marry her for that," he pointed out.

Tanizaki looked at him sadly. "You saw her. Tomoko was beautiful. She was young and full of life. She made me feel young again. When I held her in my arms and possessed her, I could feel my strength returning. I absorbed her essence and it made me feel strong. I kept going back for more of her essence and I walked more lightly every day. It was very expensive, but she filled me with life. Then I ran out of money and I begged her to let me come without paying. It was she who proposed that we get married."

Tora recalled what Tomoko's sister had told him about Tomoko's desire to be a respectable wife. He asked, "And how did the marriage work out?"

"Well, it was a disappointment. I was ashamed of her, of course, but she was a good housekeeper and since I could not afford to entertain guests, we lived very simply, just the two of us. It was not bad, but it was not good either."

Tora shook his head in disgust. "So you got a housekeeper. What happened to all the joys of making the wind and the rain and becoming young again?"

The schoolmaster blushed and looked away. "She stopped trying to please me and made excuses when I wanted to sleep with her. And I eventually preferred the peace and quiet of my study to her complaints and aimless chatter."

A bad marriage!

125

And a good motive for murder.

Tanizaki was not helping himself. So far he had told them that he kept his house so securely locked up that no one could get in and now he admitted to disliking his wife. Of course, thought Tora, it could be argued that only an innocent man would relate incriminating facts so readily. On the other hand, Tanizaki might simply be too stupid to realize what he was saying. But he was a learned man, far better educated than Tora. Still, those learned men frequently did not have good sense. That must be the explanation.

Tanizaki had watched him anxiously. "You think I did it, don't you?"

He was clearly not a mind reader either. Tora shook his head. "No. But it looks a bit that way. I'm surprised the police let you go."

Tanizaki smiled for the first time. "Fortunately that sergeant was sensible. I'm a schoolmaster and I come from a good family. That still counts for something. People like me don't murder their wives. The police could see they made a mistake." He paused for a moment. "So you and Lord Sugawara need not trouble any longer. The police will find out who did this. Thanks for stopping that madwoman, but I shall manage from now on. I'll report her attack to the police."

Tora snapped, "Don't do that! Do you want them to hear her story about how you've been mistreating your wife?"

The schoolmaster gaped. "They wouldn't believe her."

Tora was done with Tanizaki. Turning to leave, he said, "Well then, why don't you find out?" He slammed the door as he left.

16

Speaking of a Dead Man

Akitada went to see Kosehira as Tora had suggested. He knew why Tora had suggested it, but he had been right for once. Kosehira's condition had worsened overnight. Much as he dreaded running into Yukiko again, he would not forgive himself if his friend died while he sat in his study worrying about him, worrying about the case, worrying about the quick and opportune discovery of the dead Kanemori, and wondering what crimes the Fujiwara faction had been covering up.

Finding the archer's body had left him with an irrational feeling that it was not over. He wanted to ask more questions, but he suspected that the prime minister and Yorimune's family would accept the solution offered by the suicide. Any activity on his part would be more than unwelcome. He would be stopped.

So he went to Kosehira's house and sat beside a semi-conscious Kosehira. His wife Hatsuko was there, and two of his daughters. So were vessels filled with ice, and the ladies worked their fans to cool the feverish Kosehira. Their eyes were red-rimmed, and the daughters barely smiled at Akitada.

He loved Kosehira's family. Years ago, when he was in despair over Tamako's death, they had taken him into their family circle, made him one of their own, drawn him into their laughter and affection, and he had responded. That his response was shortly to be focused on the eldest daughter and turned into a romantic passion for Yukiko had been unfortunate. But what had happened since had not changed the way he felt about the rest of them and perhaps they had not turned against him either.

He attempted to speak to Kosehira, but his friend was beyond speaking and perhaps beyond hearing his words. He tried to tell him about finding the archer dead. Had Arihito already told his father? He saw that Lady Hatsuko nodded.

"It doesn't matter," she said softly.

No, they were beyond caring what had happened to the man who had attacked them. They cared only about their husband and father. Akitada fell silent.

Eventually, his restlessness made him leave Kosehira's bedside. He headed to police headquarters.

Hakeda was back in his office, staring down at an array of weapons. There were swords, knives, two large bows, a number of quivers with arrows, more arrows laid out neatly side by side, and in front a short sword, still stained with blood. Kanemori's blood,

Akitada guessed. On a stand hung the armor worn by Kanemori during his attack on the Fujiwara party.

Akitada said, "So you haven't closed the case?"

Hakeda shot him a glance. "I'm curious."

"I see." Akitada walked around, looking at the collection. The red-laced armor with chest plates and a single silk-laced shoulder guard was topped with a round, metal helmet and face plate. The armor was constructed of scales, some leather, others iron, that were sewn together with red silk that gave it the red color. The face plate was dark, lacquered metal and protected forehead and cheeks. Along with the helmet, it accounted for the fact that the attacker's face had been hidden.

It was an impressive armor, surely worn only by high-ranking officers, but it was old and, on closer inspection, showed damage and fading.

Akitada turned his attention to the weapons spread on the floor. He noted the single archer's glove made from leather and covering only the thumb and the next two fingers. Unlike the armor, it was fairly new, though it showed heavy use. The dead man's sword was longer and had a heavier blade than Akitada's own, inherited from his father. The steel looked to be high quality, but the blade had nicks. It was a weapon that had been used, though probably not recently. Kanemori had oiled and polished the sword and maintained it. Akitada had heard that they now used heavier, longer swords in battles and guessed that this one had seen service in the northern campaigns. The hilt of the sword was bound in red and black silk. It looked worn and discolored.

His eye strayed from the long sword to the short one, the bloody weapon of Kanemori's suicide.

He saw that they made a matching pair. More proof that the warrior Kanemori had died by his own hand.

He passed quickly from the metal *jitte,* used to parry an attacker's sword, to the bows and arrows.

There were two bows, one about six feet long, and the other a mighty eight feet. The eight-foot bow was used by mounted archers and had its grip below the center. The shorter bow could be used by a standing archer. Their strings were waxed ramie and they had red silk ribbons tied to their ends.

An array of arrows was laid out: three quivers, two of them filled, a third empty. The arrows with bamboo shafts were lacquered, their feathers from either pheasants or hawks, their points of metal in the narrow style of leaves.

Having arrived at the end of his survey of the arsenal, Akitada glanced at Lieutenant Hakeda again and found that the policeman had been watching him.

"Apparently Kanemori was an experienced soldier in his past life," Akitada said.

Hakeda nodded. "He must have had quite a past to own all this. Unless it belonged to another man."

Akitada looked at the armor and the weapons again. "I doubt that. These have been taken care of because they represented his life's work. I believe he fought in the northern campaign. He looked old enough."

Hakeda sighed and scratched his temple. "It makes no sense."

"What do you mean?"

"How could such a man do such a thing?" Hakeda gestured at the weapons. "These belonged to a brave and honorable man. You heard what that youngster Haseo said."

"The young are easily impressed by tales of derring-do. And a man who has killed in battle would not mind killing in time of peace."

Hakeda gave him a look. "I served. We had a strong sense of honor. We killed only soldiers."

Akitada snorted. "In my experience, once the killing starts, men lose all sense of restraint."

"This is true of the common soldier, but this man was an officer."

Akitada gave up arguing the point. Hakeda's own background predisposed him to such admiration for warriors. He said instead, "Are you suggesting that Kanemori was not the killer at Shirakawa?"

The lieutenant looked uneasy. "No. But I don't understand it. What happened to him?"

"Ah. Yes, you may have something there. I suppose we could find out."

Hakeda suddenly smiled. "You would go against the prime minister's orders?"

Akitada hesitated. It was a huge risk. Then he said, "Perhaps. Up to a point. I hate uncertainties."

Hakeda gestured at the weapons. "His whole life is here. He spent his youth leading soldiers into battle in the service of the emperor. He must've been good at it. The armor and the swords are of good quality. They are old and have been heavily used in the past, but he brought them back with him because they meant something. And he brought enough money to buy his house and live quietly, teaching archery."

Akitada considered the policeman. Hakeda was older than he, his hair a little grayer. Not unlike Kanemori, he had fought as a soldier and then returned to the capital to accept a position in the capital police.

He nodded. "What is known about him? Does he have a family?"

"He lost a wife and small son during one of the attacks by the enemy."

A lonely life.

Akitada knew about loneliness. For him, the dry work at the ministry had not been enough. For Kanemori, evidently, warfare was enough. A strange character. He said, "He must have liked violence."

Hakeda said quickly, "Not violence. Duty. And the excitement, perhaps. The skill of it. He did leave and come here to live peacefully."

"Well, we won't know what happened until we find a motive."

They fell silent. After a while, Akitada gestured to the empty quiver. "You haven't recovered those arrows?"

Hakeda shook his head. "We may not. Those physicians and monks who took care of the victims may simply have thrown them away. I expect they resembled the others. He killed until he ran out of arrows. It seems excessive."

"Yes."

"It took a strong man to use that bow." Hakeda pointed to the long bow. "I tried it. It's the kind that takes two or three men to string."

"He looked too old."

"Perhaps teaching archery every day keeps you fit."

Akitada nodded. "Eleven arrows. Six people dead and five wounded. From horseback. He must have been good."

"Yes. He aimed very carefully and he hit his mark. At least until his victims started running. When

132

they were sitting still, they were much like a stationary target."

"Who do you think was his primary target?"

"Either Yorimune or Kosehira. They were the first."

"I have talked to Kosehira. He's my friend. He's completely unaware of any reason for it. No old scores to settle. With Yorimune, there may be reasons. He has had a checkered career, especially in his younger years."

Hakeda frowned. "Too much is unknown."

"What will you do next?"

"When our coroner is finished dealing with the victims, he'll have a look at Kanemori. It's a formality, but I have to close the case properly. Other than that, I suppose I shall always wonder. No point in doing anything else. It's over. The case will be closed whether we like it or not."

Akitada nodded, but his own dissatisfaction nagged at him.

17

The Schoolmaster's Secrets

Tora walked away from the schoolmaster's house thoroughly angry. He did not like the man. Everything about him set his teeth on edge. They had come to help him because his wife had been murdered and he was frightened and upset, but, to Tora's mind, he did not deserve help..

From the start, this man had expressed little grief at his loss. Tanizaki was afraid of being arrested and he had wanted Lord Sugawara to prevent it.. He had been collecting his dues because he had formerly worked for his master and because he thought such a great man would simply order the police to leave him alone. To his surprised horror, he had been disabused of such thinking. But now he was back and free. And why? Because he was a respectable man with a good reputation. And now he did not need them any longer.

In Tora's experience, even the "good people," that is, those who belonged to the great families, were capable of evil deeds. True, the poor made more trouble and got caught more often, but all men, and some women, could commit murder if they were sufficiently provoked.

They had set out to clear Tanizaki and had—so far—failed. Instead Tora had become increasingly suspicious of the man. He decided that the time had come to find out exactly what sort of person the schoolmaster was and what kind of life he and his wife had led.

He headed for the *hinin* village that had sprung up in the far western part of the city. Here lived the lowest class of people, the ones who were classless slaves, vagrants, or untouchables who did the work that the gods had forbidden, work with dead animals and all sorts of filth. The younger men worked in slaughter houses and tanneries, making leather used for weapons and armor and saddles. The older people cleaned up after the more affluent, sweeping, washing, and carrying off human and animal soil. Some women worked as low-class prostitutes, "floating women" who walked the streets looking for business. Some eked out a living by selling talents like singing or crafts.

Tanizaki's gardener, Osamu, lived here. Tora, while very uneasy about ghosts and spirits, had no particular revulsion about the untouchables. Sure they tended to be dirty, but he had seen enough of death not to be troubled by contamination. Osamu merely tended plants and cleaned and raked.

Osamu lived with his wife, a short, white-haired woman who bowed a lot, smiled a lot, and chattered a lot. Her husband, it appeared, was recovering from his beating by the police, and their primary worry was where their next meal was coming from.

Tora parted with some money. They were touchingly grateful. It would only buy enough food for a couple of days, but they never planned further ahead anyway. Something would come along.

Tora asked first how Osamu felt. The old man complained a bit, but it seemed he was on the mend. He wanted a job, and in that context he got up to demonstrate how fit and agile he was.

"Glad to see you so well," Tora said with a grin. "But I'm here to ask some questions about your master and mistress."

Osamu sat back down and looked wary. "I'm only a gardener. I do not go into the house."

"Yes, I know. So Master Tanizaki comes outside to tell you what to do and to pay you?"

"Yes, always. Always he says, 'You're a lazy slug. Dig up the vegetable garden! Carry the wood to the kitchen! Sweep that path, Fetch water! Do not sit down! I do not pay for sitting down.' It is hard work."

"Yes, I'm sure it is. What about his wife?"

"I do not go inside!" The fear was back.

"But you take water into the kitchen?"

"I take it to the door. The maid takes it."

"I see. What about the wife coming outside to give you work to do?"

"She sends the maid."

"So the maid brought you the mirror stand to mend?"

"Yes. The maid."

"The maid hasn't come back yet."

"Sick family."

137

"I see. So when you brought back the mirror stand, how would you have returned it?"

Osamu looked blank. "Don't know. The policemen broke it."

That, as far as Osamu was concerned, was the end of the mirror stand and his pay. He was uninterested in discussing the matter further.

"I suppose Master Tanizaki usually spoke to you early before he left for work?"

"Sometimes after he came back."

"When did he leave and when did he get back?"

"Left at first light, came back for his evening rice."

"Always?"

"Sometimes not. Didn't come home. And sometimes he left again."

That was better. "What do you think he did on those evenings?"

Osamu grinned toothlessly. "Women."

"But he had a wife. A young and pretty wife."

"Yes. So?"

"You mean he liked all sorts of women?"

"Yes. Pretty ones."

Tora added this to Tanizaki's other dubious traits. He definitely wanted to know all about that man. However, there was his wife, the victim. There, too, might be interesting facts that could point to a motive to kill her. "Did the wife go out during the day?"

"To the market. With the maid."

Very proper. For a former courtesan. "She never went alone?"

Osamu looked doubtful. "Not sure. I only work two days a week."

138

Tora nodded. "What about the maid? Where does she live?"

That got him a blank stare. "In the house."

"No, I mean, where is her family? The sick family?"

"I forget." He frowned. "It's near Hosho-ji, I think."

Hosho-ji was a temple outside the capital in the south. "And what's their name?"

"Otsuki. She's called Kogiri."

"Thank you, Osamu. I hope you'll soon be on your feet again. Will you go back to work for Master Tanizaki?"

"I hope so." Beside him Osamu's wife nodded eagerly. They needed the money.

Tora decided that he must talk to the maid. Since his way would take him through the capital, he planned to stop by at the school where Tanizaki taught, in hopes of picking up more information from his colleagues.

The school was near the place where once the great southern gate to the city had stood, Rashomon. Since then the capital had spread southward and toward the east until you had to guess at its former shape. To-ji, the ancient temple still stood there, and Tanizaki's school, the Gakk-wan, adjoined it. It was a *shigaku*, a school founded by one of the great families for their own members and retainers. In this case it was the Tachibana family, but by marriage, the school now belonged to the Fujiwara clan.

In appearance it resembled most government institutions and temple compounds. A walled enclosure contained a number of lecture halls. Tora walked in through the gate, after identifying himself to a watchman

139

as a Sugawara retainer with a message for one of the teachers.

Inside, he found that he had arrived at the end of a class. Students spilled out of a hall, and teachers gathered to talk. Tora did not see Tanizaki and approached the two teachers who rested on the veranda of a nearby hall.

He bowed politely. "I have come to see if I can enroll my son," he said. "Perhaps you two learned gentlemen can tell me a bit about the school."

One teacher, a jolly, fat man said quickly, "You need permission from the Fujiwara family."

The other, an elderly man, asked, "How old is your son? And what are your plans for him?"

Yuki was seventeen and training with the guards. He wanted to be a soldier and had no mind for studying the ancient masters. Tora did not explain this but instead invented a studious child of ten. They chatted amiably for a little, then Tora asked, "Don't you have a teacher by the name of Tanizaki here? I'm told he's very good and will come to my house to teach my son."

They looked at each other. The fat teacher cleared his throat meaningfully; the elderly one smirked a little. He said, "I think Tanizaki used to go around to people's houses, but he is here now. Still, maybe he needs the money. Who knows? He seems competent or he would not be teaching here. You must ask him yourself."

This scant praise suggested Tanizaki had not made friends or overly impressed his new colleagues. Tora said, "I worry about the influence of a stranger on an impressionable child. Is he a steady family man?"

The fat teacher snorted, and when Tora looked at him, said, "Not at the moment. But he lost his wife a few years ago. So it makes sense he should look elsewhere."

Interesting! Tanizaki had not told his colleagues that he had married again. Most likely he was ashamed that Tomoko had been a courtesan. He asked, "Where, elsewhere?" guessing what the answer would be.

"Oh, the courtesans in the quarter, I'd guess." The fat man chuckled. "I'd also guess that's why he needs more money than he earns here."

His older companion was disapproving. "It's no crime for a man to look for a little companionship. Too bad those women are so greedy."

Tora, having become thoughtful, thanked them, and departed.

Hosho-ji was a magnificent temple south of the city and east of the Kamo River. It was endowed by the court and a number of villages had sprung up nearby. By asking questions, Tora tracked the Otsuki family down to a small farm bordering the river. Here they were growing a little rice and quite a large number of vegetables for sale in the markets of the capital.

When he found a middle-aged woman feeding the chickens, he asked for the maid Kogiri and was directed to the outdoor kitchen. Kogiri was a strong, somewhat squat young woman with a broad, heavily pock-marked face. She was about as unattractive as any female Tora had seen lately. At the moment, she was chopping vegetables.

Tora flashed her his smile, and saw that this still worked pretty well. Kogiri stopped her work and gaped at him. "I'm Tora," he said simply "You're Kogiri?"

She nodded, staring back mesmerized.

"You work for Master Tanizaki?"

She made a face. "No more. Grandmother died. So I left."

"I'm very sorry about your grandmother. But shouldn't you have gone back?"

"No. I stay here."

"Why?"

"He's mean and she's bossy."

A woman of few and very descriptive words!

"Did they beat you?"

"She slapped me. And she's no better than me. Worse, if you ask me. She worked in the whores' quarter before he married her."

"She's dead. Murdered."

Her mouth fell open. "M-murdered? He killed her?"

"He says he didn't. Why do you think he'd kill her?"

"They're always shouting at each other. And he has another woman."

"What other woman?"

"I wouldn't know. He goes to see her."

There it was. Tanizaki's secret.

And a motive for murder, perhaps.

"What about her? Any boyfriends?"

She spat. "Those women lie with anybody."

Clearly Kogiri had hated her mistress. Tora pressed the former maid, "But do you know for a fact that she had men? Did any men come to the house?"

"Not that I saw."

"You went with her when she went out. Did she visit anyone in the city?"

"Once she went to the place where she used to work as a whore. I told him and he beat her."

And here was another motive for the schoolmaster.

"How do you know?"

"He shouted and she cried."

"What happened then?"

"I don't know. I left."

Tora did not waste another smile on her. She was vengeful and had probably been fired either by Tanizaki or his wife. Had she told the truth? It was hard to tell, since she clearly hated both, but he was inclined to believe that Tanizaki had another woman. The teachers and Osamu had said the same. It was less likely that his wife had been unfaithful. The maid had not been convincing about this. But she had clearly overheard a quarrel between Tanizaki and his wife, and possibly he had beaten her.

18

Buddha or Devil?

Akitada slept poorly that night. He got up twice and went to sit on the veranda outside their room. Behind him, Sadako slept peacefully. They had made love, carefully, and she had held him close and murmured endearments into his ear. He was not sure if she had thanked him for sparing her another pregnancy or begged him to give her a child. He wished she could come to accept childlessness and settle for their love. To his mind, it was the perfect existence: just the two of them, making a perfect whole, the *ying* and *yang* of life.

Eventually, he put his marriage from his mind and thought instead of Kanemori. He understood what the lieutenant felt, even though he had never accepted

145

violence so totally as a measure of heroism. Kanemori had returned and gained a very good reputation, as a peaceful, even gentle man. Had all of that been pretense while he planned his revenge on the people at Shirakawa? Had the man been a Buddha or a devil?

And still, there was no link between him and any of the dead.

In the end, Akitada knew he would have no rest until he understood Kanemori. The next morning, he saddled his horse and rode back to Shikino village.

It was another beautiful day, the air crisp with the scent of pines and cryptomerias on the slight breeze. A man had died, but in the village, it was just another day. The peasants were in their fields, and their wives worked in the houses. Children and chickens scampered about outside. Older boys and girls worked alongside their parents.

They stopped to stare at him. Here and there, a peasant bowed or knelt. The nobles were a frequent sight in these parts as they traveled between their country houses and their duties in the capital. They had brought some affluence with them. The farms looked prosperous.

The village had a small wine house on the road, catering to travelers. Here Akitada dismounted and sat down at one of the rough tables outside the door. Not far from him at the other sat a solitary drinker, a middle-aged man in a hunting jacket and boots. Akitada assumed that he was passing through and had stopped for refreshment. Their eyes met briefly and they nodded to each other.

A slender young girl in the peasant garb of cotton pants and top under a blue apron came out and asked what Akitada might like. He ordered wine and, sniffing the tempting smell coming from inside, asked what was cooking.

"Just noodle soup, sir, with pumpkin and cabbage."

"It smells good. Bring me some."

She returned quickly with Akitada's wine and a bowl of steaming soup. Akitada paid and asked, "Did you know Kanemori?"

Her pretty face turned sad. "We all knew him. He came here for spiced wine sometimes." Almost defiantly, she added, "He was a good man."

"The police think he killed all those people at Shirakawa."

She looked away. "It doesn't seem right. Are you sure it was him?"

"You don't think he did it?"

"I don't know. I never knew anyone to do such a thing. Why would he do it?"

"Did he have friends he drank with?"

Her eyes went to the other man. "A few. Nice, polite men, all of them. Sociable. They'd been soldiers together."

Akitada eyed the other man with interest. He looked to be the same age and type as Kanemori. "When was the last time Kanemori was here?"

She thought. "A week ago, I think. He was alone. He brought some vegetables from his garden. He liked to share."

That would have been before the attack. Akitada studied the girl thoughtfully. Her liking the man did not prove anything. Like Haseo, she was young. And like anyone, she found it difficult to imagine the sort of cold rage that had driven the Shirakawa killer.

He asked, "When he was with friends, what did they talk about?"

"The weather, the rice harvest, competitions."

"Sometimes men who drink get into arguments. Did he?"

"Never. He was a gentle man. He would never even raise his voice."

Akitada nodded. "Thank you," he said. "I'm trying to understand what happened."

She nodded and left him to his soup. It was delicious. He smacked his lips and emptied the bowl. When he raised his eyes, the other man smiled at him and said, "She makes good soup."

A friendly man.

Akitada smiled back. "You're a frequent guest?"

"From time to time, sir. I had a friend here. He died and I came to pay my respects."

Akitada asked, "Kanemori?"

The man nodded. "I heard some of what you asked her, sir. You knew him, too?"

"No. I found him. Will you join me?"

The stranger came over. "My name's Hiraga, sir," he said, bowing slightly, aware of Akitada's rank but not unduly impressed by it.

"Sugawara Akitada."

"I knew him. We both served in the north. Old soldiers tend to flock together when they return from wars. There's not much back home that compares to what they've seen."

A brief silence fell. Akitada gestured to his cup. "Will you have some wine?" When the other man nodded, he called to the maid, who brought another cup and flask. They sipped their wine. Akitada asked "You liked him?"

"Yes. He was my friend. Not easy to know, but good at heart. He'd give you anything he owned."

Here it was again: Kanemori had been a good and kind man. Knowing the answer already, Akitada asked, "Do you believe he's the one who killed Yorimune and all those other people?"

Hiraga said, "Yorimune perhaps, but not the others."

"Why Yorimune?"

The other man hesitated. "Why are you asking these questions? I thought the police had decided on Kanemori's guilt."

Akitada liked Hiraga. He wanted to trust him. "I don't know what to believe. The whole affair was strange, and Kanemori's suicide was the strangest part of it."

Hiraga considered this. He also seemed to consider Akitada. "The suicide was not so strange for Kanemori. It is the way he would have chosen to die."

"But you don't think he did choose to die?"

Hiraga looked up at the forested hills in the direction of Kanemori's house. "I don't know what to think. That's why I came."

"And did you learn anything?"

"No. There's a young man. Kanemori was fond of him. I've seen him and asked him questions. But Haseo doesn't know either. He grieves and he's angry. The young think they can change fate."

Akitada finished his wine. "I've met Haseo. But he suffered a serious case of hero worship. That's notoriously untrustworthy."

"Why? Sometimes the young see more clearly because their eyes have not been blinded to the evil in this world."

This silenced Akitada. He had seen much in his life that qualified as evil. Did this mean that he no longer trusted anyone? Everything pointed to Kanemori having been the killer at Shirakawa. Could he conceive of the man's innocence in spite of the evidence? After a while, he said, "I would like to know more about Kanemori. Are there others who knew him well?"

The other man smiled. "There's a place just outside the capital. It belongs to a sword smith. Some of the old soldiers meet there to talk and practice their skill. They have competitions. When Jocho inherited the farm, he was already a fine smith, so he rents out the land and uses the farm to entertain his friends and customers. He knew Kanemori. And there are others. I'll take you, if you like."

Akitada accepted eagerly. Hiraga was also mounted, and so they rode together out of the mountains and back among the green rice fields near the river. When they reached Jocho's farm, Hiraga took his leave, claiming other business. Akitada thanked him and rode on alone.

Jocho's farm was a well-kept cluster of wooden buildings with thick thatch for roofs. As they got closer, Akitada could see that someone had set up practice fields with targets, and there was a wooden platform that he guessed was used to practice swordsmanship. It was occupied at present by a youngster and his master. They were using wooden swords, as had Akitada's own son not so long ago.

Akitada's visit produced more glowing testimonials for Kanemori. Jocho, the sword smith, had known Kanemori the longest.

"Ever since he hung up his sword, sir," he told Akitada. "Came back from the north when they made peace. He came to honor his parents' graves. His whole family was dead by then."

"When was that?" Akitada asked.

"Three years ago. He tried to make another life for himself and bought his house in Shikino. He found a girl, much younger than him, but she took up with another man. He decided he didn't need a family."

Unbidden, his own doomed marriage to Yukiko crossed Akitada's mind. Another aging man with a young woman who was bored and looked for more exciting partners? Perhaps there was a motive here. Was Yorimune in some way involved?

He asked, "What about this other man?"

"I don't know him. Kanemori wouldn't talk about it. She was pretty and, I think, of good family."

"Which family?"

But Jocho did not know that either. "I only heard about it afterward. He never talked about her."

"He did not try to take revenge?"

"No, sir. Kanemori wasn't the type. He blamed himself and went on with his life."

Again, Akitada was struck by the similarities between his own case and that of Kanemori. And again, here was the emphasis on Kanemori's lack of violence. That he should have ridden out that evening in order to kill six people and wound another five did not make sense to anyone who knew him.

And yet, the man had been a warrior, a soldier of repute who had killed many during the years he served. And certainly the subsequent suicide was in character. And the warrior creed was that shame must be removed by reprisal and revenge.

Akitada talked to others there. They were unanimously shocked by the charge against Kanemori. Some were former soldiers, like Kanemori, and talked of his past. He had served during the Tadatsune revolt in the service of General Minamoto Yorimichi. He had commanded a troupe of mounted bowmen who had a famous reputation for horsemanship and skill with the long bow. No, Kanemori, would never have used his skills in peacetime to kill anyone, let alone women.

19

The Wisdom of Wives

Akitada was torn between the evidence, which seemed to prove that Kanemori was the killer, and the fact that he had an admirable reputation among the people who knew him. Could a man everyone called "gentle" suddenly snap and go on a killing spree? It seemed improbable. And yet! Everything matched. Witnesses had described the killer's horse, his armor, his skill with the long bow, his horsemanship. It had been Kanemori.

He arrived home, frowning and distracted. Genba took his horse and asked anxiously, "Is Lord Kosehira worse?"

Akitada returned to his own world with a crash. All day, he had forgotten about his friend's fever, a fever that could well signal his impending death. Perhaps it had already occurred while he was riding in the east-

153

ern hills and chatting with Hiraga in the Shikino wine shop.

He said, "I'm just back from Shikino. I don't know. Have you heard anything?"

"No, sir. Nothing. Her ladyship went to call."

"Ah." Akitada hurried into the house, calling out, "Sadako? Sadako?"

She came immediately, her face anxious. "What's wrong?"

He stopped. His heart expanded at her sight. Not all was death and dying. Here was life, his life. He smiled. "Nothing. Nothing now." Then he took her into his arms and buried his face in her hair. "I've missed you. Oh, I have missed you so."

She held him. "What was so terrible?"

He raised his head. "I forgot about Kosehira. You went? How is he?"

"Not well, but alive. His doctor is trying everything to bring the fever down."

"Thank heaven for that. I was distracted. That killer we found in Shikino. Everyone says he couldn't have done it."

"Come and sit. I'll send for some wine."

"Yes, but make it tea, I think. My mind is sadly confused already."

"Are you hungry? It's nearly time for the evening rice."

He had not eaten since that excellent soup in Shikino. That had been seven hours ago. He nodded. "Yes, let's sit together and eat and I'll tell you about it."

She rose and went to the kitchen, returning with the maid. They both carried trays and bowls which they arranged in the floor near Akitada. Appetizing

154

smells rose from buckwheat noodles with bamboo shoots, and baked eggplant with fish dumplings.

Halfway through the meal and his account, a distracted-looking Tora arrived. With the informality they were accustomed to these days in the privacy of their household, he was invited to share their meal and Akitada's update. Sadako sent for more food, and for wine, since Tora had never acquired the taste for tea, thinking it merely one of the nasty medicinal concoctions that the late Seimei had inflicted on the Sugawara family.

Tora ate, drank, and listened with growing surprise as Akitada outlined the facts that linked Kanemori to the Shirakawa massacre and the testimonials as to his character. When Akitada was done, he said, "It's the exact opposite with the schoolmaster."

"What do you mean?"

"Your schoolmaster turns out to be exactly the type that would kill his wife."

Sadako protested, "Oh, that cannot be true. He is a very proper man. He and I talked often when he taught Yoshi and I was looking after Yasuko. He seemed a learned and dedicated teacher and a highly moral man. Akitada would never have permitted anyone else to come into this house and teach his son."

Tora frowned. "Even so. Maybe he was all those things here because his pay depended on it. I'd swear Tanizaki is guilty as hell. He's a different man in his own household and with women."

Akitada raised his brows. "You surprise me. Are you sure, Tora? You sound angry. Angry people rarely think straight. What has the schoolmaster done to you?"

"To me, nothing. To his poor wife, well, it doesn't bear thinking about. I got an earful from her sister."

"Go ahead, tell!"

Tora started with the gardener Osamu's tale, emphasizing the schoolmaster's tight-fistedness and his obsession with keeping people out of his house."

Akitada said, "A schoolmaster doesn't earn much and he lives in a large house. I expect he has to be frugal in the matter of servants. Also, that area is not particularly safe. I doubt night watchmen patrol it. And many men prefer their wives not leave the house." Sadako cleared her throat. Akitada smiled at her. "I'm not like most men, I think. And we live in a safer neighborhood."

Tora said, "And your lady's not a former courtesan."

"No. Do you mean to tell me Tanizaki found his wife in the quarter?"

"Yes, indeed. He's a regular there. Still, even after he married her. The man is addicted to sex. At his age!"

This time Akitada cleared his throat.

Tora blushed. "Sorry, Lady Sadako."

She lowered her eyes modestly. "I've heard of such things."

Akitada suppressed a snort of laughter. "Do go on, Tora. I find your revelations surprising, not to say shocking."

"It gets worse. The murdered woman's sister immediately said he'd killed her. So did some neighbors. It seems they fought like cats and dogs. And the victim's former auntie told me he's still visiting women in the quarter."

156

Akitada shook his head. "Ouch. You have your work cut out for you if you want to help Tanizaki."

Tora flung up his hands in disgust. "I don't want to help that man. You're the one who told me to investigate because you want to help him. Are you saying I should abandon the case?"

"Not at all. It's your case. The matter is entirely up to you."

"But I don't like the man. He's despicable. Why should I help him?"

Akitada nodded. "A dilemma."

Tora gaped at him. After a moment and a cup of wine, he said, "What if he killed her?"

"You have doubts?"

"Well, I can't prove it. And I doubt the police would act on what I've learned about him. To them, a schoolmaster isn't likely to kill his wife."

"Yes. He's a very respectable man. That's why I hired him. That's why the Tachibana school employs him. That's why his wife married him. Who can argue against such a golden reputation?"

Sadako finally joined the conversation again. "It seems to me you're both faced with the same dilemma. Tora's suspect has the sort of reputation that raises him above suspicion, and you, Akitada, have the same problem with Kanemori."

Akitada smiled at her. "Precisely, my love. You put it very clearly. We must decide if a man can be both a Buddha and a devil."

"I opt for devil in my case," Tora said.

Akitada sighed and shook his head at him. "You may not be wrong, Tora, but you cannot prove it. Your work isn't done."

Tora glared. "Then neither is yours." He paused, then added, "Sir."

"Very true."

Frustrated, Tora got up and started pacing. "But what can I do? You ask me to find a killer that doesn't exist. Everything points to Tanizaki. Surely that proves there is no other killer. Where else can I look?"

"I wonder about that maid. She left rather conveniently. Was she fired? Did she have a lover she let in the house? Did Tanizaki keep money in the house? Who knew about it? What about keys. Who had them? Check the locks to see if they could be tampered with. And then there is the character of the victim. You have concentrated on the husband. What sort of wife was she? Perhaps *she* had a lover. And go back to the neighbors. Someone may have seen something."

Tora gaped at Akitada. He said angrily, "Half of that just gives Tanizaki a better motive. If she did have a lover, he would surely have killed her. And what if the maid had a lover and was fired. That doesn't help at all. Why would she kill her mistress?"

"If she had a lover and knew of money in the house, they may have plotted to steal it. Perhaps Tanizaki's wife discovered the theft."

Tora flopped back down, looking disgusted. "All right. I'll go check all that. And you? What will you do?"

Akitada nodded. "Yes, Tora. You're quite right. I also had not finished. And I also shall continue my search for another killer."

Lady Sadako smiled with satisfaction. She had managed to instill some purpose into the two men. She was fond of both of them and did not like to see them at odds or frustrated. Akitada, of course, she loved. He had to be handled with the greatest care even though she had come to feel quite certain of his devotion. Men were easily upset when they felt a woman had manipulated them. And yet, a happy marriage meant constant alertness to well-intentioned interference by the wife. Tora's wife, Hanae, knew this also. All good wives knew it.

Akitada saw her smile and wondered at it for a moment. It was a very pretty smile. He said, "Well, this was a useful conversation, but it's late. Let's get some rest and start afresh in the morning."

Tora obediently departed.

When they were alone, Akitada gave Sadako a searching look. "You're taking an interest in these cases?" he asked uncertainly.

She laughed lightly. "I take an interest in everything you do and think, my husband." She took his hand and kissed it.

He pulled her closer. "I think of you," he said softly. "I've been impatient for us to be alone."

She placed his hand on her neck where he could feel her warmth. "Then come! Let us make love and sleep in each other's arms."

20

The Coroner's Views

The next morning, Akitada went directly to police headquarters to speak to Lieutenant Hakeda. Hakeda was at his desk, staring morosely at a stack of documents. He greeted Akitada with a frown.

"A very unsatisfactory state of affairs," he said, "when I cannot take satisfaction in having solved a horrendous murder. Surely you haven't come in hopes of another surprise witness?"

Akitada sat on one of the cushions. "No. I've been wondering if Kanemori might have been murdered."

Hakeda's jaw dropped. Then he shook his head firmly. "You saw him. I saw him. Lord Arihito saw him. Even Haseo knew it was suicide."

"Yes, but what if someone else arranged it so it would look like suicide?"

"Forgive me, but that's absurd, my Lord."

"Has the coroner seen the body?"

The lieutenant was becoming upset and defensive. "He was busy. And there was no need. We don't burden the man with suicides."

Akitada said nothing. He watched Hakeda's face, saw thoughts chasing each other in his expression, and waited.

Finally Hakeda spoke. "It can't be." But his tone was less certain. "Kanemori was a healthy, well-trained man, a great fighter. He would surely not allow someone to get close enough to kill him. And why arrange the body in the position of ritual suicide? No, sir. I cannot believe that Kanemori would not have defended himself against an attack."

"He may have been caught by surprise. He was a teacher of martial arts. All the killer would have to do would be to ask for a lesson with the short sword. A demonstration on how to hold the weapon perhaps."

Hakeda got up and started pacing. "Maybe. But there's no proof. We cannot just proceed on this idea because we don't want Kanemori to be the killer. Think what everybody will say."

"The coroner might prove it."

Akitada could see that the lieutenant was becoming thoroughly frightened by the likely repercussions of this theory. His fear made him angry. He snapped, "Might? You're just guessing, aren't you?"

Akitada remained calm. "Yes. But we have a problem, you and I. We have accepted Kanemori as a killer when by all accounts he would not have done it. And we find it hard to believe that men like Kanemori could commit such a crime. If we start with the assumption that he didn't do it, then the real killer must be someone else."

Hakeda groaned. He sat down and buried his head in his hands. "The fact that everyone liked the man is not hard evidence. And I'm not about to lay this idea before the family of the victims."

"No. At least not yet. At present, no judge would accept it. But let's try out the theory. Let's see where it leads us."

"You know the coroner will think I've lost my mind."

"Blame it on me. I'm used to being thought peculiar."

That put a smile on Hakeda's face. He shouted for a constable and sent him in search of Doctor Sugito. Then he said, as if to reassure himself, "You know, we never established a motive for Kanemori. As I've said repeatedly, 'It made no sense for him to kill those people.'"

"We haven't looked for a motive. We've accepted all of this too readily because we were glad the killing was over. Actually, there might have been a reason in Kanemori's background. All the fighting he did up north. Who knows what offenses he witnessed by some Fujiwara lord."

"You cannot have it both ways. Either you believe he's innocent or we find his motive."

Akitada teased, "And for that matter, his more recent life might also produce a motive. He's been teaching the sons of noble families."

Hakeda glared.

"And then, there's the matter of the run-away girlfriend. What if she ran right into Yorimune's arms?"

Hakeda opened his mouth, but at this point the door opened to admit the coroner. Doctor Sugito waddled in, nodding to Hakeda and making Akitada a small bow. "Morning," he drawled. "What is it? Any new corpses? Your timing's good, I'm actually free for once."

Hakeda said, "Lord Sugawara wishes you to prove that Kanemnori was murdered."

Sugito laughed until his belly shook. With a gasp, he fell on one of the cushions and laughed some more.

They waited, Akitada frowning, and Hakeda looking smug.

Finally Sugito caught his breath, looked at Akitada, and said, "Seriously?"

"Yes."

"Not a suicide then?"

"Perhaps not."

"Ah." The coroner thought. "Interesting. Something about the scene wasn't quite right?"

Akitada hesitated. "No. At least I don't think so. It's more of a feeling about the man." He glanced at Hakeda. "And the lieutenant shares it."

Sugito raised his brows. "Really, Lieutenant?"

Hakeda blushed. "It's always good to be thorough."

The coroner looked disbelieving. "You amaze me. Where's the body?"

"At Sosho-ji. We turned it over to the monks. It was the closest."

The coroner turned red with anger. "What? You let those fools get him ready for cremation?"

The lieutenant threw up his hands. "I had no reason to refuse."

"Well then, he may already have gone up in smoke."

"No. I doubt that. I'll send my men for the body."

"Good luck. He won't get here till tomorrow. The Day of the Dead. How appropriate!" Sugito gave him a disgusted look and left, with barely a nod to Akitada.

"He gets very angry," muttered Hakeda. "He hates it when someone has touched his bodies."

"Well, we must hope we're in time. How soon will he be able to start?"

"It's a holiday. And he's angry. Not until after the midday rice, I expect. He may not find anything. And that will make him even angrier."

Akitada sighed and got up. "I'll be back tomorrow."

He walked to Kosehira's house to visit his friend. To his relief, he was told that Kosehira had spent a quiet night and was still sleeping. Lady Hatsuko herself came to welcome him. She was smiling and walked with barely a limp.

"He's better," she cried. "Oh, Akitada, he's finally getting better. That fever was awful! He was talking the whole time, saying strange things. And he was so restless, we wives had to take turns pinning him down so he wouldn't open the wound again. But then he grew quiet, and I thought he'd died, but he was breathing. Breathing quietly! And then the doctor looked at him and said the fever had broken and he would be well. He would heal and he would live." Tears of joy gathered in her eyes. Kosehira had been very lucky in his choice of wives.

Akitada took her hands. He said, "I cannot tell you what a relief that is! I was so worried."

She nodded. "I know, dear Akitada. He is so fond of you."

That brought tears to Akitada's eyes. He swore to himself that he would not let the past come between him and Kosehira again.

"He's still asleep?"

"Yes. And we are to let him sleep. The doctor thinks he needs the rest. But do come and take a peek."

They tiptoed into Kosehira's room where Akitada confirmed for himself that his friend was sleeping naturally and his color had returned to normal. Then they crept out again.

As Akitada was bidding Lady Hatsuko goodbye, Arihito arrived and also heard the good news. He, too, crept into his father's room and came back out smiling. "Thank the gods," he said. "It was very bad the last two days."

Akitada told him about his doubts concerning Kanemori. "Hakeda agrees, though he's very uneasy about it. The coroner will take a look at the body."

Arihito was matter-of-fact. "Better not expect anything. The man's belly was badly cut up, and there was a lot of blood."

"Yes, but not perhaps as much as you'd expect. I don't know. My experience with that sort of suicide is limited. In any case, there won't be news until tomorrow. They have to bring the body back from the temple where they are preparing him for cremation."

When Akitada arrived home, he found a messenger from the prime minister waiting for him. The great man wished to see him. Dismayed by the summons, Akitada changed into his court robe and departed for the *Daidairi*.

His Excellency, though dressed in plain, dark clothing suitable for mourning, looked to be in a good mood, and Akitada relaxed a little.

"There you are, Sugawara," he said with a smile. "I wanted to congratulate you on having solved this horrible crime so efficiently. I should have given you more credit. My apologies. Very good news, finding this Kanemori. And even better news that he decided to take the easy way out and avoid the shameful death by decapitation. I hate those affairs."

Akitada was at a loss for words. Of course he should have expected it, but his mind had been occupied with Kanemori's character. He said cautiously, "We have not found a motive, sir. Kanemori seems to have been a man with an exemplary past."

The prime minster waved that away as a mere detail. "We'll find it. Rest assured. The main thing is that we can now go about the business of mourning our dead and looking after the wounded. And that reminds me: How is Kosehira doing?"

"I'm happy to report that he seems a little better today. And his lady is also healing well."

"Good, good!" The prime minister looked positively energized. "Well, it's back to work for me. A big day tomorrow. His Majesty will participate in the donation of food to the temples and the burning of hemp. And we will mourn our recent dead. My thanks, Sugawara. Your service will be remembered."

21

Tora is Frustrated

Tora felt both chastened and irritated by his master's admonition that he look harder for a killer who was not Tanizaki. What? Go back to that maid in case she was fired or had had a lover? The girl was too plain to have had a lover, and Tanizaki was hardly the kind of employer who would have tolerated such a thing. Had she been fired? That was possible. She claimed she had left because she didn't like working there, but servants who were fired often said things like that. And Tanizaki might well have fired her to save money. He was the sort of husband who would expect his wife to do the housework. But if she was fired, so what? That did not suggest a killer. Of course the maid herself could have taken revenge by killing Tanizaki's

169

wife, but that was surely silly. The master must be slipping.

Tora reflected for a while on the possibility that Akitada might no longer be infallible. He was getting older and the Shirakawa affair had put a lot of stress on him. And then there was Lady Sadako. Tora was very pleased with the happiness she had brought to his master, but he was also aware that her husband doted on her in a manner that was surely excessive at his age. Indulgence in sexual pleasures could sap a man's intelligence and strength at his age. And it made a mature man look a bit pitiful. Tora had long since regulated such activities with Hanae. In fact, Hanae seemed to welcome his restraint. Of course, Lady Sadako was probably starved for sex after her years of widowhood. They said widows needed sex much more after losing a husband. And she was younger than the master.

Tora sighed and returned to his own problem. He decided to take care of the easiest errand: he would check the locks and consider possible stashes of wealth in the Tanizaki abode.

To his surprise and satisfaction, he found Osamu back at work, weeding the vegetable garden. Osamu was also very pleased to see the generous Tora again.

"You want me to answer more questions?" he asked hopefully.

"Just a few. I figure you're still in my debt." Tora was rather short on cash after his generosity.

Osamu grinned toothlessly. "Ah. Well, I guess I am. What do you want to know?"

"I went to see Kogiri, the maid. She says she left of her own free will. She says she didn't like the job. Was that the truth?"

Osamu pursed his lips. "Maybe. And maybe not. The mistress and Kogiri quarreled."

"Ah. Did you hear them? What was it about?"

The old man pondered a moment. "Kogiri thought she was better than the mistress. She didn't like her telling her what to do."

Tora guessed, "Because the master's wife used to work in the willow quarter?"

Osamu nodded. "Everybody thinks they're better than someone. Me, I'm used to it. I just do what they tell me and get paid."

Tora grinned. "I fine philosophy."

That made Osamu chuckle. "And you?"

"I mostly think I'm better, but I don't say so."

Osamu laughed. "The master, now. He knows he's better and he says so. A very fine man, Master Tanizaki. Fine old family. Used to be 'good people.' And he's a learned man, too. And beautiful women find him attractive."

"They do?" Tora pictured the middle-aged Tanizaki with his belly and thinning hair. "I don't think so," he said firmly.

Osamu laughed again. "You're a very funny man, Tora. Women look past a man's appearance. They're a lot more practical about such things than men are."

Tora regarded Osamu with new interest. Who could have known that this *hinin* or *eta*, a manual laborer, took such an avid interest in human nature. "You may be right," he said. "In any case, I think your mistress married your master because she wanted to be respectable."

Osamu suddenly looked sad. "Yes. Big disappointment. I could've told her. Once a *hinin*, always a *hinin*."

"He must've promised her a fine life. Maybe he has money for fine things?"

Osamu spat. "Don't think so. He's stingy. No money there."

"Some wealthy men are stingy. They hoard their money. Keep it in big chests."

The old man thought about this. "Hmm," he said and looked at the house and the vegetable garden. "Well," he continued, "for her he was a big disappointment. The maid said he sold her fine clothes and she cried for days."

So the wife's sister had been right. Still, it didn't mean Tanizaki had no money or didn't love money for its own sake. But it seemed to rule out thieves knowing of any hidden treasures. And he had not seen anything worth selling on his visit to the house.

He said, "I assume the wife did the shopping in the market. What about locking up the house then?"

"She had a key."

"Ah. And what if she gave it to someone?"

"Why? Now, if she had a friend who'd kill her husband, I could see that."

Tora grinned at the old man with new respect. "Yes. You're quite right. Did she have any male friends?"

"Never saw any."

Well, that proved nothing. So far, his efforts at clearing up the loopholes his master had pointed out had produced only partial results. He could not really blame Osamu, who seemed grateful for Tora's past generosity and therefore not likely to keep back any information. He thanked the old man, and headed for the house where he studied the lock at the door. It seemed solid enough, but he knew he could open it with some special tools he had at home. Would a thief be less prepared? He thought not. But the door was in plain sight from the street, and any shenanigans would have taken place at night when someone was home. Tora walked around the entire building looking for places where an agile person might climb in. The only place that invited such activities was the lone window to the kitchen attic, and he saw no way to reach it unless the murderer brought a ladder with him.

Satisfied that he had done his best to clear up three of the doubtful facts his master had pointed out, Akitada left the Tanizaki premises and took another stroll among the shacks and sheds of the schoolmaster's closest neighbors.

This time, he was received eagerly by a number of the inhabitants who claimed to have vital information. Their ranks thinned dramatically when Tora confessed he had only a modest string of coppers with him. But one youngster, a youth of about fifteen with hair standing up on his head like a stiff brush, bargained for twenty coppers, promising to tell Tora what he had seen at Tanizaki's place the day before the murder was discovered.

Even though he suspected this promise, Tora parted with the coppers because it had become clear that this boy had been hanging around the house, hoping to catch glimpses of Tanizaki's wife. He seemed to have become enamored of her because of the lurid tales his friends passed around about the delights offered by the courtesans of the willow quarter.

So much for the respectability Tomoko had hoped to gain as the wife of a staid schoolmaster.

The story, once divulged, amounted to only one piece of information, and this was doubtful in Tora's view. The youngster claimed to have seen a young man at the window above the kitchen. He deduced from this that the schoolmaster's wife had had a lover.

"Did you see a ladder?"

The boy grinned. "No ladder. Bet she let him in."

"He could have been the maid's lover," Tora pointed out.

The youngster shook his head emphatically. "That ugly bitch had left long before then. Besides he was dressed in fine clothes. Such a one would never sleep with a maid."

"What did he look like?"

The boy hesitated, then eyed Tora. "He looked like you, only young."

Tora glared at him and left.

22

Day of the Dead

The first day of the *O-bon* festival dawned gray and wet. A fine, misting rain hung over the Sugawara garden when Akitada opened the shutters. Behind him, Sadako stirred sleepily.

He said, "It's raining."

"Oh. That's why it's so dark." She sat up and yawned.

Sadako looked most seductive when she was rosy and disheveled from sleep. Akitada swallowed and smiled. "It's appropriate. I think it's late. We didn't go to sleep until the hour of the rat, and there was no sun to wake us."

She was immediately wide awake and scrambled out of the bed clothes. "Oh. You're right. I must hurry. It's a busy day."

It was the day when they honored the dead in their family. Akitada felt a stab of sadness. He had lost so many. Sadako threw on some clothes and hurried out of the room. She would prepare the offerings and have them ready when they gathered at the Sugawara family altar with its ancient Buddha statue and the name plaques of their dead ancestors.

Akitada had little to do with preparations and ambled toward the bath to soak and think of his dead.

It was a painful exercise and a part of him envied the others their busy work, but he felt he owed his dead family this mourning. He tried to remember them as they had been in life and failed shamefully. No longer could he call up Tamako's face, or the small, agile figure of his little son Yori. No longer could he recreate old Seimei's cracked voice or his smile. It mattered less that both his father and his stepmother had receded into an impenetrable past. He had not been close to either. Still, they would be honored along with those he had loved. He did recall his own pain after his first wife and his little son had died. And he missed Seimei, the faithful retainer with his wise sayings who had been like a loving father to the young Akitada when his own father had rejected him. Every year on this day, Akitada sent his thoughts back into the past, and every year he grieved over his own forgetting.

Perhaps too much happiness had clouded his remembrance worse this year. He wished *O-bon* over so that he could devote his attention to the present.

The bathwater grew cold and he shivered. Too much happiness brought devastating grief.

Dressing swiftly, he went to the kitchen for his morning gruel. He saw that Sadako had lined up the offerings to the dead already. Fresh peaches and plums, golden ears of rice, sweet buns, nuts. He ate his gruel without much appetite.

Later, as every year, they gathered at the small altar, wearing their best clothes, to bow to the ancestors and to welcome them home. The children looked astonishingly mature. Yoshi, who was only twelve, had shot up lately. His studies at the university had not kept him from his favorite exercises and he had developed surprisingly broad shoulders. He looked older than his years, but he fidgeted. Yoshi barely recalled his mother, but Yasuko, now sixteen, looked sad and wiped away a tear. She resembled Tamako but was taller and would soon bring suitors to their house. At least he hoped they would be suitors and not just frivolous young men determined to add to their collection of lovers. Prince Genji and his friends had started a deplorable custom. Akitada was determined to guard his daughter against the licentious activities his second wife had engaged in.

His thoughts turned to Kanemori's doomed love affair. There was still much they did not know about the man and many places where they might find suspects. But first things first. This afternoon, the coroner would probe Kanemori's body to ascertain once and for all the manner of his death.

The day's observances closed with a family meal. Yoshi had had other plans, but his father insisted. He saw far too little of his son these days and he still hoped to bring them all closer together more regularly in a happy group like Kosehira's family. He would never forget the cheerful meals he had eaten at his friend's house in the company of Kosehira's three wives and all his children. The warmth and love in that family had played a large role in his marrying the eighteen-year-old Yukiko, Kosehira's eldest and favorite daughter. He had longed for such a family because he had never had one as a child.

He made an effort to keep the conversation light, to encourage the children to talk to each other and to him and Sadako. Brother and sister had never been close. The age difference was partially to blame, but their interests also diverged, and the years after Tamako's death had not helped. He had not known how to deal with his children and had preferred to withdraw into his grief.

The meal was not a total success, and Akitada rose from the elaborate spread with some relief. The children departed to their own pursuits and he thanked Sadako.

She asked anxiously, "It wasn't quite what you'd hoped for, was it?"

"Everything was perfect. The offerings looked particularly well and the meal was delicious."

She smiled. "Don't worry so. The children are young. They'll come around to respecting each other."

So she had guessed. He said, "I blame myself. I've been a terrible father. I may not have been as harsh as my own father was, but in some ways I've been worse. I've been cold and uncaring. No wonder they've grown up that way."

She touched his hand. "No, Akitada. I cannot believe that you're ever uncaring. You were caught up in your grief and in the demands of your work, but you've always cared for them, and they know that."

He looked at her uncertainly. "Did they say so?"

"In every way, with every glance, even when they were angry because you refused them something."

He laughed. "You're humoring me. I hope a small portion of what you say is true. But enough of family business. I must go see what the coroner finds. He's going to have a look at Kanemori this afternoon."

"Surely you hope for something quite beyond his skill."

"Yes. But there's nothing else I can pin my hopes on."

"And why do you wish this man to be innocent? You will just have to start searching again."

"If what I suspect is true, then the crimes at Shirakawa almost pale when compared to shifting the guilt to a good man and then taking his life before he can clear his name."

She turned away. "Yes, you're right, but I'm afraid. This is a monster you're dealing with and he may be protected by those in power, perhaps by the emperor himself."

"Not the emperor. No. I don't believe that. Do not worry so, my love. I'll be careful."

He embraced her, then changed into plain clothing. In a straw rain cape and hat, he set out for police headquarters.

He found that Lieutenant Hakeda had preceded him to the coroner's place of business. A constable took him to the small building where Dr. Sugito practiced his sacrilegious art. Hardly anyone faced contamination by contact with the dead more thoroughly than a coroner or a physician. Many coroners belonged to the untouchables, but Sugito had trained at the university to be a physician, a fact that made him a good deal more reliable than the pharmacists and horse doctors serving in provincial police systems.

In this case, the body was far from fresh. As he and Hakeda hovered near the fat coroner, Akitada reflected that this work would have been an even more sickening business, if the weather had been warmer. At least they were all used to dealing with the more repulsive aspects of death.

Being too fat to crouch comfortably on the ground, Sugito had the body raised. Kanemori rested on a plank. He was stripped naked and looked defenseless. The naked dead always presented a shocking appearance, and this body had begun to decompose. Livid spots had appeared on the skin, especially on his face where it had rested on the ground. It looked puffy, as did his limbs and abdomen. And there was a strong smell. Akitada shivered slightly.

The fat man didn't glance at them, but the lieutenant gave Akitada a nod. The coroner was washing the body. He moved slowly, almost delicately for such a large man, using a square of unbleached cotton and water from a bowl to cleanse even the smallest surface of skin while peering at it closely from those bulbous eyes.

"Hmm," he muttered. "The monks did us a favor. They prepared him and kept him covered. Otherwise, this would have been difficult."

Sugito gave close attention to the skull, parting the gray hair and feeling it all over. He pried open the eyelids and stared at the dead eyes. He opened the mouth, exposing the tongue, and leaned close to sniff the dead man's breath. He probed the nostrils and both ears.

Nobody spoke.

The horrific belly wounds were already cleansed of blood and looked almost harmless, except for the disconcerting bluish gleam of intestines between the gaping wounds. Akitada was both fascinated and sickened. Kanemori had missed the first time. His short sword had nicked a rib before it found the soft tissue lower down and cut into the belly.

The coroner inspected both hands and feet and then asked to have the body turned over. Two assistants, *eta,* no doubt, who had cowered in a dark corner, sprang forward and repositioned the corpse. The slow and careful cleansing resumed.

Kanemori was badly scarred. Old wounds, both from arrows and swords, marked his back, arms, and legs. The fatal wounds to the belly had distracted Akitada, but he guessed that he had missed more scars to the front of Kanemori's body, evidence of his life as a warrior. A fine warrior, for he had survived and that must have taken skill.

Finally, Sugito straightened with a groan and rubbed his back. "Well," he said.

"Well, what?" Lieutenant Hakeda demanded.

Sugito did not answer. "Turn him back!" he told the assistants.

They did, and the coroner picked up a folded piece of cotton and placed it over Kanemori's lower body. It covered his legs and private parts but left the belly wounds, the broad chest and arms, and his face bare. It had been a gesture of respect Akitada found astonishing in a man like the coroner who had not struck him as sensitive or respectful. The thought saddened him. He had been too quick to judge, too accepting of the presumed callousness of those who dealt regularly with the dead.

The lieutenant was not so easily distracted. He snapped, "Stop playing games, Sugito. Was it suicide or not?"

The coroner sighed. He pointed to a wound near the rib cage. "There's your answer, Lieutenant.." He turned away and started to waddle out of the room.

Hakeda shouted, "Damn you, stop! What the devil do you mean? How am I to guess from that?"

But Akitada had got it. At that very moment, while Hakeda was still erupting in fury, he knew.

"He was murdered," he said quietly.

Hakeda swung around, disbelief and anger mixed in his face. "How do you know? How can you know? I see the wounds he made himself. And that's all I see. What? Has he been poisoned? Bludgeoned? How was he murdered?"

Akitada looked at the coroner, who said nothing but smiled a little.

"I think," said Akitada, "Doctor Sugito has ruled out poison or bludgeoning. Kanemori was stabbed, probably with his own sword."

The coroner nodded. "I confess, I was surprised," he said. "I saw it right away but I had to make sure."

Hakeda looked from one to the other in utter disbelief, then went to bend over the body. "The wounds all look the same," he said. "How can you possibly say he was stabbed? Those are *jigai* wounds. And when we found him, his sword was in his body and he had hold of it."

"We've discussed that such a pose may be arranged after death," Akitada said.

Hakeda nodded slowly, then turned to the coroner. "How did *you* know?"

Sugito heaved an audible sigh and waddled back to the body. He pointed to the one cut that was near the rib cage. "That's not a cut made for a suicide," he said. "And it's not accidental. That's a cut made by another man standing in front of his victim and shoving a sword into his chest. Look how violent it was. It nicked a rib. Look how deep it is and how much blood is inside." The coroner peeled back the edges of the wound to demonstrate. "The other wounds came later. There is very little blood in them. A man stops bleeding after death."

Hakeda still protested, "There was plenty of blood under him when we found him."

Sugito sighed again. "He drained. That's all."

Hakeda opened his mouth again but he closed it without a word and just shook his head.

Akitada touched Hakeda's arm. "So Kanemori was murdered. Wasn't that what we suspected all along?"

The coroner said sarcastically, "I trust I can leave now? Or would you like me to supply the name of the murderer, too?"

The lieutenant glared at him and Akitada said quickly, "No, Doctor. We are grateful for your help."

Sugito grunted and waddled out.

"So," Akitada said, "we have saved a hero's reputation, but now we have a murder to solve. Isn't that what you hoped for?"

Hakeda looked miserable. "I hadn't thought that far. I was shocked that a man like Kanemori could have done what someone did at Shirakawa."

"You were right. We were in agreement there. But clearing Kanemori means that we now have an additional crime, his murder. And it needn't be the same killer in both instances."

Hakeda looked bewildered. "Surely . . . I would have thought only the real killer would set up something like this. If you're right . . . I didn't really believe it could happen and so . . . " He paused. "I follow what you're saying, but surely it isn't likely that there are two killers. This killing cannot have been accidental. And if it isn't the same killer, then there could have been a conspiracy." He suddenly looked uneasy. "Maybe a group of powerful people have been working together to plan all of it."

Akitada nodded. "It's possible. A lot of things are possible now."

Hakeda was clearly upset and started pacing. "If their intention was just to kill Yorimune, then perhaps they'll stop now. But what if this is much bigger? What if someone is trying to attack our government? I think we must let the prime minister know right away. This isn't something the capital police can handle."

Akitada understood Hakeda's panic, but since he had no idea why Yorimune had been killed and who might be involved in his murder, he thought bringing the coroner's findings to the prime minister's attention would be a dangerous mistake.

He said in a soothing voice, "I think that it's highly unlikely that there is more than one killer. And troubling the prime minister now on the Day of the Dead when he and his family are mourning his brother would be most unkind and improper."

Hakeda stopped pacing. "Yes. You're right. You know more about such things than I. I've been a soldier like Kanemori and know nothing of the *kuge*. What do you think we should do?"

The *kuge* were the highest ranking nobles in the government. Most were Fujiwara and related to the prime minister and the emperor.

Akitada said, "We can ask more questions. Quietly. It will be best not to reveal the coroner's findings for a while." As he said this, Akitada realized that they had already made one very careless mistake by letting Doctor Sugito leave without warning him against speaking to anyone about this. He said quickly, "We'd better let Sugito know right away not to talk to anyone. Has he gone home?"

"I've no idea. Surely he wouldn't talk. Do you really think there is danger?"

He was frightened again, and Akitada said, "Probably not. He did not strike me as a man who gossips much."

"I'll let him know."

Suddenly very tired, Akitada decided that nothing else could be accomplished that night and went home through the dismal rain.

23

Akiko

There was still much they had not learned about Kanemori. It was almost certain that the killer knew him well, or at least well enough to find out where he lived, and above all, well enough to get close to the man to kill him. But did Kanemori allow this person to masquerade in his armor and use his horse?

Although tired, Akitada could not sleep. New problems with the crimes had surfaced and seemed to multiply as he thought about them.

Could Kanemori have been an accessory after all?

But surely he was not a man to countenance the slaughter of women whatever reason he might have had to condone the killing of Yorimune and his male relatives.

And then there was the fact that Kanemori did not seem to have had any close friends. Or friends like this killer.

Still, a clever man may convince a trusting one of almost anything. Kanemori probably thought he was helping with a harmless entertainment.

Akitada sat up. But then he must have discovered the truth after the massacre. He must have known the very next day. He would surely have done something. But he had done nothing and yet he wasn't killed until three days later.

It was impossible!

Akitada sighed and lay down again. Tomorrow he must make a start to find out what happened. He would pay another visit to the sword smith's place. The killer was also a fine archer in his own right. Surely they met there.

On that thought, Akitada finally went to sleep.

Unfortunately the next morning he realized that the problem with asking more questions was that he could not reveal that Kanemori had been murdered. And clearly, the people who had known and worked with Kanemori would be puzzled why Akitada was still pursuing the matter when the authorities had closed the case.

Everywhere he turned he ran into insurmountable obstacles.

He turned his mind again to Yorimune. If he had indeed been the reason for the massacre—and even that no longer seemed certain—then there must be something or someone in his past who was the link between the massacre and Kanemori's murder.

He could not ask anyone connected with Yorimune's family. Indeed, just asking questions of people connected to the court was dangerous.

It was again impossible!

Then he remembered his sister Akiko.

Akiko, who frequented the halls and backrooms of the imperial palace.

Akiko, who knew how to keep a secret.

Akiko, who took enormous pleasure in meddling in his cases, having decided that she could do as well as her brother at catching killers.

He would pay Akiko a visit.

Akiko was Akitada's less favorite stepsister. She was the older one. The two were his father's children by the woman he took to wife after Akitada's mother died. Akitada had never known his mother and was raised to believe the second Lady Sugawara to be his mother. His childhood and early adulthood had been made miserable by this woman and his father had done nothing to protect him. But he had found his younger sister to be a gentle and loving child while Akiko was always bossy, a trait she had inherited from her mother. Like her mother, she valued money and power above all else, two things that were sadly lacking in the Sugawara family.

Akiko had married well. Her husband Toshikage belonged to a branch of the Minamoto family and was quite wealthy. Her sister Yoshiko had chosen an untitled farmer, but that had been after their parents' death and over Akitada's objections.

Since then, he had changed his mind about Yoshiko's choice, and he had also come to appreciate Akiko, who had raised a family with a firm, but loving hand, and who had never abandoned Akitada, looking after him and his affairs with sisterly and often irritating affection. Now he found he looked forward to seeing her, and perhaps also Toshikage, a bumbling, ineffectual, but kindly man.

The weather had cleared overnight, and Akitada walked more cheerfully to the large house his sister and her family occupied. He found her supervising her daughters in their sewing efforts. To his dismay, she scowled when she saw him.

"So there you are at last," she snapped, then took him to another room before telling him exactly what she thought of him.

"What did I do?" he asked, puzzled.

"It's what you didn't do, you ungrateful wretch! Where have you been? Why didn't you come or send me a message? Do I mean so little to you? Have you forgotten the help I gave you in the past? I expect you were going to keep it all to yourself. And I had to deal with everybody's questions about what you were doing and had nothing to say. I was mortified."

Akitada listened aghast to all this and eventually realized what she was talking about. He attempted a defense of sorts. "Kosehira was wounded. It looked very bad. I haven't really had time."

"Nonsense!"

"Well, he's a bit better, so I came right away. And here I am. What do you want to know?"

"Liar! You didn't come to bring me information. You want something."

Akiko was very bright. He should have known she would see right through his excuses.

"Well, could we sit down while I tell you?"

She relented and gestured to cushions. "I'll get some wine, or do you want tea?"

190

"Either. Don't go to any trouble. I've had something at home." And as an afterthought, "How's Toshikage?"

"Fine." She was gone.

Akiko's attitude toward her husband had always been one of pained forbearance. He, on the other hand, was besotted with Akiko. To prove it, he had never taken secondary wives, to Akiko's resentment. She had hoped concubines would leave her free to do what she wanted to do. Instead their marriage had been blessed with five children, cousins and playmates to Akitada's own. It had only been in the last years that Akiko had found the freedom to meddle in her brother's investigations. Her attendance at court had been useful to him in the past, even though she had had a hand in turning Yukiko's head with the splendor of rubbing shoulders with empresses and imperial concubines. Akitada hoped that his sister still harbored a few feelings of guilt over her part in the break-up of his marriage.

She returned with wine and a small bowl of nuts and sat down again.

He poured for both of them. "You look well," he said with a conciliatory smile.

She did look well, even though he saw a few white threads in her long, glossy black hair. Akiko was tall and slender, and clothes looked wonderful on her. Toshikage spoiled her with fine silks and pretty fans.

She still glowered. "Don't try to flatter me. You don't care what I look like."

"That's not true."

He tried to look and sound hurt and saw that she was relenting.

"How's your wife? Any sign of a child yet?"

191

"Sadako is well, and you know I don't want any more children."

"She's healthy. Strong. All those northern women are that way."

"We are happy as we are. Finally!"

She relented some more, no doubt recalling his unhappy marriage to Yukiko and the fact that she had introduced his young wife to a corrupt court. She sipped her wine and said, "You came about the Shirakawa matter."

He sighed. "Yes, that too. I need to know what they think at court."

She raised her brows. "I can tell you that they are very impressed with your speed in solving the crime. But surely you must know that. The prime minister has been heard to say that his government needs more men like you. I'm sure you'll be promoted."

Akitada made a face. "The opposite, I expect."

She stared. "Why? What did you do this time?"

That was typical. She knew him too well to think he would long remain in the favor of the court. He said, "Kanemori did not kill anyone at Shirakawa."

She frowned. "Kanemori?"

"The man who committed suicide and is believed to have been the killer."

"Do tell!"

This again was like Akiko. She did not bother to question his words. She wanted to know the facts. He told her.

She listened, then asked, "If he was such an upright man, why didn't he tell anyone about the man who borrowed his clothes and horse?"

She had found the hole in their argument immediately. It had taken Akitada days to come around to it. He sighed. "I'm getting old."

Akiko snorted. "Yes. And so am I. It doesn't matter. You can still think, can't you?"

"Apparently it's taking me much longer these days. I need your help, Akiko."

"It's not like you to whine like that. What's the problem?"

"The prime minister's acceptance of Kanemori's guilt."

"Oh!" Akiko frowned. "Well, he likes you."

This surprised Akitada. "He *likes* me? Are you joking?"

"No. I have it on good authority. Some people have been frustrated by the fact."

"At Shirakawa he ordered me to stay away from the case. I clearly did not obey."

"Oh, but he should know by now that you don't do what he wants. He was very pleased that you found the killer so quickly. He sings your praises throughout the palace."

"Akiko, have you been listening? Kanemori wasn't the killer and I need to find the real one. How am I to do this without facing the anger of the entire Fujiwara clan?"

"I would be very surprised if you let that stop you."

"I have a family and . . ."

She smiled. "And you have a new wife."

"Yes."

"You know, I should be very hurt that you have never cared about what might happen to me and Toshikage in all those years when you took chances."

"Yes. I know it. I'm sorry, Akiko, but I knew that Toshikage didn't need court influence and you seemed to be so close to the empress that she would have protected you. This is different. The victim was the prime minister's brother. They were close. I'm convinced he knows something, some reason why Yorimune was attacked."

"Hmm. Not so close perhaps. But never mind. I see you have a problem." She had a calculating expression on her face. "I may be better placed than you. I suggest you leave the matter with me for the moment."

Akitada felt relieved. "You will be careful and you'll tell me when you have information?"

"Yes." She looked pleased with herself.

"Umm, Akiko, think before you ask questions. I need to know if anyone among the family, friends, and acquaintances of Yorimune is skilled in archery and may have had a reason to kill Yorimune and his family. That's not an easy thing for you to discover."

She laughed. "I know. Now go home to your Sadako and do your duty there."

He blushed and rose reluctantly. "Don't do anything foolish. I'd never forgive myself if . . ."

She pushed him out of the room, still laughing. "It's a little late for that, dear brother. Don't worry. I'll solve your case for you."

24

The Secret Visitor

All through O-bon, Tora pondered his case. The boy's tale of seeing a well-dressed man at the attic window was new and startling, but he did not know whether to believe it. He had inspected that very attic and seen no sign of anyone having been there other than a maid, or a cook. There had been only kitchen stores. Though, come to think of it, there had been that pile of empty sacks or whatever it had been. But only a cat would sleep there, certainly not a well-dressed man. And how would a stranger have got inside, unless invited by the people who lived there? He decided to put the matter from his mind for the time being.

There was still the dubious character of Tanizaki. Any number of people had suggested or hinted that Tanizaki had a lover. And several of them had also thought Tanizaki had killed his wife. Tora's instincts were that the man was guilty as hell.

It rained all day, his body ached, and he decided to stay home with his wife and son. But by evening, the problem of the guilt or innocence of Tanizaki weighed so heavily on his mind that he decided to discuss the matter with Hanae. Their son Yuki having left for the guard barracks, they were alone together.

He rarely shared his business with his wife. She was the joy of his life and he did not want to spoil their togetherness with the bad things of the world. Occasionally they did speak of their worries about Yuki. Hanae was bitterly opposed to her only child becoming a soldier, and Tora mostly tried to calm her fears by pointing out that the capital guard was practically never involved in war. Their function was to patrol the city and enforce law and order. Yuki, of course, wished to be allowed to join whatever large military force was at the moment engaged in fighting in some distant province. He hoped for adventure, fame, and excitement. Tora sympathized. He had briefly been a soldier, though only a lowly member of the infantry. He had seen the mounted warriors then and had envied them.

The topic had come up again over their evening rice and Hanae was still upset.

So this evening, Tora decided to tell her about Tanizaki, partially to distract her and avoid any arguments and partially to reassure himself.

Hanae was fascinated. She was also gratified. Tora knew she thought him a good husband and, he hoped, a great lover, but she always complained he kept too much of himself to himself. Now she listened and asked questions, being careful to assure him from time to time that she admired his resourcefulness.

Encouraged by this, Tora confessed, "I think the master wants me to clear Tanizaki, but I've come to hate the man. I know he did it."

Hanae nodded. "There were such men when I still worked in the quarter."

Tora said quickly, "Don't say you worked there. People will think you were a whore."

Hanae smiled and patted his hand. "I know. You rescued me. I was just a dancer. But Tora, you used not to despise the working girls. In fact, I think you knew some of them very well indeed."

Tora grinned. He scratched his head. "You're right. What's happened to me? Hanging around people like Tanizaki is turning my head. Tell me what you think."

"You said something about the master using the words 'Buddha or devil'. I don't think people are either of those. Take Tomoko, the wife, for example, or her sister. Both worked as courtesans. From what you say, both were successful. That means they earned good money. Being successful in the quarter means you have to lie to men you don't like. It's always the ones you don't like, the old ones and the ugly ones, who have the money. And lying becomes a habit. So you cannot really believe everything such women say."

Tora thought about this and nodded slowly. "But Tanizaki lied, too. He promised her a good life as his wife and then he sold her clothes and made her work like a maid."

"Yes. The men also lie. But the women face a dismal future if they cannot earn enough to support themselves when they grow old and unattractive. A woman has a right to protect herself. And all that Tomoko wanted was a simple life as a married woman.

She was willing to give up her prospects to get that. I take it Tanizaki was neither rich, nor young and handsome like you."

Tora grinned. "I know a good woman when I see one." He reached for her. "Let's go to bed. It's getting late."

She freed herself from the embrace. "I thought you wanted my advice."

"Yes, I do. Should I go ahead and prove that Tanizaki did it? Because, Hanae, I don't see where else I can go."

"I think," she said, "that you must do what seems right to you. Because as long as you are convinced of it, you won't be able to think of anything else."

Tora was disappointed, having hoped for some new insight, but Hanae looked very sweet with that serious expression on her face. "Thank you, my love," he said, with an effort at enthusiasm. "That's exactly what I'll do. Now let's go to bed."

The next morning, Tora went to speak to Tanizaki. He found nobody at home there and with a sigh walked all the way to the Tachibana school. There he arrived almost at the same moment with Tanizaki and wondered where the man had been.

Tanizaki recognized him and greeted him angrily. "What are you doing here again? Yes, I know you've been asking questions about me, trying to ruin my reputation among my colleagues. Isn't it enough that you've terrorized me in my own house and spread suspicions and lies about me? How dare you come to my workplace? Is there no end to this? I shall speak to Lord Sugawara and also complain to the police about your harassment." The staid schoolmaster had turned quite red with anger and shook a clenched fist at Tora.

Tora asked coldly, "Where have you been? I've just come from your house."

"None of your business. Go away or I'll have you removed."

"Don't you want to know what I've discovered? Someone's seen a man in your attic window before your wife died. Who was that?"

To Tora's surprise, Tanizaki's flushed face turned absolutely white. "Wh-what are you talking about? There was no man. Who said that?"

Tora pressed, "I think you know about him."

Tanizaki raised a shaking fist again. "No. I don't know of any man. It's all lies and more lies." He took a deep breath. "You're saying my wife had a lover. That's what you're implying, isn't it? That's a cruel insult to her and to me. You've the nerve to sully the reputation of a dead woman. You're despicable!" He drew himself up. "Get out of my sight, you dog, or I'll call the police." And with that, he stalked away.

Tora looked after him, startled. The reaction had been much too strong, given that Tanizaki had not enjoyed a happy marriage with Tomoko who, far from being a staid and proper housewife, had been a courtesan before they married. And once again, he had overlooked the fact that this information might clear him. Apparently he was all set now to prove how much he had cared for his wife.

And he had not answered the question about where he had been earlier.

It was clear Tanizaki was hiding something. And the only way to find out what that was, was to follow the man on his evening excursions.

Later that day, Tora dressed in dark clothing and went to Tanizaki's house. In the past, Tanizaki had usually returned there after his school day was over and then left again later. He hid behind some trees along the road and waited for the schoolmaster to come home.

By the time the dark-robed figure of the schoolmaster appeared, Tora was heartily sick of waiting. Tanizaki walked to his house, used a key to let himself in, and was gone.

Tora shifted position to another tree and then crept past the back of Tanizaki's house. He was in time to see Tanizaki appear at the attic window. He peered out and Tora ducked into a patch of weeds. Tanizaki disappeared again.

Clearly Tora's questions about the man at the window had troubled the schoolmaster enough to check out what could be seen. Tora hurried around to the front of the house again.

To his relief Tanizaki appeared again quickly, relocking the door, and set off in a southerly direction. Dusk had fallen, and following him had become a lot easier. They were also soon in populated areas where others were on the streets.

Tanizaki eventually turned into the Matsubara quarter of modest houses and shops. The shops were still open. Working people mingled here after a day's work, doing some shopping for their evening meal or buying wine to take home with them. Noisy laughter and shouting came from a few wine shops.

Tora lost Tanizaki quickly. He hurried, peering into shops and down dark alleys, but Tanizaki had disappeared. Beginning a methodical search of the area, he blamed himself bitterly for not having stayed closer.

Time passed, it grew quite dark, and Tora had strayed into streets that looked surprisingly disreputable when he suddenly saw Tanizaki again. What was the proper schoolmaster doing here? Tora hurried to catch up, having decided it was better to confront him now than to lose him altogether. Just then, the door to a wine shop opened, spilling drunk and belligerent customers into the street. Some six or seven men, laborers by their clothing, suddenly surrounded him. Fists were flying, curses filled the air. Tora fought his way out of the melee and caught an elbow in the ribs. When he was free again, Tanizaki was gone. As he looked around, a ragged boy pointed at an alley. "He went that way," he said, grinning.

Tora cried "Thanks," and plunged into the opening.

He was in a narrow, winding passage filled with assorted debris. It was very dark, and he could not see far ahead in the darkness, but he pushed on bravely, dodging casks and rain barrels. There were doors into houses on both sides, but he had not heard any of them opening or closing, so forged ahead.

Then, just when Tora thought he saw light ahead from another street, something struck his back hard. He stumbled forward and fell to his knees. And then they were on him. Two or three of them. With cudgels. Tora threw his arms around his head to protect himself.

They took it out on the rest of his body.

When they stopped, one of them searched him quickly and took the string of coppers from his belt. And then he thought he heard him hiss, "Leave the schoolmaster alone, or next time you're a dead man."

Footsteps receded and it grew quiet. He lay on his stomach, dazed with pain. When he tried to get up, he made it to his knees and vomited. He felt a little better and attempted to stand, but one of his legs gave way, he cried out, fell again, and passed out.

25

Worries

Akitada walked away from his sister's home, convinced that he had just made a fatal error. He knew Akiko's enthusiasm well. She would immediately go to the palace and start asking questions. He had created the very situation he had hoped to avoid and now he had also involved his sister and her family.

It was too late to stop her. He must hope that she would use her head. On an impulse, he turned into the street to police headquarters. He was suddenly uneasy about the coroner again and hoped Hakeda had spoken to the man and cautioned him.

Hakeda was out, but the coroner was in. A new body occupied him. This one was an old man dressed in rags.

Sugito was waiting for his assistant to undress the dead man. He saw Akitada and grinned. "Well, sir, have you found your clever killer yet?"

Akitada cast a warning glance at the assistant. "No, Sugito. It has turned into a difficult situation. May I see you outside for a moment?"

The coroner grunted his irritation but walked outside with Akitada. Akitada said quickly, "I trust Hakeda has warned you against talking about the Kanemori matter."

The coroner chuckled. "He did. This morning. Hakeda's amazingly nervous for a former soldier. What does he think will happen? Most people don't pay attention to such things."

"You're quite wrong there. So you have not mentioned anything to anyone?"

"Well, hardly anyone. I may have said a word or two to some friends in the wine shop afterwards. Purely as a matter of medical interest. Why are you concerned?"

Akitada did not know what to say. He was suddenly very angry. Hakeda had failed to caution this man in time. He snapped, "For one thing, you may have alerted the real murderer that we shall be looking for him again."

The coroner pursed his lips. "Well, you must be quick then. You and the good lieutenant. Though mind you, my friends are hardly likely to know the man."

Muttering under his breath, Akitada stormed out.

Halfway down the block from police headquarters, he calmed down. Part of the fault had been his own. He should have spoken up before Sugito left that day. Now he must hope for the best and follow the man's advice of being quick to identify and arrest the real killer.

For lack of a better idea, he decided to visit the sword smith again. He thought if he phrased his questions carefully, he might elicit more information without giving away that Kanemori had been murdered. What he wanted to know and had not asked before was who had befriended Kanemori recently.

It was becoming clear that the Shirakawa killer had planned his actions carefully. That planning had included finding a suitable person to serve as his substitute. These elaborate arrangements were, like the masquerade and the crime itself, slightly mad. Somewhere there was a man who had cause to hate Yorimune sufficiently to go to such extremes. Someone who was both clever and strange in his habits. Such an unusual character should be memorable enough for the sword smith to remember him.

Jocho was sitting on a stump behind his house, watching two younger men as they worked at an anvil and stoked the fire. He rose to meet Akitada.

"Welcome, my lord," he said, bowing. "Any news about Kanemori? None of us can imagine what came over him." He looked both distressed and hopeful.

"None, I'm afraid," Akitada lied. "Just tying up loose ends, so to speak. Like you and his other friends I'm trying to understand what happened to him." The last was true enough. "Forgive me for interrupting your work. I can wait."

"I'm not busy. This is work for younger muscles. Let's go inside."

Inside Akitada sat down and looked around while Jocho gathered a flask of sake and two cups. The sword smith's house was well-furnished, even with some luxurious touches like finely wrought candle holders and braziers. Cushions and *tatami* looked new and the reed blinds were trimmed with silk. He was clearly a successful man.

Jocho sat down and poured. Not surprisingly, the wine was also good. Akitada complimented him.

"I have no use for money, so I spend it," Jocho said with a smile. "My son outside is learning the craft and, I hope, will be well able to provide for himself and a family when he has one."

"A contented life." Akitada nodded with a smile. "It occurred to me that you take pleasure in the association with men who practice the skills of battle. I was told of your generosity in making your farm available to them."

Jocho chuckled. "It wasn't so generous. It was selfish. When my father died, I was the only one left. And I had no wish to take up farming. This is better. As a youngster I wanted to be a soldier, but that never happened. What you see is my second childhood."

"You're a fortunate man," Akitada said and meant it. "I came back in hopes of learning more about Kanemori."

Jocho shook his head. "I told you all I know. I still can't believe it."

"Yes, it seems strange. I wondered if Kanemori was tricked or forced in some way to do this."

Jocho frowned. "I cannot imagine such a thing. Kanemori wouldn't have done it, even when forced. As for tricking him, how would one do this?"

"I don't know, but I wondered about his associates. Someone he met or even someone from his previous life."

The sword smith thought. "There are former soldiers in the capital. Some come here regularly."

"Do you know their names?"

For the first time, Jocho resisted. "I'm not getting anyone into trouble," he said firmly. "They're all good, decent people."

Akitada was becoming heartily sick of all the good, decent people. He said, "If so, nothing will happen to them."

But Jocho shook his head stubbornly. It was clear that he no longer considered Akitada one of the good and decent men.

"Well then, forget your regulars. What about a stranger who might have shown interest in Kanemori recently. Maybe someone he had met, some new acquaintance."

The sword smith pursed his lips. "I don't think so. Not here anyway. I know everybody who comes here."

Akitada sighed. "I wondered if someone could have followed him home." He rose and said, "Thank you for the wine. If you should think of something, will you let me know?"

Jocho nodded and rose. He bowed Akitada out. "Sorry I couldn't be more help," he said.

*

Akitada returned to the city and stopped at Kosehira's house. As he entered, he met Arihito. The handsome young man's face looked drawn and tired.

Akitada asked anxiously, "Is your father worse?"

Arihito smiled. "No, no. He's back to complaining bitterly about the doctor who treats him and insists on bed rest. He considers his family co-conspirators with the doctor, and he calls him a sadistic quack."

Akitada laughed. "You look tired. How are you?"

Arihito ran a hand over his face. "I *am* tired. Running about all day asking questions about the massacre and sitting up all night at Father's bedside. Is there news?"

Akitada debated only for a moment. Arihito deserved the truth. "Come," he said taking his arm, "let's go somewhere private."

Arihito took him to one of the eave chambers. "Nobody comes here," he said, gesturing at assorted storage containers, rolled up *tatami*, stacked cushions, and bric-a-brac. He took two of the pillows and they sat.

Akitada looked at the expectant face, knowing the news would frustrate Arihito as it had frustrated himself and Hakeda. "This is information that may be dangerous, so keep it to yourself."

Arihito nodded. Looking even more eager.

"Kanemori is not our killer." He let that sink in.

"What?"

"Kanemori was murdered. The suicide was faked by someone else."

Arihito frowned. "How do you know? How can you know? I was there. I saw the body."

"The coroner took a closer look. Kanemori was stabbed between the ribs. It's something he could not have done, and it killed him. The other wounds happened later. His killer arranged the scenario we saw."

Arihito stared at him for a moment. "But that means he would have got Kanemori's blood on him."

This surprised Akitada. How quick Arihito was. "Yes," he said. "Not that the fact is much good to us unless we find him and the clothes he wore."

"But what about Kanemori's armor and horse? Or did he kill Kanemori before the massacre?"

"There are still problems. But Kanemori's armor, while striking for its red color, is not unique. And everything else the killer wore was ordinary military equipment."

"And the horse?"

"A black leg need not really be black."

Arihito gazed up at the rafters and thought. "Yes," he muttered. "The killer is probably military or police. But it's complicated. He must've planned well ahead of Tanabata. It means we have new questions to ask. The killer knew Kanemori." Arihito lowered his eyes and looked at Akitada. "If this is what happened, all we have to do is look for one of his associates. It must be someone who also knew Yorimune and had cause to hate him."

"I agree. But that's where it gets dangerous. The prime minister has closed the investigation. They have buried their dead. They are satisfied that the killer is dead also."

Arihito frowned. "But it isn't closed. The killer is alive. You must tell them."

Akitada said nothing.

Arihito waited, then said, "They never established a reason for Kanemori to have killed anyone."

"No."

"You think they know why Yorimune was attacked? They know who killed him?"

"Yes, I think they know why he was attacked. And they may know the killer."

"Oh."

After another silence, Arihito said, "Let's tell Father."

"No. Please. I only told you because you deserve to know. The fewer people who know at this point, the better."

Arihito looked uncertain. "But you'll go on with it?"

"Yes. I've already talked to the sword smith again. It's tricky to ask questions without revealing why. Let me see what I can do. You need some rest. I'll come back when I have news."

Arihito nodded. "Thank you for telling me. You can rely on me. I won't mention the matter to anyone."

Akitada said, "Be very careful. This is dangerous."

He trusted Arihito, but the problem was that he could not be at all certain that the coroner's chat with his colleagues had not already spread far and wide. On his way home, he glanced over his shoulder from time to time. He did not know what he expected to see, but he felt very uneasy.

26

Tora's Anger

When Tora became conscious again, it was no longer dark. He blinked at the stained wall of a house, some trash, and assorted weeds. It was all he could see without moving, and moving seemed a bad idea. He lay still and tried to remember.

There was a sudden rustle next to him and then a horrible face appeared in front of his eyes. A bloated, red-skinned ogre with slavering lips and blood-shot eyes stared into his face. The ogre had a repulsive smell and smacked his fat lips in anticipation.

Tora jerked away and screamed, with horror as much as pain.

The ogre also shrank back and hissed. Then he asked in a rough voice, "You're alive?"

Tora found his own voice. "Go away! Leave me alone. I've done nothing to you."

The ogre belched. "You got any wine?"

"No wine. Nothing."

The ogre belched again and spat. Then he settled down next to Tora and leaned against the wall. The smell grew more rancid.

Tora took in the stained rags his visitor wore and reconsidered. No ogre but a shiftless drunk looking for more *sake*. Just an old drunk, his greasy gray hair tied on the back of his head with a piece of rag. His hands and bare feet were nearly black with grime, and he had the unhealthy physique and skin color of someone who eats little and drinks a lot.

With these considerations, bits of his memory returned. He had been attacked and had passed out. Several; times during the night he had come to, but each time he had been aware of nothing but agonizing pain. He had eventually dozed off, slept a little, and woken to more blinding agony. Until now.

It must be nearly morning.

The drunk asked, "Got any money? I know a place where they'll sell me some strong stuff. I'll share."

"No. I'm hurt. Go get the constables."

The drunk turned his head a little and stared down at him. "You asking me to fetch the constables?" He chortled, choked, then gasped, coughed, and became speechless.

Tora wheedled, "Please. If you get help, I'll buy you some wine."

The drunk found his breath and got an idea. He got on his knees and felt around Tora's waist. He muttered a curse when he found the coppers in his sash gone. He took Tora's shoes, causing Tora to cry out

212

with pain, and shoved them inside his rags. Then he climbed to his feet, stood swaying for a moment, before he lurched off.

Tora shouted after him, "Just tell someone. You're welcome to the shoes,"

The drunk did not reply.

It grew quiet. The narrow piece of sky between the two buildings brightened a little, and Tora struggled into a sitting position to examine his injuries. The movement was not only exceedingly painful, but he got dizzy and vomited again, this time all over himself. When his stomach settled, he found his arms and hands trembled uncontrollably, and a vicious pain stabbed his chest and back. Broken ribs perhaps. He wanted to lie down again, but made himself stay sitting, merely moving fractionally to find a less painful position. Then he began to examine himself. His arms seemed whole at least, though they too were painful and slow to respond. His back and hips had taken the brunt of the beating, but one lower leg lay at an odd angle and was unresponsive.

A sudden fear that this injury would cost him the leg made him fall back with a sob.

Quite a while later, he had struggled back up and started to shift his body toward the entrance of the alley. This was a slow and painful process and involved half crawling and half sliding along on one hip, dragging his injured leg behind him. All of his body hurt, but the leg was the worst. He would move a few feet and then rest. It was cold in the predawn, but sweat soon covered his face and trickled down his back.

Time passed slowly. It got a little lighter, and he could hear voices in the distance. He tried shouting for help. The chances of getting it were slim in this neighborhood, even if someone heard him. It was more likely they would rob him again, of his clothes next, and then, disappointed, they might well finish him off.

Somewhere along the way, he suddenly recalled the words of one of his attackers.

"Leave the schoolmaster alone!"

His attackers had not been random thugs after all. No, clearly he had given himself away as he was following Tanizaki, and Tanizaki had led him into this quarter and into an ambush. The thugs had been hired to teach him a lesson and warn him off. They had done a great job. And yes, there had also been a warning they would kill him next time.

The effect of this on Tora was to make him furiously angry. He was angry that he had been outwitted and angry that Tanizaki thought he could be frightened. He wanted to get his hands on the bastard and teach him once and for all the respect he clearly lacked. He was also angry he had not been believed.

It made perfect sense, but he was helpless and as weak as a kitten, and that infuriated him further. The effect of all this pent-up rage was that he took less notice of his pain and gained the entrance of the alley far more quickly than he could have hoped.

And here he finally attracted the attention of an old woman sweeping in front of her shop. She stared, then shook her fist at him, shouting some abuse. It seemed all very unfair, and Tora began to wonder why so many evil people lived in this quarter. He stared at her and she stared back. Then she raised her broom and started toward him.

To sweep him away?

Or beat him to death?

As she came closer, he finally caught her words and realized that she thought he was a drunk.

She stopped before him and looked him over. The angry expression changed to one of alarm.

"You hurt?" she asked.

Tora nodded and gestured to his broken leg.

"A drunken brawl," she said with a nod, becoming hostile again. "Serves you right!"

"No, no, Grandmother ," he begged. "They jumped me and robbed me. Last night. In this alley." He pointed over his shoulder.

"What were you doing in there?" she asked suspiciously.

He was at a loss how to explain, then said for lack of a better idea, "I was looking for Tanizaki."

"Ah! Him. Wrong street."

Tora blinked. "What?"

"Two streets that way." She pointed. "Nice house with cherry tree in front."

Tora closed his eyes in gratitude and smiled. "May Buddha bless you."

She snorted. "No good! How you gonna walk there with that leg?"

"Please fetch some help," he pleaded. "They'll pay you at my place."

"Where's that?"

Tora told her the street. "The Sugawara mansion."

She raised her brows. "You work for the good people?"

"Yes. Please hurry."

"I'll send my grandson." She turned and shuffled back to her house. A moment later, a child appeared, still munching on a bun. He approached and studied Tora. "How much?" he said, after swallowing and wiping his mouth.

"A half piece silver if you hurry and bring them back with you."

The boy's eyes widened and he took off at a run.

Tora prepared to wait as, one by one, curious people came to look at him and ask stupid questions. He prayed the men who had beaten him up were not among them.

The wait, while miserable and painful, gave him a chance to think about what had happened. The attack might have been random—he had clearly strayed into an unsavory area—but the words whispered to him proved that he had been attacked on Tanizaki's orders. Or at least on orders by someone who wanted Tanizaki protected. And that made Tanizaki guilty.

So much for the master's efforts to clear his precious schoolmaster's reputation!

As his broken leg throbbed and his whole body ached, Tora simmered with a righteous indignation directed at everyone connected with the case.

They finally came, the boy running ahead, shouting and pointing, Genba and Saburo hurrying after him, their faces anxious.

The boy was grinning and jumping about. "A piece of silver! He promised!" he cried, pulling Genba's sleeve. Genba reached into his sash.

Tora snapped, "Half a piece! The little snotnose lies."

The boy screeched, "It was a long way and I ran."

The grandmother came back out and joined in the conversation. They attracted a small crowd very quickly.

Only Saburo remained silent. He knelt and inspected Tora's leg with surprisingly gentle fingers. Then he lifted Tora's shirt and looked at the bruises. The chatter died down as they all leaned closer to look.

Genba cursed volubly.

Saburo asked, "Where are the constables?"

The curious dispersed quickly. The old woman took the boy's arm and started pulling him away. Tora groaned, "Pay him his piece of silver and take me home."

They did, carrying him between them, awkwardly since Genba was much taller than Saburo.

And then there was Hanae, looking anxious, and then the master and his lady, and the others.

The master asked, "Dear heaven, Tora, how did this happen?"

Tora glowered at him. "It happened because your precious schoolmaster's a killer who sent his thugs after me. It happened because you didn't believe me! It happened because you think you know everything!"

Tora saw that the master was taken aback. He shook his head, then told the others, "Send for the doctor. We'll talk later when you're more comfortable, Tora." He left then, taking his lady and some of the others with him.

When the door had closed, a shocked Genba said, "How can you speak like that to the master, Tora?"

Tora did not bother to answer.

27

Searching the Truth

As it turned out, the day they brought Tora home continued eventful.

A shocked Akitada waited anxiously in his study for the physician to tend to Tora and make his report. He listened carefully to Saburo's tale on how and where they found Tora.

Saburo was voluble on the dangers in that neighborhood and expressed surprise that Tora had strayed into it. Akitada ignored this. There was a certain amount of jealousy between the two men because Tora had been chosen to investigate the Tanizaki murder. Besides, Saburo thought it very unlikely that Tanizaki could have been involved in any way in the attack on Tora.

Saburo had joined Akitada's family of retainers much later than either Tora or Genba, and four years after this his mother, Mrs. Kuruda, had arrived to stay on as housekeeper, terrorizing the whole household, including Akitada. Saburo's background as a former monk meant that he took on secretarial duties once handled by Seimei. But he wished more than anything to investigate crime.

Of all Akitada's retainers, Saburo was the most uneasy. He lived in constant fear of his mother causing trouble with her sharp tongue and of being dismissed for his past spying activities. Thankfully, Mrs. Kuruda had mellowed greatly with age, but Akitada did not approve of spies and Saburo knew he was distrusted.

Now in Akitada's study, Saburo said, "How could Tora speak to you that way? He must have some head injury."

Tora did indeed have old head injuries. They caused occasional pain but did not seem to have affected his mind.

Akitada said, "I think he was in a great deal of pain. It was hours before he was found."

But Tora's anger had upset Akitada. It was so unlike him. Not that he was ever particularly respectful. The bond between them was strong and close and Akitada relied on that friendship and loyalty. Pain might account for some shortness of temper, but this had seemed personal. What could have happened to break the trust?

It had something to do with Tanizaki, of course, and Akitada was beginning to wish he had never met the man. Tora had been convinced of Tanizaki's guilt without having much more than vague suspicions to go on. Whatever the situation was, the attack had been caused by the tasks Akitada had set him. They had exposed Tora to mortal danger. Did this mean

220

Tanizaki was guilty? Possibly. It certainly meant Tora considered his master to be responsible for what had happened to him.

The physician, a small, elderly man, bent with age and chronic pain, finally came. Akitada asked quickly, "How is he?"

"Well, the worst of it is the broken lower leg. He says they hit him with cudgels. I have straightened the bones in his leg and wrapped it, but he cannot stand or walk until it heals. And he may always have a limp. It was a brutal beating."

Akitada bit his lip. "Thank you. Will you take a cup of wine, Doctor?"

The physician accepted. He sat down and sipped. "He's a strong man," he said consolingly. "And he has a fine wife and son to look after him. I'll return to make sure the leg heals. As for the rest, he's badly bruised and may have a cracked rib or two. At the moment, he feels like all of his body is broken."

"Can I speak to him?"

The physician chuckled. "I wouldn't recommend it just yet. He's in a foul mood. I've given him something to make him sleep. Maybe later today?"

After the doctor's visit, Akitada and Saburo went to report the attack to the police. The captain in charge listened attentively, then shook his head. "We have almost nightly reports from that quarter," he said. "It's a bad part of town. Many poor people and men who can't find work. We'll look into it, but from what you tell me, there isn't much to go on."

Akitada had not mentioned Tanizaki. Given Tora's mood and the fact that he claimed to have heard the threat after his beating, he had too many doubts about the schoolmaster's guilt.

221

What had happened to Tora faded from Akitada's mind around the time of the midday rice. His sister Akiko arrived. He had just been on his way to check on the wounded Tora, when she ran up the stairs to the main house, silk robes and embroidered coat gathered in her hands so she would not trip in her hurry.

"There you are," she cried. "I have some news."

She made for his study, Akitada following, curious about what could have provoked so much speed. Akiko was still wearing her best court costume and normally took better care of her fine clothes.

In his room, she fell on a cushion and drew a deep breath. "I practically ran the whole way," she gasped.

"From the palace? You could have taken a sedan chair."

She frowned. "I thought you were in a hurry."

"Yes. Thank you. What happened?"

She waved a hand. "Pour me some wine and let me catch my breath."

He did, and she drank, then sighed. "I hope you appreciate the things I do for you."

"I do, I do. What's the matter?"

"They know about the coroner's finding."

Akitada sank down on his own cushion. "So quickly? How did you find out?"

Akiko held out her cup for a refill. "The usual gossip by the men who attend the empress. You really are careless. They know that you demanded the coroner take a closer look. If this matter is as dangerous as you think it is, you should have planned to leave town right away."

He stared at his sister, then refilled her cup. "I cannot leave. Where would I go? Besides, I have duties in the ministry. And what of my family and my people? Tora was attacked last night and has a broken leg. That leaves only Genba and Saburo to look after Sadako and the children. Saburo is no longer very strong and Genba is getting old. Neither is much of a fighter any longer. I cannot leave Sadako and the children to face the punishment intended for me."

"Was Tora involved in this affair?"

"No. Not at all. A different matter altogether, or perhaps just being in the wrong place."

She sniffed, then glared at him. "Well, you certainly walked into trouble. Prepare yourself." When Akitada said nothing, she said, "Perhaps there will only be a reprimand. No doubt, the prime minister will want a public denial of the report from you."

Akitada snapped, "I will not lie."

"Not even for the people you love? You surprise me."

Akitada said nothing. He did not know what he would do. Could do.

Akiko got up and shook out her silken skirts angrily. "I'm going home." She paused, "Oh I almost forgot. When I asked about the funerals, one of Her Majesty's ladies recalled an old story about Yorimune's wife."

"What story?"

"It probably means nothing, but his first lady was a Taira."

"So?"

"Oh this happened a long time ago, when she was a young woman. She was raised with a Yamada relative who was her father's ward. This girl was found dead

223

in the Taira pond and the Yamada family broke off their friendship with Motoko's family. I think they demanded blood money."

"Interesting but too long ago." Akitada thought a moment, then asked, "What happened? I assume someone killed the girl."

"It's still a mystery. She was found drowned. Your friend Kobe investigated. Apparently they called it suicide."

Akitada considered it, then shook his head. "Young women have been known to drown themselves. It's probably not connected. Anything else?"

"One of the young men who got killed was also courting Arihito's bride."

"Ah! Which one?"

"Fujiwara Toshiyuki. Another branch of Yorimune's family. They say he didn't have a hope because the girl had fallen for Arihito."

"Hmm. I don't know. Keep your ears open. There must be some other connection."

"I doubt I'll be welcome when they realize what you have done."

"Akiko, I'm not attacking the Fujiwara clan. I'm looking for their killer."

"You and I know this, but clearly they don't. Be careful. Now I must be off. Let me know what happens. And give Tora my best."

Tora was awake and alert. Hanae knelt beside him, looking anxious. "He's still in a lot of pain, sir," she said, then bit her lip. Tora glared.

Akitada went to sit on his other side and said mildly, "You're very angry with me. Please tell me what I did."

Hanae's hand flew to her mouth.

Tora growled, "It's your fault I'm a useless cripple."

"Ah. Please explain."

Tora did, with a flood of angry detail. Hanae cried out from time to time and once put her hand over Tora's mouth. Tora flung it away and continued. What it all amounted to was that Akitada had sent him into danger because he refused to believe that Tanizaki was a murderer.

When he ran out of words, Akitada nodded. "Yes. I see that now. How do you know Tanizaki sent the men who attacked you?"

With great satisfaction, Tora told him what the attacker had whispered before leaving him.

Akitada did not speak right away. He thought, then nodded again. "Yes, that seems to suggest Tanizaki was behind this. I'm surprised. I didn't think the man had it in him to be a criminal."

Tora was slightly mollified. "I've always said the quiet ones are the worst. It's a big mistake to trust those very proper people. Give me a poor bastard any day, even if he drinks, curses, and whores."

Hanae whispered, "Oh, Tora!"

He grinned at her. "In a manner of speaking, I mean. A lot of poor fellows haven't been blessed with wives like you."

"Well," said Akitada, "I'm most heartily sorry that I've sent you into danger. Please forgive me."

Tora suddenly looked embarrassed. "Never mind. It was my fault, too. I should have been more careful."

"But you were following Tanizaki at the time?"

"I thought I was. I lost him. I went down that alley thinking it was a shortcut to the next street. But I'd lost the bastard a few streets back."

"How do you know?"

"Oh, the old woman who found me knew where he lives."

Akitada's brows rose. "Where he lives? You mean he has another house?"

"Yes. I guess. Anyway, they knew him in that quarter."

"But that is very interesting."

Tora glowered. "It's not much good. I'm laid up here and can't do anything about it."

"But I can. Please tell me exactly where you were and what the old woman said."

This surprised Tora. "I thought you were too busy?"

"I'll take the time to find out who attacked you."

Tora blinked. "But it's my case, you said."

"It seems to me you have made all the progress already. All that's left is to make an arrest."

Tora brightened. "So you agree Tanizaki's guilty?"

Akitada hesitated a moment, then nodded. "He's guilty of something. And I must say I'm ashamed I hired the man. His character appears to be deplorable."

Tora smiled. "You'll tell me what happens?"

28

A Strange Household

A kiko's report had been disturbing. Apparently the coroner had managed to spread the news of Kanemori's murder more efficiently than they had hoped. But so far nothing had happened and that was reassuring. Akitada was glad that Tora's situation gave him an excuse to put aside the Shirakawa case. He felt guilty for having exposed Tora to the attack and was intrigued and angered by Tanizaki's involvement. Apparently you could not trust schoolmasters any longer. It was a sign of the times. There was corruption everywhere.

Akitada paused only long enough to tell his wife he was going out. He saw sudden fear in her face and added, "It's Tora's case. That business of the schoolmaster. I'm going to have a talk with him."

Visibly relieved, she smiled. "Give him my best."

Clearly Sadako had also been mistaken about schoolmasters. Akitada did not enlighten her.

It was still broad daylight and another pleasant clear day. Akitada did not think carrying a weapon was indicated, but he decided to take Saburo with him. Saburo was pleased.

As they walked into the city, Akitada asked, "Did you know Tanizaki well when he worked for us?"

Saburo considered the question. "He wasn't easy to know, sir. He kept to himself and spoke mostly with Yoshi, you, or your lady."

"Who wasn't my lady then," Akitada said with a smile. "She liked him. I didn't tell her about Tora's report. I'm surprised myself. How could I have been so wrong?"

There was a short pause, then Saburo said, "I followed him once."

"Why ever did you do that?"

Saburo grinned. "I didn't trust him. I never trust men who act as if they have something to hide. All of us tried to talk to the man. He was cold and secretive. He only talked to his betters. Since he worked in your house, I thought it best to check him out."

"Very commendable. And where did he lead you?"

"He liked to drink after work. And once he went to the willow quarter." Saburo chuckled. "Normal enough. I decided he was just another intellectual who thought he was better than the rest of us."

"Hmm. Something is very wrong about him."

"Yes. Tora might be better off if I'd kept watching Tanizaki."

228

They reached the quarter where Tora had run into trouble. The streets looked ordinary, the houses neat, and the pavements swept. These were the places where lower level clerks lived or well-to-do dancers and musicians. Such people were not quite respected, but neither had they tumbled into poverty. Saburo stopped a passer-by to ask where the schoolmaster lived and got a blank stare. But when he asked for him by name, the man grinned and pointed to a house.

"A man by that name visits that house, but he's not always there. A woman owns it."

Saburo thanked him and the man walked away. Saburo said, "Maybe this is a love nest. Surely the schoolmaster's love life is surprising for a man his age."

"Let's find out. The neighborhood looks safe enough. I wonder how Tora could have found thugs here."

Saburo shook his head. "It wasn't here. Around the corner and two streets down the quarter changes. I should've been with him."

It was probably a hint that Saburo was dissatisfied with having been retired from his spying activities but Akitada said nothing. The house the man had indicated was modest in size but well-kept with handsome shutters that gave it an air of secrecy. Saburo knocked on the door.

It was opened by a mere child, a very pretty girl of perhaps ten or eleven. She was heavily made up and wore a pink silk dress.

Saburo's eyebrows shot up. "Is your mother home?" he asked.

"Auntie's gone to the market," she said, then bowed prettily.

Akitada asked, "What's her name?"

229

The girl stared at him and hesitated. "I can't tell," she said softly. Looking from one to the other, she started to close the door.

"What about your uncle?" Saburo asked quickly.

She said, "No uncle." The door closed.

They looked at each other. "Well," Akitada said, "we have the right house, but do we have our Tanizaki?"

Saburo grinned. "I think so. I bet this 'auntie' is in the business in the quarter. The schoolmaster is leading a double life, and not a very respectable one."

"You may be right. Tora also reported Tanizaki's visits to the willow quarter. The dead woman used to work there. And that little girl looked as if she were being groomed to become a courtesan." He made a face. "So young!"

"They start them young, then sell them to the highest bidder. 'Auntie' has an investment in her. She looked happy enough in her pretty pink silks."

Akitada nodded. "Come, we'll walk over to that canal and wait for a bit on the bridge. That way we can keep an eye on the house."

The bridge was arched, and from its top they could watch the canal and the backs of the houses adjoining it, where maids and housewives were washing clothes or vegetables and children were trying to fish. People frequently stopped there for a rest, but in this case, it also offered a nice view of the auntie's house and the street approaching it.

They leaned on the railing and waited. It was not very long before a young man in very colorful clothing strode into view and walked into the house without knocking.

Akitada said, "I wonder who that is."

"A customer?"

"Not for that child, surely."

"For the auntie? Or else he's also working in the quarter. Some men prefer male companions."

"Yes..*Wakashudo*. He dresses like one of them. And he's a little too young for the auntie."

A short while later, the auntie appeared herself. A middle-aged female walked purposefully up the street with a full market basket over her arm. She was dressed neatly in black silk and wore her hair in a bun at the back of her head.

"That's her," Saburo said and started forward.

Akitada touched his arm. "Wait."

The woman bustled up the walk and was about to enter when the door opened and the young man appeared. He took her heavy basket, she patted his arm, and both disappeared inside.

"Let's go," Akitada said.

They returned to the house and knocked again. This time, the young man opened the door. He stared at them and asked, "What do you want?"

Since they were both neatly dressed, though far more soberly than he, and wore hats, it was a rather rude greeting. Akitada snapped, "We want to see the owner of this house."

His voice sounded official, and the young man became uneasy. "What's it about?" he asked, looking from one to the other.

Akitada glowered at him. Close up his clothes were almost blinding. He wore a short robe printed in purple and yellow and a green underrobe that reached his knees where it met a pair of full, dark red silk trousers. "Who are you? Do you live here?"

The young man retreated a little. "I'm called Yasumasa. My mother owns this house. What's the matter?"

"Get your mother."

They followed the young man into a neat room overlooking a small garden. The young man pointed to some cushions and said, "Please be seated. I'll get Mother."

The middle-aged woman they had seen before came in quickly. Her son was not with her. It was clear she made efforts to look attractive. Her eyes were lined in kohl and her lips rouged. Akitada could smell the scent used to perfume her clothes across the room. Perhaps she had been attractive once, but she was near fifty and her features had coarsened, her figure had thickened, and her expression was petulant. She was astonished to see them but bowed and said in a high voice, "This insignificant person is honored by your visit. How may I be of service?"

"We're looking for the schoolmaster Tanizaki," Akitada said. "He is said to live here."

Her eyes widened briefly. "I regret deeply that a mistake has been made. There is no one here by that name. I live here with my maid and a little girl."

"Who is the young man who let us in?"

"My son. He doesn't live here." She bowed again and smiled a little. "I apologize. He's a show-off."

The young man's clothing seemed to support that. Akitada frowned. "And you don't know the schoolmaster Tanizaki?"

She bowed again and stood with her head lowered. "I regret. It must be a mistake. Very sorry, sir."

They were getting nowhere "What does your son do for a living?"

"He helps me in my business. I own the *hananoya.*"

It was the name of a brothel in the willow quarter and explained her make-up and scent. She was a former prostitute who had done well for herself. Akitada said, "Call him in here."

She went to the door and called her son's name. There was no answer. Saburo followed quickly, moved her aside, and left to look for him. She protested, "What are you doing? This is my house."

Akitada said nothing.

She turned to him, her voice angry. "I'll call the constables! You cannot do this. I have done nothing. My son has done nothing."

Saburo came back and shook his head. "He got away, sir."

"No," his mother cried. "He left for work. It isn't right that you come here and threaten us. I shall report this."

Akitada bit his lip. She was within her rights. He said, "One of my friends was attacked last night by some men with cudgels. He nearly died and may be crippled for life. We are looking for the men who did this."

She drew herself up. "It certainly wasn't my son. He was working with me all night."

Akitada nodded. "In that case, we must look elsewhere." He did not bother to apologize.

Outside, Saburo said, "She was lying. That whole set-up was suspicious."

"Perhaps. Come, we'll go home and report to Tora. It's his case after all."

29

Visiting an Old Friend

When Hanae opened the door to them, she looked distressed.

"What's wrong?" Akitada asked.

"Oh, it's Tora." She brushed back some hair that had escaped her bun. Hanae was a small female and usually tidy, graceful, and quick. Today she looked as if her appearance were the last thing she was concerned about. "He's getting up. He'll kill himself."

Akitada smiled. "I doubt he'll kill himself. The doctor said the main thing was the broken leg, and that was a clean break. He's probably just getting restless."

She wailed, "But he'll hurt himself."

Akitada raised his brows at this but said only, "Well, let's have a look at him. Maybe he'll take an interest in what we have to tell him."

"I hope so," Hanae said. "He's been impossible in his present mood. I've been so frightened."

They found Tora upright, balancing on a crutch, hopping back and forth in his room in a very determined manner. When Akitada and Saburo walked in, he turned to them and announced, "I can do this. I've seen the cripples in the streets. They're very good at getting around. You'd never believe how fast they can move. And they lost their legs altogether."

"Are you trying to lose yours?" Akitada asked.

Tora's face fell. "I have to move. It's horrible just sitting or lying on the floor, being useless. People aren't meant to do that."

"Nonsense."

Saburo said, "Tora's right. People die if they don't get up and move now and then."

"How do you know that?" Akitada asked suspiciously.

"I was a monk once. Whatever you may think, sir, monks take an interest in such things."

Tora was grinning. "Thank you, brother. You've got that right. See, Hanae, Saburo knows what it's like."

Akitada relented."Well, you must be careful and not overdo it. And under no circumstances take any risks of falling."

"I'll be careful. I promise. Do you have any news?"

They all settled down, Tora with his crutch beside him.

"Just wait till you hear," Saburo told him.

Tora heaved a sigh. "So you solved the case, I figured you would. Thanks for telling me." He turned his head away.

Akitada asked, "What's the matter? Are you in pain?"

"Of course I'm in pain. They broke my leg and beat me black and blue. They should've killed me and spared everybody the trouble."

Akitada teased, "The police are already badly overworked and you want them to solve another murder?"

Tora did not respond.

Akitada tried again. "The doctor can come back and give you something to make the pain better."

"The doctor's a quack. He knows nothing. I'm done for."

Hanae gasped.

Akitada said firmly, "Nonsense. You'll be fine. Now listen to what we've found out."

Tora turned away again. "You always knew I couldn't do it," he said accusingly.

Akitada was becoming angry, but a tiny feeling of guilt stirred. Had he really treated Tora so shabbily all these years? "That's not true! Really, Tora, you're being no help at all. We haven't found the killer, but we did find out who lives in that house."

Tora was finally interested. "Not Tanizaki? Then who lives there?"

"A middle-aged female. She wears paint and says she owns one of the houses in the willow quarter. And she has a son who works there. We met him. He's a snappy dresser. Does any of this help?"

"She owns a brothel? What's her name?"

Akitada glanced at Saburo. "Great heavens, we forgot to ask. But she said she owns the *hananoya*."

A slow grin spread over Tora's face. "You forgot to ask her name? What if her name's Mrs. Tanizaki?"

"Er, no. It isn't. She claims she doesn't know any Tanizaki."

Saburo said quickly, "But that woman's a liar, and her son is a crook."

Tora nodded slowly. "That woman's Miyagi-san, the auntie of the house where Tomoko and Nariko worked. She's in it up to her eyebrows."

Akitada chuckled. The old Tora had returned. And Tora's comment was funny: the woman they had met had plucked her eyebrows and painted new ones on her forehead in the fashion of court ladies and courtesans. He said, "I'm glad this story makes sense to you. Saburo and I were puzzled."

For a moment, Tora looked suspicious, but then another thought struck him. "Her son . . . you say he's an adult and a sharp dresser?"

They both nodded.

Tora clapped his hands. "Then he may be the man at the window."

"What man at what window?"

"The man the kid saw at the window of Tanizaki's house the day before we found Tomoko's body."

Akitada and Saburo exchanged a glance. "You didn't mention it," Akitada said. "Can your informant be trusted about this?"

"I think so. Mind you, I didn't really believe it because there was no way to get inside and the maid had been fired or left. But he could've been admitted by Tomoko."

Akitada nodded. "Yes, you're right. You think it may be significant?"

"Yes, I do, sir. It proves I was on the right trail. That woman and her son are involved in the murder. I bet the son was having an affair with Tomoko."

Saburo said, "It makes sense. They met at the brothel before she married Tanizaki. Then when Tanizaki lost his appeal as a husband, she got back together with this Yasumasa."

Tora agreed eagerly. "Exactly! That's what happened! And Tanizaki caught them together and killed her. There! You got your killer."

Akitada blinked at this summing up. "I agree we're almost there, Tora, but this requires more proof. I'll have to leave the solution to you. I don't have the time. Saburo can perhaps do the walking for you. You might check with the neighbors again, Saburo." He got up.

Tora still had the smile on his face. "Yes. Don't worry, sir. I'll work out all the details with Saburo. Tanizaki's not going to get away."

Outside, Akitada told Saburo, "That was well done. It's given him back his courage."

Saburo looked unconvinced. "He's still too sick. The police should be able to solve it now. That young man could be questioned."

Akitada smiled. "Eventually even the police will solve it. Meanwhile, try to give Tora a hand."

Sadako was pleased to hear that Tora was in good spirits again. Akiko's news she already knew about, because the two women had talked after Akitada had gone to see Tora.

239

She asked, "What will you do now? Is it very dangerous for you to go on?"

"I think my sister exaggerates. I doubt anything will happen. At most they'll call me in to give me a warning."

"And will you give it up then?"

Akitada sighed. "I don't know. If I do, it will nag at me the rest of my life."

She said firmly, "Then you must make every effort to solve it."

"I don't know where to begin."

"Akiko mentioned Superintendent Kobe."

"I doubt that old case is relevant."

"Perhaps not, but sometimes it helps to talk things over with someone who will take an interest."

She was right. Sadako had a knack for being right about such things. He said, "I owe him a visit anyway. It's been months since I saw him last. I shall go right now."

Kobe lived in relative poverty in a small village near Saga west of the capital. He had retired as police superintendent several years ago and had chosen to spend the rest of his life with Sachi, a blind shampoo girl from the amusement quarter. His wives and grown children had bonded together against him and forced him to resign his properties to them.

After years of early enmity between Kobe and Akitada, the "stolid bureaucrat" and "spoiled aristocrat" who meddled in police business, they had developed a grudging respect for each other and gradually moved on to friendship.

Kobe was nearly twenty years older than Akitada and had aged during the years of his troubles with his family. When his beloved Sachi had died, the joy of life had left him. Akitada had visited from time to time, but the change in his old friend depressed him, and the visits had become rarer. On this occasion, he did not know what to expect.

He rode through the western part of the capital and into the green and golden countryside. The streets in the city had been crowded. There had been others on horseback and on foot, but when he left the capital behind, he had the road to himself. Only once or twice did he hear the sound of hoofs behind him but the riders must have turned away.

To his relief, Kobe seemed in good health. He was still tall though a little bowed, and his hair and neatly trimmed beard and mustache were nearly white. He found him outside his farm, feeding rice to the ducks in the lake. The lake had been made when Emperor Saga had dammed a river to irrigate his rice lands. All around there was beautiful and fertile country, and Kobe owned a small parcel of it, all that was left to him after he had given the rest of his property to his family.

The joy with which the former superintendent greeted him shamed Akitada. He knew he should have come more often. But Kobe had not visited either.

Kobe teased, "You're most welcome, but are you deserting your lovely bride already? I would have come to see you but knew better than to trouble such happiness."

This shamed Akitada even more. It had been over a year since Sadako had become his wife.

He said awkwardly, "I must seem quite besotted at my age. I've neglected my friends dreadfully."

"No. Never say so to me. You know my story well enough. I wouldn't trade my late and all too short happiness for anything. Come, let's go back to the house. I have some decent wine and there's fresh fish for our meal tonight. I caught it myself. And a place to sleep if you can stay."

"Next time I'll stay. At the moment I may be in some trouble and dislike leaving Sadako and the children alone."

Kobe raised grizzled brows. "You've been meddling again in matters that are none of your business?"

Akitada chuckled. "I'm afraid so. I got involved because Kosehira and his wife were attacked."

"Not the Yorimune murders?"

"Yes. I came to tell you about it and to take your advice. I'm at my wits' end. If I can solve the case, I may spare myself considerable unpleasantness."

Kobe nodded. "I'm a selfish man. Nothing ever happens here and I like a good story."

Kobe's house was part of a cluster of farm buildings. He had rented out his land to peasants and lived on a share of the rice crop and his modest pension as a retired official. Akitada was relieved to see that Kobe seemed to manage better these days. The farm buildings were in good repair, and the inside of the house, a spacious, well-built one, was furnished with Kobe's favorite things. Books were stacked on bamboo shelves, hunting and fishing gear hung on one wall, a handsome scroll on another, and the doors stood open to the view of lake, hills, and the distant pagoda of *Daikakuji* , the temple founded by the Saga emperor more than three hundred years before.

They sat together companionably on the veranda with their wine, and Akitada described what he had found at Yorimune's Shirakawa house that dreadful day.

Kobe listened without interrupting until Akitada paused for breath. Then he asked, "How are Lord Kosehira and his lady?"

"Kosehira almost died but he seems on the mend now. His lady got an arrow in her leg and is doing well. I've been working with Arihito, their eldest."

"The intended bridegroom?"

"Yes. He escaped injury but was very upset. He'd taken a fancy to the young woman. She died."

Kobe sighed. "I feel for him. He's a nice young man, I recall."

"Yes, and very bright. As you must've heard, a man called Kanemori is being blamed for the massacre."

Kobe sat forward. "Don't tell me he didn't do it."

"He did not." Akitada explained about the apparent suicide and the coroner's findings. "And now I'm afraid Yorimune's family is very angry with me."

Kobe nodded slowly. "They're protecting Yorimune's memory from scandal."

"Yes. But it makes no sense. They should want to find the killer."

"They think about the future. As for Yorimune: it was his karma. That man was evil. My advice is to let it rest."

"I can't. I need to find the killer quickly before they stop me. What can you tell me about Yorimune? You must know more than I."

"You're hoping to find the killer's motive, but there are far too many people who had reason to kill Yorimune and didn't. You need a recent incident, but

243

Yorimune has led a quiet life these past ten years. Earlier, yes, he behaved shockingly. But none of the people he injured ever took revenge."

Akitada grimaced in frustration. "I know, but there must be something."

Kobe refilled their cups, "I know little of what's been going on in recent years. I'm sorry."

Akitada was deeply disappointed but reminded himself that he had come for a visit. He turned the conversation to everyday matters, and they chatted about Kobe's fishing and hunting, and about Akitada's family. He told Kobe about Tora being attacked and they discussed the schoolmaster's case. Kobe had no illusions about Tanizaki's probity. He sided with Tora and thought the man had probably killed his wife in a fit of jealousy.

He said, "You say he was a widower without a family? Old men take young wives to make children. They feel inadequate and want heirs along with sex and companionship. I think in this case, the schoolmaster found out that the young courtesan he had purchased to be his wife and bear him sons had betrayed him. He killed her, outraged by her behavior."

It made sense, and Akitada accepted the reasoning, but something still troubled him about the case.

Silence fell until Kobe said, "About Yorimune now: I once met his wife. Many years ago."

Akitada nodded. "Yes, I meant to ask you about that. My sister Akiko mentioned a story about some young woman drowning in that family. It seemed unconnected to the massacre, but she did say you investigated the case."

Kobe smiled. "I was quite young then and trying very hard to impress those in power. But it was a sad tale and I still feel bad about it when I think back. Nothing to be done of course, but that lovely girl was murdered."

"Murdered? Akiko says it was a suicide. She drowned herself in the family pond."

"Yes, but it might as well have been murder. They drove her to it, that family."

"The Taira family? Yorimune's wife was a Taira."

"Quite right. It happened in the Taira mansion in the capital. Now it belongs to the emperor through one of his wives, but back then, Taira Masamori lived there with his wives and children. The girl who died was a Yamada and had been sent there as a companion to the oldest Taira daughter. The one who later married Yorimune. The girls were the same age and the Yamada girl was a famous beauty. All the young men kept visiting. I always thought there was a good deal of jealousy between the two young women, and after the death, the Taira parents spoke badly of the girl. They claimed she had affairs with several young men and they had planned to send her back to her family. It was her disgrace that supposedly caused the girl to commit suicide."

"What did you think?"

Kobe looked thoughtful. "The coroner said the dead girl was not a virgin. In the end, we had to accept the Taira explanation, but the Yamada family was very upset. She was their only child and they'd hoped she'd make a fine marriage because she was beautiful and talented. I think they may have hoped to interest the emperor."

Akitada sighed. "There's too much of that. What about her family? Did they make trouble?"

245

"At first, yes. But I think the Taira smoothed things over. The girl's family is gone now. There were no heirs and a distant relative inherited."

"I see. No help there. What do *you* think happened at Shirakawa?"

"I don't know, but I think it's dangerous to pursue this too far. Not only is there the killer, who seems to have gone to an extraordinary amount of trouble to remove Yorimune, but you say those in power are covering up the reason for the murder."

Akitada nodded. "I think so too, but surely we should not close our eyes to injustice when it becomes dangerous."

"Well, I merely said what I thought." Kobe smiled. "You'll do as you see fit. Now let's go eat that fine fish."

The fish was indeed a delicacy. Akitada did not leave until after sunset. He rode back on the same lonely road and because of the late hour he became uneasy. There were highwaymen about near the capital, and he carried only his short sword.

After a while, he picked up the sound of another horseman. The hoof fall was strangely uneven, as if the horse was lame or had lost a shoe. He slowed down to see who was following him, but the other man slowed also. Ahead lay a stretch of woods where it would be to dark to see an attacker. Akitada urged his horse into a gallop.

The road became uneven among the trees, and he had to pull back on the reins when his horse stumbled over a root and almost threw him. He paused to listen. There was only silence. Relieved, he continued his journey more slowly.

He had almost reached the end of the forest, when something whirred past his shoulder and hit a tree with a twang.

An arrow!

Bending low over his horse's neck, Akitada spurred it on. They reached the open road in a mad gallop and did not slow down until the lights and houses of the capital received them.

30

The Summons

Later Akitada thought that he had needlessly panicked. After all, there was a good deal of hunting going on in the area, and Kobe himself hunted. Besides, if the arrow had been meant for him, surely his attacker would have tried again. It was a matter of being too much involved in the Shirakawa case. In any case, he decided not to tell Sadako about it. And then events drove the incident from his mind.

The day after the visit to Kobe, Akitada was sipping his morning tea and talking to Sadako about Kobe when he had visitors.

There were five of them. Two were high-ranking officials. The other three belonged to the mounted palace guard. The former wore their black

249

silk robes and hats with stiffened ribbons; the latter were in uniform.

Genba had no time to announce them. They followed him into the room and dismissed him.

Akitada rose. "What is going on?" he demanded.

One of the two officials nodded to Sadako. "Without the lady, if you please!" he said peremptorily.

Sadako rose, looking frightened, and walked out.

Akitada was becoming angry. The anger helped subdue a nagging fear that he might be unable to control what his visitors had in mind. He said, "How dare you walk into my house and order my wife and my retainer around?"

The officials did not react. Neither did they lose their stern expressions. The one who had spoken said, "You are to come with us."

"Why are you here and where am I being taken?"

"You will be informed when we get there."

"On whose orders?"

"His Majesty's."

And that ended his feeble objections. You did not argue with an imperial command. Akitada glanced down at his ordinary robe, slightly worn and stained and asked, "May I change into suitable clothes?"

The second official's mouth twitched unpleasantly. He said, "You won't need anything but what you have on. Not even a hat."

Akitada cast a helpless glance around his beloved study. Then he obeyed. They walked out, the two officials in front, followed by Akitada, and the three guardsmen brought up the rear. It looked like what it was, an arrest.

They attracted stares from people as they entered the confines of the *daidairi*. The seat of the government and of the imperial palace was busy at this time of day. Akitada kept his eyes straight ahead, hoping no one would recognize him. It was a shameful way to be summoned.

He did not know who had issued the summons but suspected it had been the prime minister himself. That did not mean that he would shortly speak to the great man.

As he suspected, the two officials turned down the street that led to the building housing the board of censors. The censors represented the most direct method of dealing out punishment to government officials because their duties included investigating officials of the fifth rank and above, reporting their misdemeanors, and impeaching them. The censors investigated wrong doings, but they could also simply act on instructions from above. It was ironic that Akitada had finally and against great odds reached the fifth rank. Whatever the situation, he was in serious trouble.

They entered the small building that housed the important and terrifying men who had already in the past dealt harshly with Akitada. He had no friends among the censors, if he had friends anywhere.

There were three of them, old men with white hair, though different in other ways. One was portly, his eyes almost disappearing in folds of flesh, the second was tall, thin, and beak-nosed, and the third was so bent with age that his face wore a permanent expression of bitter suffering.

The fat one dismissed Akitada's entourage. Akitada knelt and bowed his head to the floor. When he sat up again, he met three pairs of eyes that regarded him coldly.

The thin one asked, "Do you know why you are here, Sugawara?"

He knew but said, "I do not."

"You have interfered in an investigation and spread rumors that threaten the government."

Akitada looked blank. "With utmost respect, your Excellency, I am not aware of this. Could a mistake have been made?"

"No mistake. Both Lieutenant Hakeda and the coroner Sugito have testified against you."

Akitada's heart fell. Not only was he in trouble, but he could well imagine the fear that had caused Hakeda and Sugito to reveal what had happened. To be sure, Hakeda had already been frightened, but Sugito's attitude had promised a certain amount of defiance. On second thought, Sugito would have considered the entire matter trivial, told them what he had found, and his insistence on the facts would have brought the coroner even more severe punishment.

And it had all been Akitada's fault.

Akitada's sense of responsibility for a moment obscured the fact that whatever was about to happen to him would affect his family and his whole household. He stared at the censors at a loss for words.

The fat censor nodded. "I see you understand. It has been decided that it will be best to let the rumor die down on its own."

Hope rekindled. Perhaps it would only involve a reprimand. He tried not to think further. He was merely glad that he might be let go to return to his family, to Sadako.

But hope is invariably a foolish thing, a forlorn thing, something to be dashed quickly and thoroughly.

The thin censor said, "You will travel to Shikoku on the emperor's business." He took a sheaf of papers from his sleeve and extended them. "Here are your orders. You may peruse them at your leisure during your voyage."

Almost blindly, Akitada took the papers. He looked from one man to the other, hoping that there would be more. When nobody said anything, he asked, "May I return home to get ready for the journey?"

"No," snapped the thin censor. "You'll leave now. Your escort is waiting." He cast a disparaging glance at Akitada's robe and slippers. "The season is sufficiently warm. Later you may order winter clothing to be sent to you."

Winter?

Appalled, Akitada asked, "May I at least write a note of explanation to my wife?"

"Your family will be notified. Now go!"

Seeing no hope in the stern faces, Akitada turned and went.

31

Journey into Oblivion

His escort consisted of two officials and ten soldiers. The two officials were lower-ranking and unknown to him. The soldiers wore the uniforms of the palace guards. None of them was an officer. They had a horse waiting for him. When one of the officials gestured, Akitada got on and they set off, five soldiers in front, then he, then the two officials, and finally the other five soldiers. Nobody spoke. Everybody looked grim.

Their silence was enervating and grew more so when they crossed the Katsura River and took the southern highway out of the capital..

As his home and family disappeared behind them, Akitada thought of escape. He could spur his horse suddenly and make a break for it. But it would be pointless. They'd capture him quickly. It had not escaped his notice that his horse was elderly. He grew desperate when he thought of leaving wife and children behind without so much as a word. Perhaps he would never see them again. Would they really be notified? If so, what would they be told?

He wondered what was to happen to him. The orders in his sleeve suggested that he would not be killed somewhere and left to rot by the wayside, his death blamed on highway men, but they were no guarantee by any means. Perhaps they were intended as false reassurance so he would be compliant.

They reached Yamazaki by evening. At the landing stage on the Yodo River a boat was waiting, proof that his abduction had been well planned. Here he and the officials dismounted.

Akitada asked one of the officials, "Where are we bound?"

There was no answer, just another gesture for him to hurry and get on board.

They were the only passengers. The soldiers stayed on land and watched as the boat moved into the current, then they turned their horses and headed back toward the capital.

He was offered food and water, again wordlessly. He knew the journey would continue on the Yodo River, and that river led to the Inland Sea. His heart contracted with fear. Was it to be Kyushu all over again?

Or a quiet drowning on the way?

As the light faded, he finally thought of the orders in his sleeve and took them out. Breaking the seals, he scanned the contents rapidly. Not Kyushu, but Shikoku. Shikoku Island was the largest of those in the Inland Sea. It was much less remote than Kyushu but still far away from home. He took some hope from this. But then he recalled the censor's comment about winter clothing and quickly abandoned it. He would be days getting there and months getting home.

If he would return at all.

He read the rest of his instructions more carefully. He was being charged with advising the provincial governor of Sanuki Province on legal matters in a dispute between local landowners. This was reasonable enough, given his experience and rank. He was familiar with the laws pertaining to land ownership and he had served as governor so he knew about local administrative problems. By an ironic coincidence, his famous ancestor, Michizane, had once served as governor of Sanuki Province.

The timing and the manner of his departure said something altogether more disturbing. He was being removed from the capital before he could proceed further in the investigation of Yorimune's death and the killing of his family. It had been meant to be a surprise and he had been prevented from sending messages or speaking to anyone. Nobody knew where he was.

He was not the only one who believed that Kanemori was innocent. There were also Arihito, Lieutenant Hakeda, and the coroner. What was happening to them? And would his family be silenced in case he had spoken to them?

This fear sickened him to the point of nausea. He crept to the side of the boat and vomited the food he had eaten.

One of the officials asked, "Are you sick?"

Did they care?

He mumbled, "Something I ate."

The man laughed. His companion said, "Go to sleep."

He would not. He would not make it easy for them to drown him in the river.

Night fell quickly. The boatmen lit lanterns. The river traffic was still lively, with lights glimmering here and there, on boats and at stopping places on the shore. They passed Wada and a little later the reed fields of Sumiyoshi. Ahead lay the towns that catered to sailors and lords alike by offering the services of prostitutes and courtesans. Here they encountered boats that were lit up with many colorful lanterns. Musicians played and elegant men and women sat together, eating and drinking.

Akitada was prepared to fight for his life if they tried to throw him overboard. He knew all about death in these waters. It had not been far from here that they had pulled a drowned girl from the river when he had come this way before. That had been more than 10 years ago. He had been younger then, and Tamako had still been alive.

The night passed without incident and they reached Naniwa. The journey had been quick, moving downstream while rowing, and it was barely dawn when they left the boat and walked quickly to one of the ships tied up in the harbor. Again, Akitada marveled at how well his abduction had been planned.

One of the officials went to speak with the captain, identifying himself and his charge. The other stayed close to Akitada.

Akitada said, "I have no luggage, no clothes but what I'm wearing."

The man said, "It will be provided," and immediately fell silent again.

"Are you coming with me?"

"No."

The other official returned with the captain, a rough-looking man, and Akitada was helped on board. The officials stayed on shore and watched as the ship cast off and its rowers moved it into open water. Akitada stood and watched them watching as the sun rose and turned the land green and golden and lush and the sunlight shimmered on the many-colored roofs and pagodas of Naniwa.

The two small black figures eventually moved away, and the land receded into a golden haze. The sailors spread the sails, and the ship slipped smoothly into the waters of the Inland Sea.

He was the only passenger.

For a while he stood at the rail and watched the sailors and their captain. They were a scruffy lot, looking more like pirates than legitimate mariners. It occurred to him that those who had sent him on this journey would be likely to use a pirate ship for the purpose. There was less chance that the captain and crew would talk.

And every chance that they would not hesitate to murder their passenger.

His sleepless night had taken its toll. When they brought him a meal of rice, fish, and vegetables, which he devoured after having had nothing the previous day but the food he had vomited into the river, he became very sleepy. He tried to fight off this exhaustion by walking back and forth in a small area of the deck where this was possible. The weather was clear and the wind seemed to be with them. The ship moved rapidly, throwing up spray as it cut through the waves. It appeared the sailors did everything to maintain their speed by constantly adjusting the huge sails. Eventually the captain came and told him to stay inside because he was getting in the way.

Akitada obeyed. He sat down and occupied himself with thinking about his situation. The capital of Sanuki Province was Takamatsu. It was on the northeast coast of Shikoku. This part of the inland Sea was full of many islands, some very small. It was also notorious for the many pirates who used these islands for their headquarters and launched attacks on shipping from them. There was, of course, no guarantee that they were actually going to Takamatsu. The captain and crew of his ship probably belonged to the local pirates and had been hired to carry him away from his home and family because he had become a threat to someone close to Yorimune.

Eventually exhaustion overcame him and he slept, but nothing happened. Over the next two days, he watched the pirates. They ignored him and seemed bent on getting to their destination as quickly as possible. Why the hurry? Surely it was because they might run into other shipping and wished to avoid contact. A meeting with another ship might offer Akitada a chance of escape. But in that case, why not kill him quickly and toss his body overboard?

Days passed into nights and still the wind held and the ship moved smoothly across a quiet sea. Akitada dozed, jerking himself awake from time to time.

On the third day, he woke to shouts and movement. For a moment, he was completely disoriented. He was looking up at a gray sky with seagulls diving and shrieking above a flapping sail. The sail swung away and dark figures passed at a run with more shouts.

He sat up slowly, feeling stiff and chilled to the bone. What was happening? Where were they?

It became clear that the sailors were reefing the sail and the ship's movement slowed. He stood up and almost fell again, unused to the heaving, twisting motion of the deck. Staggering to the rail, he peered ahead. Land. Mountainous land and low clouds. Either they had reached their destination or this was where he would end his life.

Or both.

The captain joined him. Akitada nearly jumped. The man looked truly villainous with his long hair blowing and his scarred face. He only pointed. "Sanuki!"

Akitada looked. "So we're here?"

The man nodded, then grinned wolfishly. "You get off."

Akitada hoped the grin meant he was glad to be rid of his passenger and collect his fee. It did not seem likely that he had come all this way to drown him within sight of land.

Ahead lay a harbor with fishing boats. A few people were on shore. The ship dropped anchor, and one of the boats came to meet it. Akitada was transferred much like a package being delivered by being passed over the side to drop down into the boat. He fell but was caught and helped to a seat by one of the men in the boat.

They took him to land, somewhat drenched by having to wade ashore the last few feet. It did not matter, for the rain started just about then. He stood on the shore in it, looking after the ship as its sails unfurled again and it moved away into the haze of rain and clouds, sails flapping wildly when it turned, then filling with the wind. His last link to home receded quickly into the general grayness and was gone.

Someone plucked at his sleeve.

An elderly man in poor clothing asked, "Gentleman going to Takamatsu?"

What else could he do? Akitada nodded.

"I take you."

"Thank you. That's very kind of you." Akitada glanced around, looking for signs of a city, some roofs or pagodas rising above the wooded hills before him. There was nothing but the rain.

"A piece of silver?" the elderly man suggested.

Foolish to assume that in Sanuki Province people would perform services out of kindness. Suddenly new problems arose, insurmountable problems. He had very little money, having been snatched from his home. A piece of silver was little enough, but he did not know that he had even that much on him. He reached to his belt, feeling for his money pouch. It was there, but felt sadly slim. He would have refilled it before leaving his house, but the officials had not allowed him time. At least the pirates had not relieved him of it.

He dragged it out, suddenly uncomfortable in the small crowd his arrival had attracted, more ragged creatures who stared at his hands hungrily as they opened the pouch.

There were two pieces of silver and some loose coppers, perhaps enough to buy a meal or two. How was he to survive?

Suddenly cautious, Akitada asked, "How far is it?"

The old man looked vague. "An hour," he said and checked Akitada's feet. "Maybe two."

Akitada still wore the thin cloth slippers he used at home. They were already wet and filthy with mud. He sighed. Perhaps a piece of silver was a fair price. He passed it over to the man, who grinned happily, tucked it in his shirt, and turned, gesturing for him to follow. They would walk.

The road was good, perhaps very good in dryer conditions. But Akitada's footwear and his rain-sodden clothing made walking a misery. They turned away from the coast and into pine woods. The trees rose dark and forbidding on either side. There was no other traffic and no signs of habitation beyond the fishermen's huts on the shore. His guide did not seem very chatty. It was probably not a sign that the natives were unfriendly but had more to do with the weather. For his age, he set a remarkable pace, and Akitada was soon out of breath.

Eventually the old man turned his head. "You wanna rest?" he asked.

Akitada bit his lip. "No. I've been resting on the ship. Carry on."

The old man nodded and increased his pace.

Time passed. They seemed to have reached the end of the forest, and the road began to descend. Akitada overcame his shame and said, "Stop!"

The old man stopped.

"How much farther?"

"You wanna rest?"

"Yes. And I want some answers."

The old man looked blank. "Answers?"

"Are we going to Takamatsu?"

263

"Yes. Takamatsu." The man pointed vaguely ahead. "Just there."

"Where?" Akitada strained his eyes but saw only the road and trees and low gray clouds overhead.

The man waved his hand impatiently in the same direction. "There. You'll see."

The road had to go somewhere, but suddenly the distance became a serious matter for concern. Akitada limped to a rock and sat down. The rain had long since penetrated to his skin and he shivered.

"How big is Takamatsu?"

"Big! Many houses. Temples. Beautiful! You'll see."

"The governor lives there?"

"Yes, yes. He has a beautiful house. Many servants. You go there?"

"Yes." Akitada got back to his feet. "Lead on!"

The trees parted after a while and revealed a vast plain. And there was the city. To be sure it was smaller than the capital, but nonetheless Akitada saw substantial buildings. And beyond it the plain stretched with rice fields and many small villages and farms.

The old man said pointedly, "I told you."

"Yes. Thank you."

"There's the tribunal." The man pointed. Akitada saw the flag flying over one of the closer complexes of walled buildings. As provincial capitals went, this one was a civilized place. They were approaching the city from the north, and typically, the government center was northernmost.

The old man said, "You need me to take you?" He clearly had little confidence in this odd visitor who had decided to arrive at dawn and in a rain storm and without servants.

264

Akitada said, "No. I can manage now."

Without a word the old man turned and started back.

Akitada walked on in the rain. His shoes were disintegrating and small stones cut the soles of his feet. The wind buffeted him and his wet clothes clung to his skin, making him shiver with cold. Now his teeth began to chatter. And it was not even autumn yet.

He touched the documents inside his jacket. No doubt they were soaked like the rest of him. The august signatures might be unreadable by now. Their rapid planning had not allowed for more than getting him removed as quickly as possible. Perhaps more instructions might be sent later. Meanwhile, it would be difficult to explain himself to the local people.

And that might have been part of the plan all along.

32

Consternation

The messenger arrived late in the afternoon. By this time, Sadako was in a panic.

It had started normally enough. Akitada received officials frequently. It was work-related, she thought. He had been called back to the ministry on some urgent matter. She busied herself with household chores. But unwelcome thoughts nagged: they had been unusually rude when they told her to leave the room. As if something unpleasant had been on their minds.

When Akitada had not returned for his midday meal, she went to see Genba to ask him about the visitors.

"Genba, those men who came for my husband. Do you know who they were?"

Genba seemed glad to see her. "No, my lady. I've been worried about it. They weren't friendly, you see. The gentlemen who work with the master are all quite pleasant in their manner."

"Yes." Sadako clenched her hands. "Who can it have been? It's not like him to go away this long without saying anything."

"Did he expect trouble?"

She hesitated. Fear suddenly twisted her heart. "Maybe. It's a case he was working on. If so, the prime minister himself must be behind it."

Genba looked shocked. "The prime minister? Dear heaven! We must tell Tora and Saburo right away."

She clenched her hands again. "I'm probably wrong," she said. "Nakatoshi might know something." Nakatoshi was one of Akitada's close friends, a man he trusted, and one who knew much of what was happening in the government.

Genba nodded. "Yes, but first the others."

They walked to Tora's house, where they found Tora and Saburo in close discussion. Their arrival caused surprise. Lady Sadako rarely troubled the private quarters of Akitada's retainers. This was not because of her position in the household, but because she herself valued privacy and hesitated to disrupt that of others.

Hanae immediately showed signs of nervousness by scurrying about to rearrange cushions and fuss about offering refreshments.

Sadako said quickly, "No, don't bother. And forgive me, Hanae, but I'm so worried about my husband."

That struck the right note. Hanae recognized a common bond. Wives knew what that was like. She glanced at Tora, who had become alert. "Tell us," she said.

With help from Genba, Sadako explained about the strange officials with their military escort.

Tora started to struggle up. "It's that damned massacre," he said. Hanae pushed him back anxiously. He resisted for a moment, then submitted with a grimace. "They got him. And I can do nothing. Look at me! He's in danger and I'm a cripple. The last time he was in trouble, I was twenty years younger, had both my legs, and was able to fight. Now I can't even walk."

"Don't fret," Saburo said. "Genba and I can walk. We'll find out what happened."

Tora was not consoled. "You don't understand. We're like brothers, the master and I." He shot a glance at Sadako. "Begging your pardon, my lady, but we've been that close even though he's high-born and I'm a peasant's son."

Sadako touched his hand. "I know, Tora. I've been grateful for your affection for Akitada. He has depended on it all his life, even though he doesn't always show it."

Tears came to Tora's eyes. He looked away, ashamed of them. She squeezed his hand. "We'll find a way to help him, all of us," she said.

The others muttered agreement. Saburo said, "I'll report his absence at the ministry. The talk may raise some concerns in the prime minister's office. They'll have to take notice and give us some answers."

Tora said, "They'll lie, the bastards. They're behind it."

Saburo nodded. "Maybe so, but we're expected to raise an outcry, and you never know what you might learn as a result."

Tora looked unconvinced, but Sadako said quickly, "I think that's a very good plan. And go to see Nakatoshi in the Ceremonials Office. He's Akitada's friend. He may have information."

Genba said, "What about Lady Akiko? She knows the ladies that serve the empress."

Sadako cried, "Yes, of course. I'll go see her right away."

Genba offered, "I'll go with you, my lady. For safety."

Tora had watched and listened. Now he burst out, "And what about me? I sit here and do nothing? It isn't fair." In his agitation, he moved his injured leg and cried out in pain.

Hanae scolded, "What good will you be if your leg gets worse and has to be cut off?"

This shocked everybody. Tora lay back and closed his eyes, and Sadako said, "We'll do the walking, Tora, and we'll come back to tell you what we learn. Meanwhile, you can think about what may have happened."

Genba and Lady Sadako found Akitada's sister on the point of leaving for another visit to the palace. She listened with raised brows to their account of Akitada's "arrest".

"Well," she said dryly, "I suppose he's done it this time. It sounds official. If so, it may be difficult to find out what has happened to him. Akitada has reached a rank where he cannot be publicly reprimanded and demoted. They probably mean to have him disappear."

Sadako turned absolutely white and started swaying. Her sister-in-law took her arm and shook it. "Stop that. It's likely only a temporary disappearance. We must think what to do. I suppose I'd better go on to the palace to make a protest. Why don't you come with me?"

"The palace? I can't," Sadako whispered. "You mean to speak to the empress?"

"Yes, if she'll see us. What about Kosehira? I hear he's better. We'd best tell him also. You can do that, Genba. The more people know about this, the more likely it is that they won't send him into exile to some god-forsaken island."

Sadako was still very white but pulled herself together. "Yes," she said. "We should have thought of that. I'm afraid we're all sadly confused and shocked. Akitada has always said you're a very smart woman."

Akiko was startled. "Really? That's a surprise. I've always thought I was quite a bit smarter than my brother, but of course, being a man, he would never acknowledge it."

This made Sadako smile a little. "Men," she said.

"Yes. So stop worrying. Women must always be prepared to extricate their men from the problems they get themselves into."

Sadako sighed. "I must go and explain to the children."

Saburo called first at the ministry of justice. He did not expect to learn anything there but planned to create a general sense that something shocking had happened.

271

In this he succeeded quite well. His demands to be told what work Akitada might be engaged in brought him quickly to the minister's office.

This man, a somewhat complacent Fujiwara noble, became agitated at the thought he might be left to cope by himself. He promptly dispatched junior officials to question colleagues and superiors throughout the *Daidairi*.

Saburo next visited Nakatoshi. Here he was invited to sit and share a cup of wine, while Secretary Nakatoshi questioned him and attempted to deduce what might have happened.

"I wish your master had consulted me, Saburo," he said. "I might have talked him out of whatever it was that he did to upset someone."

Saburo asked, "Upset whom? Who is behind this?"

Nakatoshi sighed. "I don't know, but this could hardly have been done without the prime minister's knowledge."

Saburo raised his chin. "Then I must speak to the prime minister."

"You won't be admitted. I'm afraid I wouldn't be either. But let me try to find out where he is. That may be easier."

For this, Saburo settled. But he continued to visit ministries and bureaus to ask questions. Mostly he encountered blank stares, or idle curiosity, and the occasional smirk. Akitada had not made many friends in his long career.

Saburo returned late to Tora's house to share what he had learned. This amounted to nothing, and Tora's frustration grew. His son Yuki, having heard of his injuries, had come home. He was outraged by the attack on his father and wanted to hunt down the thugs. Tora wanted him to return to his duties with the guards before he got in trouble.

"You'll just make things worse," he said. "We're worried about the master. We don't know what happened to him or where he is. I've thought and thought, and not one idea has come to me. Years ago in Echigo Province I simply went after him. I found him, too, though it was hard. But I had both my legs then."

Yuki offered his services.

"No," said his father. "I want you back at your duties. Now!"

Yuki pouted and left.

Saburo looked after him. "He's grown up, that boy. He looks like you."

Tora's face softened. "He's stubborn," he said, but he smiled a little.

"As for your adventures on Sado Island, you knew where your master was then. He could be anywhere this time. Even in the capital."

They were still brooding over this when the messenger arrived.

Wearing formal court dress, he asked to see Lady Sugawara and handed her a letter. This she opened and read. Then she thanked the messenger and told him there was no answer.

When the man had gone, she hurried first to see the children. Akitada's daughter Yasuko had been weeping, but Yoshi simply looked puzzled. "Was it a message from Father?" he asked.

"No. It's from your father's superiors. He's been sent to Sanuki Province to solve a complicated legal case."

Yasuko brightened. "Then he's all right!" she cried.

Sadako said firmly, "Apparently so."

Yoshi got up. "I've a lecture to attend. You can send a message if there's more news."

Sadako nodded and watched him leave. The boy was at an age where he did not waste time imagining things happening. He simply returned to the familiar and mostly enjoyable pursuits of his day.

Yasuko was frowning again. "Father did not say goodbye. That isn't like him. Not when he was about to travel so far away. How long will he be gone?"

Sadako glanced at the letter again. "They don't say. I'd better go tell the others."

The news was met with disbelief.

"He's been sent where?" Tora asked.

"Sanuki Province. They claim there's a legal problem and he should return when it's settled." She paused. "Where is Sanuki Province?"

Saburo said, "On the Inland Sea. Shikoku Island."

Tora muttered, "Well, it's not Kyushu this time, but what good is that? I cannot go there."

Sadako was touched by Tora's misery. His loyalty to Akitada ruled his every thought.

After a moment's hesitation, Saburo said, "I can go and bring him back."

"Maybe. If what they say is true," Tora pointed out. "For all we know they've thrown him into another mine."

They still worried over this when the stable boy brought young Arihito to Tora's house.

Arihito bowed to Sadako, then stared at the bedridden Tora. "What happened to you?"

274

After they explained, Arihito said, "I heard a rumor that Akitada's been arrested."

More explanations followed. In the end, they decided to postpone a trip to Sanuki Province until Arihito had verified the truth of the official explanation.

33

The Governor

Because Akitada approached Takamatsu from the north, he reached the governor's headquarters before seeing much of the city. The rain had finally stopped, but it had left him looking like a battered crow. He had lost his hat, and his old robe hung on him, heavy with rain water. One foot was bare, and the shoe on the other was torn. His topknot had come undone and wet strands of his hair clung to his face and neck.

The gate to the tribunal had not been opened yet, and he joined a small group of petitioners, mostly in straw rain-coats and belonging to the peasant class. They looked at Akitada with considerable amazement. His appearance made no sense to them. They stared,

277

they whispered to each other, then an argument arose between them as to how to account for this strange arrival. Finally, the bravest stepped forward and asked, "What's your business, friend?"

"I'm here to see the governor." Akitada gestured to the sky. It was fully light by now, though the rain clouds still hung low over the town. "Why are they so late opening the gates?"

Someone sniggered and said, "His Excellency sleeps late. Big party."

Akitada was still considering this, when sounds behind the gate announced the start of the day. The two wooden sections creaked open, moved by sturdy guards. A third guard eyed the group unenthusiastically. "What do you want?" he demanded. "We've got no time for nonsense. If you waste the governor's time, there'll be a beating."

Two ragged men decided to leave. The rest waited.

Akitada, miserable though he was, felt stirrings of outrage. What sort of behavior was this? It offended against every rule laid down on the subject of proper administrative process. Though he had planned to wait his turn, he now stepped forward and snapped, "Immediately admit these men! It is their right to petition the governor."

The guard stared at his sodden appearance with a frown. "And who the hell are you?" he finally demanded with a nasty smile. "Got caught in the rain? Homeless? A vagrant? We'll see about that. Show me your papers."

Akitada had no papers beyond the official documents and they were meant for the governor's eyes only. He said, "Take me to your governor and I'll explain."

The smile widened. The guard shouted to his comrades, "Did you hear that? This scarecrow is giving me orders."

They had a good guffaw. The waiting men moved away from Akitada to show that they had nothing to do with him.

Akitada glowered. "You'll be sorry. The governor will not tolerate your behavior."

The first guard stopped smiling. He took a step forward, seized hold of Akitada's arm and tried to twist it so that he would fall to his knees. Akitada kicked him in the knee-cap. It hurt, but even with a bare foot he managed to do enough damage that the guard cried out and let go of his arm. But then all three fell upon him, carrying him to the muddy ground and belaboring him with their fists and knees. One vicious punch struck him near a temple and dazed him.

Akitada knew he had made a mistake and deserved this. He concentrated on protecting his head and not crying out with pain. For a moment, he thought he might die, here in the rain and mud of Sanuki Province, and no one would ever know. What he had already learned about this administration made that entirely likely.

But the sodden documents saved his life after all. They fell out and one of the guards saw them, recognized the official seals, and shouted a warning. The beating stopped, and an agitated conversation ensued. They got off him and one guard asked him, "Who are you? Are you a messenger?"

Akitada did not answer. He was busy checking the damage to his body as he slowly got to his knees.

279

His arms and legs hurt but seemed all right, but he had a blinding headache.

Another guard muttered, "This could be trouble."

"Get up!" the first guard said in an aggrieved tone. "You nearly broke my knee. And you didn't announce your business. What were we to think?"

One of the waiting men, sensing a shift of power, came over and helped Akitada to his feet. "Are you all right?" he asked, peering at him anxiously.

Akitada nodded and said, "Thank you." He told the guards, "I am Sugawara Akitada. I've been sent with orders from the prime minister in the capital. There's been an accident on landing."

The guards gaped at him and then at each other. The guard he had kicked said, "Sorry, sir. Nobody told us to expect you. If you'll follow me."

He walked with a pronounced limp, and Akitada limped after him. It would have been funny if his body had not been so painful and if he did not fear that his ordeal was far from over.

The governor, Fujiwara Munesuke belonged to a minor branch of the *kuge* family who ruled the nation. He was short and rotund like Kosehira and several other members of that family, but still quite young. Akitada judged him to be in his mid-thirties. He had a beard, neatly trimmed, and surprisingly small, delicate hands. Akitada's sudden arrival astonished him to the point of near-speechlessness. It was clear he was out of his depth about how to deal with this unexpected intrusion into his comfortable life. No one could possibly expect a ragged senior noble to appear dripping water and mud on his shiny wood floor.

"Um," he said, after inviting Akitada to sit. "Yes. Hmm. I see. Very strange. Sugawara, you say? Um, what do you do?"

Akitada understood this correctly to refer to his rank and influence. "I'm senior secretary in the Ministry of Justice at the moment, but I have served as governor several times. Upper fifth rank."

The governor stared. "B –but . . . what happened to you? Where's your escort? You're wet, dirty, and barefoot."

Akitada almost smiled. "I'm also bruised from a beating by your guards. Nevertheless I am who I said I was." He shoved the wet documents toward Munesuke.

The governor looked at them with distaste and called his secretary. "Clean those off and open them!"

The secretary obeyed with a shudder, and the governor peered at the content. Then he looked at Akitada again. "I suppose I'd better find quarters for you and some clean clothes. And food and a bath."

Akitada nodded with a straight face. "Yes, that would be best."

Things improved greatly after this. He was shown to a room in the governor's house, and went to soak in a hot bath. One of the servants shaved him and retied his topknot. The clothes provided fit reasonably well and were of good quality. Akitada assumed His Excellency had rummaged through his own collection of robes and trousers. Rank had its privileges.

But the main problems remained. He had no money. How was he to escape and get back home? Home, where Sadako and the children waited. The hurry with which he had been packed off meant that further instructions could well arrive soon. He was by no means out of danger.

281

Akitada considered his situation. If he had money, he could try to simply walk away. As this was not possible, his best option was to abide by the prime minister's instructions while learning as much as possible about the people and conditions here. Such a delay went against every instinct. Not only would he simply be waiting for whatever additional hardships were planned for him, but his family and others were in danger at home and a ruthless killer roamed in the capital to strike again if and when it pleased him.

A servant brought an invitation to join the governor for the midday rice. Akitada went and thanked Munesuke for the clothes.

The governor waved his gratitude away. "I shall advance you funds, but I must warn you that local merchants have only a poor selection in silks and brocades. I do have some excellent seamstresses, however."

Akitada was surprised by such generosity. "You're very kind. I accept gladly. For the moment I'm quite comfortable and anxious to begin my work." He eyed the array of fragrant and tempting dishes laid out before him and had to restrain himself not to fall on the food like a starved tiger.

Munesuke had a fine cook and clearly appreciated good food. After briefly describing his post and its peculiarities, Munesuke said, "The complaints that bring you here are quite ancient. They predate my administration. People had come to accept things. But there was a death recently, and now an heir is making trouble again. He turned to His Majesty for assistance." The governor looked aggrieved. "A Taira is involved, I'm afraid. They're thick as flies in this region and all about the Inland Sea, and they behave as if they owned the land outright."

Akitada was familiar with the behavior of the provincial nobility. The Taira, like the Minamoto, were a clan that traced its descent to earlier emperors whose sons had accepted commoner status, but never forgot their imperial blood, and ruled their extensive lands like kings. They kept armies, which the government used to fight their wars. To Akitada's mind, they were a threat for the future.

He said, "I should like to see the documents in the case and meet this heir."

Munesuke grinned. "Of course. Rather you than me. I shall enjoy having you take this matter off my shoulders. But enough of work. Tell me what's new in the capital. I've been stuck here for six years now."

"Six years? You weren't relieved after four?"

Munesuke made a face. "No. Seems I did too good a job. That's something I shall have to change." He laughed.

Akitada was beginning to like this man. He wondered if he was changing with advancing years: the old Akitada would have considered such an attitude reprehensible. He had always tried to be the proper, obedient, hard-working official. It had got him nothing. Not even wealth. Governors traditionally enriched themselves by overtaxing the peasants and playing games with the accounts. Appointments like this tended to be rewards given to officials in the capital who had been found agreeable or were related to the ruling *kuge* family. In his case, they had wanted to get rid of him.

He asked, "Is this a poor province?"

Munesuke understood at once and burst into laughter again. "Not really, but there are the Taira. A great nuisance because they or their vassals own half the province. That leaves little for a poor governor."

"I'm sorry. And apparently they also squabble and cause extra work?"

Munesuke clapped his hands. "Exactly! You understand the problem perfectly. I'm very glad they sent someone experienced. You'll set things straight in no time." His face fell a little. "Of course that doesn't really get rid of them."

Akitada still believed that it was not really what the prime minister had intended, but it was possible that he had hoped to solve two problems at once: he got rid of him while also acceding to Munesuke's request. He relaxed a little and reminded himself that he must not become careless. He made an effort to mention some court events in the capital, then asked, "You did hear about the assassination of Yorimune and his family?"

"Yes, of course. A terrible thing. Though I couldn't stand the man."

"Oh? Why not?"

"A bad character. You must've heard talk. Of course, rich young men get into trouble sometimes. Too much wine and too many pretty women. It's understandable. But Yorimune was a cruel fellow. He liked to hurt others. He enjoyed pain. Used to torture dogs and horses when he was younger. Very nasty."

Akitada gulped. "I didn't know."

"Oh, yes. Believe me, there are many who'll be glad he's dead. Mind you, it's a pity about his wife and daughters.

34

Waiting

After Arihito and Lady Sadako had left, Akitada's three retainers discussed the situation.

Genba, always inclined to see the best side of every issue, pointed out that it had been quite proper for the government to notify them and that surely they would not have done so if there was anything wrong.

Tora snapped, "You're a fool, Genba. They didn't even give him time to tell his family and pack a few things. They don't expect him to come back."

Genba flushed painfully. "I know your leg hurts, Tora, but surely there's no need to call me names."

Saburo said, "Genba is right. We must have hope. I think the message from the prime minister may be a response to my enquiries yesterday. That's good news. The prime minister would not admit to being involved if they intended to kill the master." He smiled at Genba.

Tora muttered, "I wish I could get around. Maybe I can hobble a bit on this crutch, Saburo and I could go and make sure he's all right."

Saburo shook his head. "No. By the time we got there he might be someplace else."

Discouragement descended again.

By noon, Arihito returned. He had told his father, and Kosehira had sent messages to friends and acquaintances, among them the prime minister. The prime minister had responded with reassurance that Akitada would return as soon as his assignment was completed.

Saburo said, "That was good of your father. What does he think?"

"He doesn't know what to think, but he's very angry. He's drafting a letter of protest to the emperor."

"Surely that's dangerous. If he offends His Majesty, it will harm your family."

Arihito made a face. "If you mean that any resentment might affect my sister's standing at court, Father doesn't care. He's angry with Yukiko also."

"This can't be good for his health."

"I think it's given him new strength." Arihito sat down and accepted a cup of wine. "The whole business is shocking," he said. "Akitada didn't know where they were sending him?"

"No. Nobody knew. I bet he didn't know why they took him away without giving him time to change his clothes, take some money, or speak to anyone."

Genba said, "It must've been frightening."

Tora muttered darkly, "I thought they meant to execute him. I still think maybe they did."

Genba cried, "Oh, no! Surely not."

Tora glowered. "You may recall it was quite a common thing in the north. And what will happen to the ones who did it? Nothing. They'll blame it on others."

Genba shook his head, "You mustn't think the worst, Tora."

Arihito said firmly, "Nothing like this can happen here in the capital or to a man like Akitada. We'll get him back."

Tora threw up his hands, "He's in Sanuki Province, sir. Anything can happen there . . . if he's really in Sanuki Province."

Arihito tried to persuade Tora that Sanuki Province was quite civilized and that everyone was working to bring Akitada back to the capital. He said, "Let's wait for more information. The best thing to do is to find the real killer and I have an idea where to look."

Genba said, "Be careful, sir. You may be next."

"They don't know I know," Arihito said with a grin and left.

Saburo glanced at Tora. "You want to try to do something about Tanizaki?"

"To hell with Tanizaki!"

Nobody said anything for a moment. Then Genba got up and said, "I wish you and Saburo would think about that schoolmaster, Tora. The master would not want to leave such a man to do more harm. He was very upset about what happened to you and blamed himself."

Tora looked surprised. "He did? Did he say so? I mean did he really say that I might have been right all along?"

"Yes, Tora." Genba left to take care of his chores.

Tora was embarrassed. "You know," he said to Saburo, "I may have been wrong for speaking the way I did to the master and the rest of you. I'm sorry I acted the way I did."

"You've been in a lot of pain. We knew. The master knew also."

"That's no excuse."

"Pain can make you crazy."

Tora looked at Saburo's scarred face. Even a beard did not hide all the horrible scars. "Yes, brother," he said with a nod. "You know all right."

Saburo grinned. "Getting back at those who hurt you may go a long way toward soothing the pain."

"Right! So let me fill you in on what I know about that bastard Tanizaki."

Saburo listened closely to Tora's account of Tanizaki's offences, asking occasional questions. He seemed interested in the youngster who had seen a man at the attic window.

"That was just before they found Tomoko dead. I think it was Tomoko's lover, and Tanizaki found them together and killed her."

Saburo asked, "Then why didn't he kill him too?"

Tora considered this. "Maybe the lover got away in time. Or . . . consider this: that man was someone Tanizaki paid to kill Tomoko. He sent the thugs after me. It would be just what he'd do."

Saburo nodded slowly. "It could be."

"Exactly. I bet he found the killer in the same neighborhood where that woman lives with her son. Maybe it was her son at the window. They're all in it together. We've found a whole nest of murderous snakes."

"Don't you think it's time to get the police to look into it?"

Tora snorted. "Haven't you been listening? They won't touch Tanizaki. They think he's one of the 'good people'."

"Well, he isn't really. He's just a schoolmaster."

"And if they decide to believe him instead?"

"Well, I suppose I could go talk to him about it. See what he says?"

"For a former spy, you're pretty dumb. If he gets suspicious, he'll run and we'll never find him again."

Saburo said nothing. After a moment, Tora apologized, "Sorry, brother. I'm out-of-sorts with this leg. I should be doing things."

"Never mind. Tell me what you would do, and I'll do it."

"You'll never find that kid who saw the man at the window. You don't know what he looks like."

Saburo jumped up. "I'll find him. Leave it to me." He was out the door before Tora could stop him.

Arihito went to see the sword smith, Jocho. He was outside his house stacking fire-wood and received Arihito politely but coolly. "Lord Sugawara was here a few days ago. I couldn't give him any more answers."

Arihito thought Jocho's phrasing a little odd. "What did he want to know?"

"He asked about the men who come to my place. I told them they would never murder women."

Arihito said quietly, "I think he wondered if any of them might have murdered Kanemori."

"What?"

"Kanemori was murdered. He didn't kill himself."

Jocho goggled. "That's impossible. I thought you and Lord Sugawara saw him yourself."

"Yes, but the coroner says Kanemori died from a sword wound he couldn't have inflicted on himself."

Jocho sank down on a tree stump and stared up at Arihito. "Murdered? But why didn't his lordship say so?"

"He was afraid if the story got out, people might get hurt. But somebody talked and he's been arrested."

The sword smith gasped. "What? Why? Who would do such a thing?"

"Someone who's protecting the killer."

That left Jocho speechless. He sat shaking his head in disbelief.

"Well," Arihito demanded, "are you going to help me or not?"

Jocho said, "There's someone who asked questions about Kanemori. But that was quite a while ago. He said he'd served up north and heard stories about him. Said he admired him. I pointed Kanemori out and later I saw them talking. I saw no harm in it. I still see no harm in it."

"Is this man still here? What's his name?"

"I haven't seen him since Kanemori died. And he never gave me his name. People don't always. They just come to watch and if they feel like it, they make friends."

"If you ask me, that's a very careless way of running a school for people who train to kill others."

Jocho bristled. "They're soldiers, not killers. Nobody who comes here has ever committed a crime. You've got a very poor opinion of the men who fight to protect the nobles in their comfortable lives."

Arihito blushed. The man had a point. "Sorry," he said. "But it's possible, just possible, mind you, that you sent Kanemori's killer to him."

Lady Akiko returned late from the palace. Sadako had sent Yasuko to bed when she started to fret again about her father's absence. They had run out of busy work and distractions, and Sadako herself was falling into a depression. She greeted her sister-in-law with almost effusive pleasure.

Akiko regarded her with narrowed eyes. "Are you going into another panic?"

Sadako pulled herself together. "No. But I keep thinking of all the dangerous things your brother did in all those years before we met. And a few since."

"Well, then you should know that he always falls back on his feet like a cat. How else could he keep doing the things he does?"

Sadako laughed weakly. "Do you have any news?"

"Well, there is little. Our new little emperor has no understanding of the situation, and his grandfather, the prime minister, apparently wants the death of Yorimune forgotten and has expressed displeasure that people keep raking it up again."

"That's not good."

"You must be patient. There's a great deal going on at the moment. The coronation will be soon, and

291

already people are planning appointments and advancing their daughters to serve in the imperial palace."

"But He's just a child."

"He'll grow up. He can play with his intended spouse until he does."

Sadako shook her head.

"There was one thing," her sister-in-law said. "I've a good mind to follow up on that. Akitada isn't the only one who solves crimes."

"Oh, Akiko, do be careful."

"Naturally. Do you want to know what I heard?"

"Yes."

"Well, there was an old case of murder or suicide involving a companion of Yorimune's wife. It happened more than twenty years ago, and Akitada didn't think much of it. But I heard that Yorimune was the one responsible for the girl's death. He was pledged to Taira Motoko, but her companion caught his eye. They say the girl returned his feelings. What do you think of that?"

"It's very long ago. Are you saying that Motoko killed her companion out of jealousy?"

"That I don't know. But I shall find out. I know someone who was there."

Sadako smiled. "You're a lot like your brother, Akiko."

Lady Akiko laughed. "It's exciting. I may solve the case before Akitada returns."

35

Bonsai

For the first three days, Akitada existed as a virtual prisoner, albeit in some luxury. He wore the governor's clothes, slept in the governor's house, ate the same food, and enjoyed the service provided by his staff. However, he still had no money and any efforts at leaving would have been noted immediately. Under the circumstances, he thought it best to submit.

While the governor went about his duties and pleasures, Akitada stayed in his house or worked in the tribunal's archives. He had made up his mind to resolve his assignment as quickly as possible and then demand passage home.

On his first day, somewhat to Akitada's surprise, the governor offered to add a letter to a package of provincial mail. This cheered him considerably. There was at least a chance Sadako would receive it. Alas, it would take a week or more, even though official government mail received special attention, being carried by the fastest ships and mounted messengers.

He wrote to his wife, telling her he was well and would return as soon as his assignment was complete. He made every effort to be reassuring, because he knew how upset and frightened she must be. And he avoided carefully any reference to the matter of the massacre or his search for the killer. Similarly, he did not add any messages for Arihito and referred only briefly to Tora's injuries.

Then he set to work on the land dispute between the Yamada and Taira families, consulting provincial documents and law books, and asking questions about the people involved. This work occupied him from early morning until it was time for the evening rice with the governor. Their conversations consisted of Akitada asking more questions about the case and Munesuke talking about local amusements.

Munesuke was an interesting character. Akitada had asked him early if he had brought his family with him to Sanuki. The question had made the governor laugh.

"Why would I do a stupid thing like that? My three wives and eight children would plague me day in and day out. No, they're in the capital, where they prefer to be in any case."

Akitada, recalling his lonely days when he served in Mikawa Province and his new wife Yukiko refused to join him, asked, "Don't you find it very dreary to be so alone?"

294

Munesuke looked astonished. "But I'm not alone, my dear Akitada. I have a most enchanting creature to keep me company in the women's quarters here. She's a local girl but well educated. I'm becoming quite fond of her and may take her home with me. As a concubine, of course, since her family is of no account."

Akitada met the enchanting creature one morning as he headed to his bath. She had just finished and emerged wearing only a thin silk underrobe that did little to hide the smooth curves of her young body. Not at all embarrassed, she smiled and bowed, murmuring, "Good morning. Isn't it a lovely day?" and then passed him on her way to her rooms.

It *was* a lovely day, but Akitada closed his eyes and ears to it and delved into dusty manuscripts. He longed for Sadako.

The case in contention consisted of multiple cases. Four claimants had squabbled for over a century. Two families claimed to have opened up new rice lands by clearing a wilderness, and both had petitioned to receive these lands as permanent property. At some point the issue became more confused when one family decided to donate the embattled land to a temple, probably in hopes of strengthening their claim. This sort of move tended to be in name only. The donor retained the use of the land and shared a portion of the harvest with the temple. The legal battle continued, now having a third claimant in the temple. Some two generations ago there was a settlement, when the land became the dowry of a young woman who married the heir of the fourth claimant.

Two of the families involved were Taira and Yamada.

Akitada recalled his sister's story of the drowned girl and Kobe's memories of his investigation into her death. They were different people, of course, living in a different time, but the fact that he had encountered the same two family names struck him as strange and possibly fateful.

He put the matter from his mind, afraid that the drowned girl might cloud his judgment of the old legal case. As he worked with the old documents, he made copious notes and consulted legal books. This occupied three days. On the fourth day, he asked Munesuke to arrange for an interview with the current claimant for the land. This man was Yamada Yasuhito, owner of a modest property in Sanuki Province.

The governor sighed. "You won't like it. He's demented. Are you sure you need to meet him?"

Akitada said firmly. "Yes. I'm sure. I have a pretty good idea whose land it is, but the man has renewed the suit and is apparently adamant. I see that he petitioned the court four times over the past twenty years. I want to know what makes him so sure he has a claim."

Consequently, Munesuke arranged for Akitada to pay Yamada Yasuhito a visit. He supplied a horse and a servant to accompany him. The distance was not great, a mere hour's ride through rather beautiful Sanuki landscape. Summer was ending. It was still warm, but already the fields and the foliage on trees and shrubs were beginning to look tired and worn. Peasants were tending to their second rice crop. The land looked fertile but not all fields seemed to have adequate water sources. The farther he got, the fewer cultivated fields he found. Peasants' huts looked poor and derelict.

Many people seemed to subsist on small vegetable patches.

Eventually the Yamada estate hove into view. It was an impressively large compound, but on closer inspection in a very derelict state. Outbuildings were in ruins and the walls around the main house had collapsed in places. Most disturbing was the fact that the place looked deserted. There was nobody in sight.

Akitada dismounted before the main house. Its veranda looked unstable, but someone had been mending the steps to the door, which stood open.

"Wait here with the horses," Akitada told the servant. Then he climbed the stairs cautiously and walked to the door.

"Ho?" he shouted, "Is anyone home?"

This brought no answer and he entered the house. He encountered large, dim, empty spaces, once quite elegant with carved pillars and painted ceilings, but now empty and dusty, sunlight falling through closed shutters, marking the worn floors with thin bars of gold.

He traversed the whole main house and emerged onto the rear veranda without encountering a soul. Before him lay a beautiful garden. Whoever had planted it had aimed for an impressive display in autumn. Chrysanthemums grew among shrubs, some already in bloom, others heavy with buds. Behind them maples were just beginning to turn red, pink, or golden. Birds twittered in the trees, and insects buzzed. The gravel path was neatly raked. The contrast to the rest of the property could not have been greater.

As he stood and wondered about this, he finally heard the sound of sawing coming from the back of the garden. Stepping down the rickety steps, he walked toward it.

He found a small, white-haired figure belaboring a fallen branch, cutting it into small logs.

Akitada called out a greeting. The old man paused, straightened, and raised his hand against the sun to peer at him.

"Who are you?"

"My name is Sugawara. Where could I find the owner of this house?"

A look of utter astonishment passed over the old man's face. "*You* are Sugawara? You can't be." He blinked. "I must be seeing things." He ran his hand over his eyes and peered again. "No, you don't look like him a bit. I've seen his picture. Who are you really?"

"My name is Sugawara Akitada. I'm looking for Yamada Yasuhito."

"Akitada? Oh. Are you related to the great Michizane then?"

Akitada smiled. Even in this derelict place there was a humble gardener who knew of his ancestor. "I'm a descendant," he said. "It's good of you to remember my ancestor. I believe he served as governor here at one time."

The old man nodded eagerly. "So he did. A great man. I'm Yasuhito by the way. What brings you here, Akitada?"

Now Akitada was astonished. So this was Yamada himself. Even fallen on bad times the man observed rank. He considered himself an equal and therefore used Akitada's given name. Akitada bowed.

"Forgive me, Yasuhito. I did not expect a Yamada heir to be sawing wood."

298

Yasuhito laid down his saw and wiped his hands on his threadbare shirt. "I have no servants left. Except for an old woman who comes and cooks a meal for me every day. I'm not ashamed. Even great men have gardened. I've always loved it, so I spend all my time tending this plot. The rest can go to hell. Come and see my little trees."

Surprised by this frank answer, Akitada followed him around a wing of the house. There someone had built shelves and on the shelves rested many small containers with tiny trees. They looked like trees in shape, but none rose above a foot, and yet they had their leaves, tiny leaves, and their needles and cones.

Akitada exclaimed in wonder and delight, bending to each specimen to study it. He found that the intricate branches had been wired and made to grow in picturesque shapes. He had seen similar constraints placed on full-grown trees by avid gardeners who attempted to create special views in their gardens, but never had he seen anything so tiny and intricate.

"How wonderful," he said. "That little maple is turning red."

Yasuhito looked gratified. "Of course it is. They're like the big trees in every way, only small."

"You're an artist!"

Yasuhito's smile was smug. "Thank you, Akitada. It's good to meet a man of taste and acumen. But you're the great Michizane's descendant after all. I knew you would understand."

Akitada understood nothing. This man lived in utter penury and occupied himself with tiny trees.

"Do you live alone?" he asked, wanting to know Yasuhito's circumstances without offending him.

"Yes. I'm an old man. They're all dead. I'm the only one left."

"I'm sorry."

"I'm used to it. Better this way. Can you see a wife putting up with this?" He waved a comprehensive arm toward the house and pointed to the little trees. "She'd have left me long ago. As it was she died in childbirth. The child also."

Akitada was beginning to think that this man ought not to care so much about the embattled land. He stood puzzled, looking around him at everything.

"Why are you here?" Yasuhito asked.

"Your law suit against the Taira."

"Ah!"

"Perhaps you no longer care?" Akitada asked hopefully.

"I don't. It's the principle. Someone needs to teach them a lesson. The monks too. Let's go sit on the veranda. There's no wine, but I make a very refreshing tea from leaves and berries."

"Yes. Thank you. That sounds good."

The "tea" was unusual but palatable, and Akitada was quite thirsty after his ride. He said, "Tell me about your claim."

Yasuhito went over the sequence of what had happened to the rice lands that used to go with the estate. The events were essentially what had been recorded, but the old man managed to imbue each transaction with evil intentions by his adversaries.

Eventually Akitada asked, "How did this enmity arise in the first place?"

"Hmm." Yasuhito thought, frowning. "Before my time. My cousin owned the land before me. When

the grief killed him, I inherited. The trouble with the
Taira started before me."

Akitada again got the strange feeling that this
meeting had been fated, as perhaps had his presence in
Sanuki Province. "What grief?" he asked.

"Oh, it's an old story. Must be twenty years
now. My cousin Tokihira had no sons, but he had a
beautiful daughter, Yoshiko. He sent her to Taira
Masamori to be raised with his daughter. Masamori was
an imperial adviser at the time and promised to intro-
duce both girls to the emperor. My cousin, poor man,
built the hopes of his family on Yoshiko being chosen
as consort. But Taira Masamori reneged on his promise
to bring her to the emperor's attention. There was some
scandal about the girl and she committed suicide. My
cousin accused Masamori of Yoshiko's murder because
she was a greater beauty than his own daughter. His
accusation came to nothing, my cousin died, and the
land, what there was left of it, became mine."

"Your cousin had no other children?"

"None alive. Not by his wives. There was a boy,
fathered on a local woman. He got in trouble and my
cousin bought him a place in the capital guard. That's
the last anyone heard of him."

"And his wives?"

"All dead now."

Akitada sighed. "It's a sad story. I've looked at
your case. In fact, I was sent here to verify facts. I wish I
could give you hope, but when your cousin passed his
lands to the temple, he lost his rights to them."

Yasuhito growled, "He didn't give those monks
the land. It was done in name only. It's done everywhere so as not to pay taxes. They were still his fields."

301

"Ah, but that depends on an oral agreement.
I'm afraid, the temple has confirmed their ownership.
They claim they bought most of the land and your
cousin donated the rest."

The other man sagged in disappointment.
"That's what they told me, but it's a lie. The devils
lied."

Akitada said firmly, "Perhaps. I'm inclined to
believe you. It's possible that with the passage of time,
the agreement was forgotten and someone at the temple
documented the land as temple property. In any case,
we have no legal grounds to get back what your cousin
foolishly and illegally arranged to avoid taxes."

Yasuhito muttered, "It was done to keep those
rapacious Taira from getting their hands on it."

"That also may be, but I'm afraid the land is
gone."

Yasuhito nodded. He looked down at his gar-
den. "It doesn't matter. I'm old. I have little time left. I
shall spend it in my garden."

Silence fell. Akitada felt very sorry for the old
man. After a while, he asked, "Did the Taira offer
blood money for Yoshiko?"

The other man looked pained. "No. My cousin
demanded it as she was in their care, but they said his
daughter had behaved badly and was responsible for
her fate. He never believed the story they told him.
Something happened to Yoshiko, but Taira Masamori
only cared about his own daughter. After my cousin
died, she was forgotten."

"Perhaps not. Is anyone in her family still
alive?"

"No. Her mother became a nun. She also
died." Yasuhito got up with a sigh, looking longingly at

his collection of small trees. "Thank you for coming. Do not worry. I'm an old man. I need very little."

36

The Boy

By the time Akitada's letter arrived from Sanuki Province, a number of things had happened. Arihito had sought an audience with the prime minister. He had been received and treated with the utmost respect and concern. The prime minister had asked about his parents' condition and sounded relieved that the news was good. He had expressed his condolences on the death of the young woman promised to Arihito. And he had listened with interest to Arihito's confession that he sided with Akitada about Kanemori's innocence and hoped that Akitada had not been punished for his insistence.

The prime minister assured him that the Sanuki assignment was purely a matter of the Ministry of Justice following up on an old case.

Arihito did not believe this, but he was encouraged by the prime minister's friendly demeanor. He returned to his search for the man who had asked about

Kanemori. Here, however, he had no luck. The mysterious stranger seemed to have disappeared.

Tora's leg healed slowly, but he managed quite well with a crutch and later a walking stick. Saburo carried on the search for the boy in Tanizaki's neighborhood.

The tailor couple welcomed him eagerly and expressed regret when they heard about Tora's accident. Saburo saw their poverty and made them, uncharacteristically, a small gift of money. When he asked them about the boy who had watched Tanizaki's wife, the husband chuckled. His wife expressed outrage. "He's no good, that one. Only twelve and always touching the young women and girls. And his language! His mother's a slut who takes men into her place. I guess he sees enough and wants to try it out."

When her husband guffawed, she gave him a dirty look.

Saburo was mildly shocked by the boy's behavior. He had spent his formative years among monks and remained untouched by lust until he was nearly seventeen, and then it had been another monk who had enlightened him about certain pleasures. Now middle-aged and married to a middle-aged woman with a daughter, he had become somewhat prudish about such things.

He asked, "What does he look like?"

The wife grimaced. "Short and ugly. With bushy hair standing straight up."

The husband said, "He's got a scar. Near his ear."

But even with this description, the boy remained elusive as Saburo roamed the poor neighborhood asking questions. Attitudes toward the schoolmaster established that he had kept to himself and few people knew what happened inside his house, though they had seen the murdered wife going to the market and the maid getting water and washing clothes in the canal near the house. The maid had disdained them as much as the Tanizaki couple had. Nobody liked the people in the big, old house much. One interesting item emerged: Tanizaki had been seen in the company of a tall young man in one of the wine shops.

Saburo also came across the half-mad old crone Tora had met. She seemed to spend most of her time sitting near the communal well, muttering and mumbling to herself and occasionally cursing the women who came for water.

He approached her with a bow. "Honored grandmother," he said. "This ignorant person asks humbly for your advice and enlightenment."

She stared at him. "Who are you?"

"I'm Saburo. I used to be a monk. I'm sorely in need of wise counsel."

She glared, then suddenly grinned toothlessly. "You're a liar, but sit down."

Saburo bowed again, sat, and said, "I really used to be a monk."

"More fool you, then."

He said humbly, "Yes, grandmother."

She pointed a dirty finger at his face. "Did they do that to you?"

"Yes, grandmother."

"Some of them are worse than murderers."

"Yes, grandmother. I left. I was afraid I'd become like them."

"What do you want to know?"

307

"A woman was murdered not far from here. In one of the big houses."

She nodded. "The schoolmaster's wife." She gestured with a dirty hand toward the well. "She'd come a few times to get water. After that lazy maid of theirs ran away."

"Did you talk to her?"

She nodded. "She wanted a child so he'd leave her alone." She cackled. "The old fool wanted a son."

Saburo thought this interesting. Had Tomoko been so desperate to give her aging husband a child that she had turned to a younger man? He asked, "Did you ever see her with another man?"

She cackled. "You've got a dirty mind. No. Too afraid of the schoolmaster."

"Do you have any idea who killed her?"

"Of course not. Do your own work."

Saburo looked discouraged. "Sorry. I'm helping a friend. They nearly killed him for asking questions."

Her eyes sharpened. "Tall fellow who grins a lot? Thinks all women should get weak in the knees?"

"That might be him. Why?"

"He asked. I told him. Don't bother helping that one."

"What exactly did you tell him?"

"I told him the first wife died. They all died." She paused and stared into the distance. "I'll be dead myself soon. Not soon enough in this world."

Saburo bent to pat her hand. "I'm sorry my friend didn't listen, grandmother. Do not grieve."

She snatched his hand with her own claw. "Beware of sons!"

Saburo had no sons he was aware of, and not even a daughter, for the one his wife had brought into their marriage was not his. It did not matter. He was content and had grown fond of the girl. He smiled and nodded. "I'll bear it in mind, grandmother."

She gripped his hand with painful strength. "Remember that schoolmaster! Be careful."

He thanked her again and pressed a coin into her hand when she released him. As he walked away, he wondered if she was mad. She was old, and for old people memories of the past become garbled. Why were sons so bad? It was all puzzling, but the old woman had mostly spoken calmly. It was up to him to make sense of her words.

His main objective was still to find the boy who had seen a man at Tanizaki's attic window. Casual questions had brought him only head shakes and comments about those boys being everywhere and nowhere when there's work to be done. One woman finally said she knew him and his name was Yoichi.

Then one day, luck was with Saburo. Behind the ruined gate of an abandoned temple, he came across a group of ragged boys of about the right age. They were engaged in a game of dice for coppers. One of them had accumulated a sizable number of these. He was a stocky, ugly youngster with hair that stood up stiffly.

Saburo moved closer on silent feet and saw the scar. The boys jumped up in fear. Only the one with the heap of coppers remained calm. Saburo said, "You must be really good at this."

The boy, who was small for his worldly demeanor, grinned. "You want to play?"

Saburo nodded and sat down beside him.

The others looked wary, but took their places again. The one with all the coins asked, "You got funds? Let's see them."

Saburo pulled out a fat string of coppers and their eyes grew round. "Five coppers a throw?"

The boy nodded and glanced at the others. They shook their heads. It was too rich for them.

Saburo introduced himself.

The boy said nothing.

"Come on. I don't play with strangers."

One of the others said, "He's Yoichi," and got a scowl from the young gambler.

"Well, then, Yoichi, let's see what you can do," Saburo said, counting off five coppers and placing them on the ground.

Yoichi selected five from his pile, then called out a number and rolled the die. His skill was apparent, as was the fact that the die was imperfect. He won and collected Saburo's money. Saburo picked up the die and checked it. Looking hard at the little gambler, he called out a number and rolled. To the boy's dismay, he also won and took Yoichi's money.

The watching boys gasped and whispered. Yoichi frowned.

Saburo picked up the die again and held it up for them to see. "You see this side? It's been filed off. It means the die will usually roll like this." He cast it. The boys gasped again, then turned their eyes on Yoichi. They shouted, "You bastard," "You cheated," "Gimme my money," and ganged up on him. Yoichi snatched up his winnings and ran.

Saburo was faster. He grabbed the back of Yoichi's shirt and held him. The coins spilled across the ground. "Take your money!" he told the boys, "and then go."

They took the money, hesitated a moment, but then ran off with a few choice promises of revenge shouted to Yoichi.

Yoichi struggled. He turned a furious face to Saburo and hissed, "I'll kill you."

Saburo grinned. "No, you won't. You cheated them. If you don't behave, I'll turn you over to the constables."

Yoichi behaved.

"Now then," Saburo said, "let's have a cup of wine, and you can tell me all about Tanizaki and his wife."

37

Flight

Akitada returned from his visit to the Yamada claimant in a thoughtful mood. The conversation with the strange old man had turned his thoughts back to the Shirakawa matter and he pondered the possibility that an injustice done in the past might survive so many years—at least twenty of them—and not resurface until now. He had rejected the idea as unlikely, but it nagged at him.

And while the story of the unhappy Yamada daughter had a way of inserting itself into the investigation, it was not even clear that an injustice had been done. By all accounts, even Kobe's memory, the young woman had indeed engaged in an affair. The temptations had been there. No doubt her beauty had attracted many suitors, something that must have rankled with

313

the Taira family. There was no proof that she had been raped. Her father had pinned all his hopes on the girl being invited to serve the emperor or at least make a good marriage. With those hopes dashed, it was natural that he should have turned his anger against the family who had her in their care. It had been easier to blame them than his own child.

But there were more pressing matters. The puzzling land dispute had been resolved. It was time to report and make his way home as fast as possible. That evening, Akitada reported to the governor, who declared himself entirely satisfied.

"Now we shall have some time to enjoy ourselves," he said gleefully. "I'll show you the pleasures of Takamatsu. You've deserved a round of all the best eating places and those delightful houses of assignation. Our women here are most attractive and you may find them quite talented also."

Dismayed, Akitada said, "You're very kind, but I must return immediately."

"Not at all, my dear Akitada. I've been assured by the prime minister that you are to take your time. There's no urgency at all."

With considerable desperation, Akitada said, "But I have a family. I left them without notice. No, no, you and the prime minister are very kind, but I insist. I must leave tomorrow and with the fastest ship available."

"You disappoint me. But there is no ship, and the weather will not allow it anyway. Calm yourself. Your family has been informed. There is no need."

To continue his protest would be useless and make things worse. Akitada forced a smile. "If you're sure I'm not a burden to you, I'll accept your kind hospitality a little longer."

Fujiwara Munesuke clapped his hands in glee. "Wonderful. Tonight we'll attend a banquet in our best eating place. It's near the market and serves the most delightful fish dishes you ever tasted. You'll love their fried eel, and they make wonderful udon noodles. We'll have those with a sea bream, or maybe octopus. A feast! I can taste it now." He smacked his lips.

Akitada expressed his gratification and then left the governor.

He would have to suffer through the banquet, but afterward, in the dark of the night, he would steal away and make his way to the coast, where he would hire a boat to take him to the nearest shipping port among the many islands of the Inland sea. There he hoped to catch one of the fast ships that carried people and cargo to the mainland.

That afternoon, he put his report in order. A copy was already in the governor's hand. Then he laid out the plain brown robe he had arrived in, now nicely cleaned and mended by the governor's servants, and counted his funds. The governor had lent him a sum in the beginning, but later he had been paid by orders from the capital. Akitada had enough to buy his passage back on a ship and pay for incidental expenses. It had been careless of them, but then they had probably trusted in the governor's watchful eye and the belief that it would take Akitada much longer to unravel the convoluted land case.

For the evening's entertainment, Akitada put on one of the robes lent to him by Munesuke. It fit quite well, though the rich brocade was more colorful than anything Akitada normally wore. He reflected that, when in Takamatsu, one must adjust to the local customs.

They were carried to the evening's entertainment in the governor's best sedan chair, an ornate affair with four uniformed bearers that would have been a credit to an imperial prince. Munesuke was in high spirits. It was clear he enjoyed the good life and the chance to impress Akitada.

The restaurant was in the foothills not far from the main temple. They arrived at sunset and were seated on an open terrace overlooking the city and countryside below. The evening was clear with a slight refreshing breeze wafting a scent of pine to mingle with the incense perfume on the terrace. Beautiful women in gowns of different colors seated them, chirping joyfully at the pleasure of being allowed to serve the important guests.

The guests numbered eight and, from the introductions, Akitada gathered they constituted the local dignitaries: several merchants, well-dressed and clearly successful, the headmaster of a local school, the abbot of the big temple in town, the commander of the provincial guard, and a provincial nobleman.

The last was Taira Tadanobu, a landowner distantly connected to the Taira family in the capital. He was a tall, red-faced man with a habitual frown.

Akitada found himself seated between Tadanobu and the aged abbot. Good food and wine appeared in rapid succession, served by young women who sat close to them and promised favors beyond what was required during a meal. The merchants were highly entertained by this, as was the governor. Akitada and his two neighbors turned to each other instead.

Tadanobu asked what had brought him to Sanuki Province. When Akitada explained, the abbot, who had been listening, said, "Ah, yes. I believe that land belongs to my temple now. I trust that has been established? The claimant has been most abusive."

Abbot Shuan must be in his eighties. He was a frail, hunched individual with deep-set eyes in a head that already resembled a skull. But the eyes still flashed and the voice was strong and resonant. Faces turned toward them.

Akitada said calmly, "Yes. Whatever the true circumstances may have been at the time, the deed is incontrovertible. Yamada Yasuhito has accepted the situation. He is, however, very poor, and has surely a claim on your temple's generosity."

The governor cried, "Yes, I've always said so. Monks should look after their benefactors when they're in need."

There was vigorous nodding at this.

Abbot Shuan flushed. "I had no idea that he was poor. We shall look into it."

Akitada turned to Tadanobu. "I believe the situation was brought about by a quarrel between the Taira and Yamada families."

"Not by my family. The Taira clan is large. But I know a little about it, since we're neighbors."

The abbot shook his head. "Leave it be. It's not good to rake up old embers."

Tadanobu nodded. "Yes. It's too long ago, Abbot. Nobody cares any longer." He said to Akitada, "Tell us instead about that shocking attack on Fujiwara Yorimune and his family."

Perhaps the abbot felt uncomfortable that his temple had unfairly profited from the Yamada misfortune, but Akitada wondered if there might be another reason. For the moment, however, he answered Tadanobu. "Before I left the capital, they had blamed the massacre on a former soldier who committed suicide after the murders."

Tadanobu snorted. "They always accuse warriors of brutality, but when their precious fortunes are in danger, they like to call on our troops."

"You may be right."

"I'm glad you agree," Tadanobu said approvingly. "It's depressing that so few of our court nobles respect the provincial gentry."

"Calling on the provincial lords for that sort of support comes with a high price."

Tadanobu bit his lip. "So what do you think happened?"

"The attack seemed . . . excessive. Mad, in a way. The innocent died along with the guilty."

The abbot sucked in his breath sharply. "So you think Lord Yorimune was guilty?"

Akitada deflected this dangerous question. "Someone thought so." He changed the subject. "I think you both know the old story of the Yamada daughter. What do you recall of the family?"

Tadanobu said, "That branch of the family died out. The man who has the last piece of land now is a distant relative. Very poor, of course. They all were. Tokihira was the last of the original line. Disease wiped out his family except for one wife and a daughter. Taira Masanori offered to take the girl into his family and help her make a good marriage. When she drowned, her father blamed it on Masanori. It came to nothing."

Akitada murmured, "A fascinating and very sad tale."

"That's why they decided to take back the donated land," the abbot pointed out.

Tadanobu said, "Tokihira died soon after. Too many disappointments! A hard karma."

"There was a boy," the abbot said, frowning. "He doted on the child and meant to adopt him. That came to nothing when the youngster got too close to the daughter. I always thought that's why they sent her away."

Akitada was interested. "What boy was that?"

The abbot sighed. "Just a boy. Belonged to one of the servants. Tokihira thought to adopt him. He became a soldier, I think, and died in one of the wars. It's not a story to tell at this cheerful gathering."

Akitada smiled. "I did ask for it. But you're right. So much misfortune!"

The conversation turned to other matters and became more general. The governor suggested games and songs, much to Akitada's discomfort. He had never been good at this sort of thing.

The evening ended well after dark and they returned to the governor's mansion and their beds. But Akitada rested only until all sounds of activity in the house had died down. Then he put on his plain brown robe and the pair of boots he had bought with funds issued to him, shoved his papers and a copy of the report inside his robe, and walked out into the garden.

From there, he made his way as silently as possible to the back gate and hence into the larger compound of the tribunal. He had noted that the stable yard had access to some fields where the guards exercised their horses. All was quiet here. The guards, if any, dozed near the main gate.

Again he slipped out without being noticed and took the road leading to the harbor. It was better weather than last time he had passed here, but he was not out of trouble yet. He could not rely on the good nature of the governor once he realized that Akitada had disobeyed.

When he reached the coast, he found several large fishing boats at anchor. He bought passage to the nearest island on the sea route home and left Sanuki Province behind as the sun rose over its mountains.

Akitada fretted most of the way during the long homeward journey. Finding passage on one of the many ships that traveled the Inland Sea regularly, carrying tax goods, government officials, new from distant provinces, and merchandise had been a simple matter. But he now felt guilty about the way he had left. Munesuke had been kind to him and might get into trouble.

The ship reached Naniwa in two days and nights. Passengers normally made the slow journey up the Yodo River by boats that had to be towed against the current. Akitada instead rented a horse.

He arrived at Yamazaki at dark, crossed the Katsura River at Shimasaka, and entered the capital as a watchman called the hour of the hare.

38

Tanizaki Fights Back

Yoichi, the unattractive and unpleasant twelve-year-old who had spied on Tanizaki's young wife, quaffed wine like a sodden drunk. Saburo decided to feed him when he began to worry that the wine might dull his powers of recollection. For such a runt, Yoichi also put away a good deal of food.

In between swallowing and chewing he told Saburo about Tanizaki and his wife.

"He used to screw her in the garden until they saw me looking over the fence." He smacked his lips. It was not clear if the greasy eel accounted for it or if he was salivating in retrospect. "She had to put him in the mood. I could've shown her a thing or two."

Saburo regarded him with distaste. "Have you ever seen her with another man?"

"Not like that. But that guy in the window. I saw him with the schoolmaster."

"You did? When was that?"

"Coupla times. Can't remember. Once before she was killed. You think the guy killed her?"

"I don't know. What do you think?"

The youth thought. "Nah! I think the schoolmaster did it. He beat her once. I could hear her crying. I think he knew about her and the guy."

It was likely. But there was a connection between the mysterious visitor and the schoolmaster. And Saburo was convinced that he was the auntie's son. He asked Yoichi, "Ever been to the willow quarter?"

The boy shook his head. "No money."

"Want to go?"

The boy's eyes lit up. "You'll pay?"

"No. You're too young for a dissolute life."

"I'm not. What's 'dissolute'?"

Saburo laughed. "Come on then. You can look around."

Yoichi went eagerly. On the way, he regaled Saburo with a detailed description of Tanizaki's wife's physical parts and Tanizaki's pathetic performance, adding details from his own conquests.

In the amusement quarter, Saburo made straight for the *hananoya*. It was still early, but he counted on the auntie being a good businesswoman who arrived long before her customers. They were in luck. The first person they saw was the flashily dressed young man. Saburo stopped.

Yoichi, who had been staring into all the windows that would later hold beckoning women, followed Saburo's eyes and cried, "That's him! That's the one. He's the one I saw."

But the young man had heard him. He recognized Saburo and took to his heels.

The boy was for chasing after him, but Saburo knew it was pointless and unnecessary. He proposed leaving Yoichi to continue his exploration on his own.

Yoichi demanded additional payment and Saburo paid.

When Saburo reported that Yoichi had been found and had identified Yasumasa as the man at the window, Tora was delighted. "We've got the bastard!" he said, rubbing his hands. "Let him try to get out of that."

Tora was up, dressed, and walking back and forth using a cane. Hanae hovered. "He's going out," she said. "I can't keep him in any longer."

Saburo smiled. "You've done enough. He's better. Let him go. It will help."

She shook her head helplessly. "Well, I suppose it's time. I wish his lordship were here. He could settle this thing about the schoolmaster."

Tora glowered. "I'll settle it. It's my case." He gave Saburo a glance. "Mine and Saburo's."

They left together, walking a bit more slowly to accommodate Tora, and went to see Sergeant Saeki at police headquarters.

The sergeant received Tora with unaccustomed friendliness. "It's good to see you up and about, Tora," he said. "They told us about your bad luck."

"Bad luck? You're joking! I was attacked by a bunch of thugs your sort of policing leaves free to rob and maim the good citizens of the capital while you pander to your well-respected murderers."

Saeki flinched. "You're not still going on about that?"

"You bet! We got the slimy bastard for you. Tell him, Saburo."

Saburo told the sergeant about Yoichi and his observations at Tanizaki's house, and the schoolmaster's meeting with the suspect."

Saeki expressed doubts. "Those boys would lie about their mother for a copper."

Tora cursed him roundly. "Oh yeah? The bastard ran when he saw us. Come on, Saburo. I told you there's no justice here. I bet the schoolmaster has greased his hand."

Saeki turned pale. "Get out!" he roared, attracting the attention of several constables.

Tora limped out.

"You know," Saburo said to the sergeant, "this will look bad for you. You'd better do something."

They returned home in silence. Tora went into his house and closed the door firmly behind him.

Saburo sighed.

The following morning, Tora approached Saburo in the courtyard. "I've been thinking," he said.

Saburo, dressed to go out, smiled. "Are you back on the job then?"

"Of course. I just needed to look at the evidence without constant interruptions."

Saburo snorted. "Working with you is a thankless job. I hope the master gets back soon."

"I didn't mean you. Hanae turns into a tyrant when she thinks I'm too weak to fight back. Husbands have a lot to put up with. Let's go before she thinks of something else to keep me home."

Saburo chuckled. "Where are we going?"

"To that school. The one for the sons of the nobility. The one that employs men like Tanizaki."

"To what purpose?"

"I'm going to let them know what sort of man he is."

Saburo frowned. "Is that wise?"

Tora snapped, "What would you do?"

"I don't know, Tora. All right. Let's try it your way."

They walked on in silence, but then Tora stopped suddenly. "Why would anyone be visiting a woman whose son is his wife's lover?"

This statement confused Saburo, but he managed to unravel it. "Maybe he didn't know?"

"But if he didn't know, why did he kill her?"

"He either didn't kill her, or he had other reasons."

Tora pondered this, then shook his head. "I've got to see his face when I tell him. He's guilty of something. Nothing else makes sense."

"That's true."

"So let's get on with it."

They continued their journey glumly.

At the school, Tora asked a student where he might find Tanizaki. The student led them to a classroom. Tanizaki's voice could be heard coming from inside.

Tora flung open the door and walked in. A dozen students of assorted ages sat in a half circle before Tanizaki who occupied the dais and was holding forth on Kung Fu. His mouth dropped open at the interruption. Saburo followed Tora, content to watch what would happen.

Tanizaki blustered, "What is this? How dare you?" He noticed the smirking student who had shown them the way and still hovered in the doorway. "You, Hisashi, run and get the school guard."

Tora grinned evilly. "Yes, run and get the other masters also, and bring the headmaster with you. The more the better."

The student ran.

Tanizaki got to his feet. He was flushed and shaking with fury. "The police will hear about this. You have been told to leave me alone. I'll bring charges against you."

Tanizaki's students were spellbound.

Tora said, "I'm here to tell you that your game is up. We know what you've done. We know all about the woman you live with, the old slut who used to sell her body in the willow quarter and now runs one of the brothels. How will your colleagues feel about that?"

The students' eyes grew round. Someone snickered.

Tanizaki sputtered, "All lies. Just like everything else you've said. You're a liar and bully. You'll find out you can't vilify your betters."

"You've paid thugs to have me killed. Not your fault they only broke my leg." Tora leaned heavily on his cane. "But you won't get lucky again. It's over, Tanizaki."

Tanizaki controlled himself with an effort. He stepped down from the dais. "Nonsense," he said. He told the students. "You're dismissed. I cannot go on after this intolerable interruption. Go home and study your notes."

For once his students were slow to obey. They looked at each other, grinned, shuffled their papers and writing boxes needlessly, and shot hopeful glances at Tora and Saburo.

Tora smirked. "You can send them away, but there'll be others in a moment and they'll hear all about you and Yasumasa. His mother won't be able to protect him when the police find out that he was in your house when your wife was killed."

Tanizaki turned absolutely white and swayed on his feet. Saburo thought he was about to faint. He said, "We have an eye witness who'll testify that this Yasumasa was in your house the day of the murder."

Before Tanizaki could answer, the door flew open and people burst in. In front was the school's guard, followed by Tanizaki's colleagues.

One of the latter demanded, "What is going on here, Tanizaki?"

Tanizaki bowed. "I'm sorry, Headmaster, these men came into the room and attacked me with false accusations. I beg to have the police called. They have persecuted me for the past month now."

The headmaster eyed Tora and Saburo and nodded. "Clearly madmen and troublemakers," he said. "Guard, take them off the school grounds, and hand them over to the constables. A night in a cell will discourage such behavior."

The guard, a burly giant of a man, grinned, and seized both Tora and Saburo by an arm.

Tora tried to free himself. He shouted, "Be careful, Headmaster. Tanizaki's a murderer!"

It was no use. They allowed themselves to be marched out. When they were outside the gate, Saburo told the guard, "You can let go now. We're peaceable men. That teacher lied."

327

The guard shook his head. "We'll let the police decide who's lying."

To their dismay, the constables were already coming purposefully toward them. A short time later, both Tora and Saburo sat in a small cell.

39

Return

Dawn was breaking in the east in a thin golden line behind the black trees and curving roofs when Akitada knocked at his own gate.

He had to knock twice before the sleepy stable boy put his head out the small side gate to peer at him. "What?" he asked.

"Come on, Toshio, open the gate!"

There was a sound of surprise and the head disappeared. The gate opened and Akitada rode in, dismounted, and handed the horse over to the gaping boy. "Don't wake anyone. Let them sleep."

He walked into his own house with a feeling of unreality.

In his study he took off his outer clothes, then, wearing only his undergown, he walked on bare feet to

329

Sadako's room. He hoped she had not decided to invite his daughter or a maid to sleep with her.

She had not.

He slipped under the silk quilts, and buried his face in her perfumed hair.

Sadako sat up with a cry.

"Calm down, my love," Akitada said softly with a chuckle, "it's only me."

"Oh!" she cried, quite loudly. "Akitada?"

"Ssh! You expected someone else?"

"You're back?"

"So it would seem. Are you displeased?"

"Oh, Akitada!" With a sound that was half laugh and half sob, she was in his arms, and he made love to his wife like a starved man.

Afterward she lay in his arms and murmured, "Most husbands would have some explanation for such a long absence."

"I thought it best to prove my faithfulness first."

"I see. But what happened?"

He told her, in abbreviated fashion. "And what news do you have?"

The sun was making its way through the shutters and outside birds were singing. Akitada kissed his wife's ear.

"Mmm. Tora is about to solve the Tanizaki murder." She nuzzled his face.

"Really. Good for him." He reached for her again. "Oh, Sadako, I've missed you so."

"And Akiko's trying to find the Shirakawa killer."

He sat up. "What do you mean?"

"She says she knows someone who knows who it is. Someone who was there twenty years ago when some young girl was murdered."

Akitada got out of bed. "So, clever Akiko has worked it out. I must see her right away."

"You can't. You only just got home. You haven't seen the children yet."

Akitada was, in fact, too tired, but his fear for his sister was greater. "I'll talk to them later. I have to stop Akiko. Let's hope I'm not too late."

"Why, Akitada? What have you learned?"

He rummaged in his clothes chest and assembled an outfit. "That old man with his little trees," he said, starting to get dressed, "He told me the same story as Kobe. Yorimune seduced or raped his bride's companion. The girl drowned herself or was murdered and her family lost everything. It makes for a powerful motive to go after Yorimune and his whole family."

"It sounds terrible, but so long ago?"

"Yes, I don't understand the delay either, but if Akiko has identified the man with this motive, he won't hesitate to kill her."

Akitada came out of his house to find his people had gathered outside for a joyous welcome and many questions. He answered briefly, then asked Genba, "Where are Tora and Saburo?"

"Still trying to get the goods on Tanizaki."

"Ah. Good for them! I can't stop now but I'll be back shortly."

His friend Nakatoshi arrived before he could leave. He cried, "What a wonderful surprise! I came to ask for news of you and here you are."

Akitada had no choice but to invite him in. "Forgive me," he added, "but I have little time. I'm worried about my sister and was just about to go see her."

"She won't be home. I passed her on my way here. She was in full court dress and said she was going to see Her Majesty."

"Oh." It was a great relief. Akitada had traveled all night and not slept much the night before.

They went to Akitada's study. Sadako sent for wine, and Akitada told his story again, then said, "I should report at the *Daidairi*, but I decided to make my return as quiet as possible to see if I can find the killer before I'm discovered. Perhaps I can ease my way back into the prime minister's good graces. My treatment in Sanuki Province gave me some hope in that regard."

Nakatoshi smiled and nodded. "I understand he never meant to punish you. He just wanted you gone for a short while."

"It could well have been considerably longer." Akitada felt some resentment. "And meanwhile a killer has been loose, a man who doesn't care about people's lives. I'll never forget the shocking sight of that massacre."

Nakatoshi sighed. "Surely it was the act of a madman."

"Yes, but this same madman then killed Kanemori and staged his suicide. He's someone who plans carefully and then kills as if in a frenzy. He dressed up in armor before the massacre and he remembered to blacken the horse's leg."

Sadako said, "He was protecting himself."

"Yes. He intended to get away with it. That makes him more dangerous. And he has courage. He was alone at Shirakawa. What if the men at the party had decided to fight back? Arihito, in fact, tried to do so."

Before Akitada got much further in his analysis of the killer, Arihito himself rushed in. "So what I heard is true. You're back! How did you manage that?"

Dismayed, Akitada said, "You heard about it? Already? It's not even midday."

Arihito said, "All up and down your street servants are talking."

Akitada sighed. "Never mind. It can't be helped. You're just in time. We're talking about what I've learned of the murderer. Sit down and have some wine. I trust your parents are well?"

"Yes, and they'll be so pleased you're back. And I have some news also."

"You saw the sword smith?"

"I did indeed."

"I've always thought that smith must know the killer. He's an experienced warrior. His skill with horse and bow proved that."

"Well, Jocho didn't want to admit it, but in the end he confessed that there had been someone who had asked about Kanemori. The man claimed they had served together. I'm afraid the smith sent him to Shikino village."

"As I thought. Did he mention the name Hiraga?"

"No. He didn't know his name. And he hasn't seen him since. I thought that significant."

"Yes, it is. It means the killer had decided Kanemori would make a suitable scapegoat. The name doesn't matter. He probably lied to me."

Nakatoshi looked puzzled. "Who lied? The smith?"

"No, the killer."

After a stunned silence, Arihito asked, "You talked to him?"

"I think so, but I may be wrong. And it won't help us find him. My information suggests he may have targeted more than one person at Shirakawa and may plan to kill others."

Sadako gasped. "Not just Yorimune?"

"Yorimune, his wife, and their daughters. Perhaps also you, Arihito. The rest only because they were friends or servants of the people he hated most. And perhaps because by then he enjoyed the thrill of killing."

Arihito looked shaken. "Hireko was just eighteen. She was gentle and kind. Everybody loved her. And why her sister? Or her mother? What had they done?"

Akitada said gently, "Hireko was Yorimune's daughter. I think the motive for all the deaths lies in a story I was told in Sanuki Province." He explained about the old man with his tiny trees and his memory of an old injustice done to some remote relative.

Arihito listened in disbelief and protested again, "It makes no sense to kill so many innocent people over an old incident that doesn't seem to have been a crime. And what did it have to do with Yorimune?"

"I don't know yet. It may only have concerned Yorimune's wife. It was clear in the tale that she was blamed for the Yamada girl's death. Yorimune was her accepted suitor and she is thought to have got rid of a rival. Yorimune's reputation suggests that he is likely to have seduced or raped the Yamada girl. She was a well-known beauty. The tale paints an ugly picture of marriage politics, female jealousies, and ruthless male aggression."

Arihito groaned and put his head in his hands. "It wasn't like that with us."

"I know, Arihito. Don't forget that we've been assuming all along that the killer may not be sane."

Sadako tried to change the subject. "I think your sister is looking into the same story. She said she found someone who knows what happened."

Akitada nodded. "Yes. Tomorrow morning I'll have a talk with her. Today we have time for a little celebration. Let's have a nice meal and finish our discussion."

Sadako hurried off to see the cook. Though produced in a hurry, the meal was a success. They talked about Akitada's journey as they ate. By the time they were done, Arihito had cheered up a little. He said, "If you're right, we need to find out who the killer is in relation to the dead Yamada girl. He must be quite old. That happened twenty years ago."

Akitada winced. "I think he must be in his forties," he said. "Not so very old. I'm more interested in the sort of man he is. His behavior is, to say the least, peculiar. At Shirakawa he seemed to kill efficiently. Yorimune and his family were targeted and killed with great precision, though he missed killing your parents. I think you, Arihito, only escaped because you didn't sit still. You tried to stop him. You interfered with his concentration and saved some lives. The fact that he stopped only when he ran out of arrows shows both determination and a fury that amounts to madness."

Nakatoshi shuddered. "That man is very dangerous."

Arihito turned white as he remembered the carnage. "We thought Yorimune had arranged some thrilling entertainment. Who would expect a fully armed warrior on a horse in the middle of summer's outing?"

"Yes," said Akitada. "That's another curious fact about him. He isn't satisfied with taking his revenge; he wants people to remember it. The killing of Kanemori was similar. It wasn't enough to stab him. He had to set it up elaborately to look like a warrior's suicide."

Nakatoshi said, "But that was because he wanted him to look like the murderer."

"He could have strangled and hanged him. Or pushed him off a cliff. No, that suicide was arranged very carefully to impress us, to make us talk about it. We were shown an honorable warrior's death. It was meant to make the slaughter look noble."

"That's mad," Nakatoshi said. "Who does things like that?"

"Someone who was close to the Yamada girl and harbored thoughts of revenge for twenty years," Akitada said. "Time and circumstances may have driven him to madness. We'll have to find him soon before the killing goes on. But tomorrow is another day. Akiko may have some useful information."

His guests left a short time later. Akitada spent some time dozing at his desk in case the news of his return had reached the prime minister, but nothing happened, except that Tora, Saburo, and Kobe arrived, having their own tale to tell.

40

Kobe to the Rescue

Tora and Saburo's situation had seemed hopeless at first, since the local constables refused to send messages and were not impressed by the fact that they worked for Lord Sugawara, a ranking official in the ministry of justice.

Around midday on the day after their arrest, the thick wooden cell door finally opened. The guard stood back and said, "Are they the ones, sir?"

Half afraid, they rose from the dirty straw and watched in disbelief as a grizzled, somewhat bent figure stepped into the opening, peered at them, and then smiled broadly.

"Indeed, they are, Guard," he said in a familiar booming voice.

337

Tora gasped, "Superintendent? Is that really you? How did you find us?"

Kobe walked in, looked around, sniffed, and said, "This place stinks, Guard. You should really keep the cells better. Take us somewhere else where we can talk."

The guard looked ashamed and obeyed. They went to the guardroom and sat down on worn but fairly clean *tatami* mats. The guard left them there, and Kobe answered Tora's question.

"I heard about Akitada being sent away. I'm sorry I didn't come sooner, but news is slow to reach us in the country. His lady mentioned what you've been doing, so I asked some questions at police headquarters. Seems I still have some friends there." He chuckled. "So tell me what you've been up to."

They did.

Kobe shook his head. "That schoolmaster's really something. Your master told me about him. Tora's quite right. I think that man's a liar and maybe something worse. I don't recall a Sergeant Saeki, but I think we'd better go and have a talk with him."

Tora whooped with joy.

Saburo asked, "How can we leave? We're prisoners."

"So you are. Oh well, I'll tell them you're needed as witnesses. True enough, as it happens."

The guard made no objection and seemed glad to be rid of them and the former superintendent, who kept pointing out flaws in his jail. They walked together to the Left Jail, where Kobe was received with all honors by those who had served under him and stares from new officers and men. A lieutenant was in charge, a man not much younger than Kobe. He took them to his office and sent for Sergeant Saeki.

Kobe looked around. "You've done well, Tamai. I knew you would."

The lieutenant grinned. "Thanks to you, sir. I'm happy to see you well."

Kobe gave an outline of the situation and Tora and Saburo told their story again. The lieutenant's eyebrows rose. He frowned. "That Saeki! I knew it. The man's still a raw recruit. I'll get to the bottom of this. I suppose we'd better also send for the boy Yoichi."

Tora tried hard not to smirk. Saburo studied the ceiling. Saeki reported, stood stiffly, and saluted with military precision. When his eyes fell on Tora and Saburo, he lost some of his assurance.

"Umm," he said, "er," and fell silent.

The lieutenant snapped, "These men reported certain facts to you about a murder?"

"Yessir."

"Well?"

"I listened, but they had no case, sir. We often get people who make accusations. We investigate and when we find there's nothing to it, we send them away."

"You decided there was nothing to their accusations against schoolmaster Tanizaki?"

"That's correct, sir." Saeki was turning red under this questioning and shot uneasy glances at Kobe. "The accused is a learned professor at one of the noble academies in our capital. He's descended from a noble family. Since then many poor and bad people have moved into his neighborhood. So when the honorable professor's wife was murdered, I naturally investigated. These two men . . ." he nodded toward Tora and Saburo, ". . . have persisted in trying to pin the murder

339

on her husband. There was no evidence whatsoever and I sent them away. Repeatedly." By this time, Saeki had found his confidence and sounded aggrieved.

"Did they tell you that there was a witness?" asked the lieutenant.

"They mentioned a boy who might have seen someone. All very vague, sir."

"Did you try to find the boy?"

Saeki fidgeted. "It's impossible to find any boy in that neighborhood, sir. They run when they see a constable."

"Ah." The lieutenant sighed. "Well, they found him. And they can produce him. And he saw a young man at a window of the house the very day of the murder. Then they found the young man, and the boy has identified him. What do you say to that, Saeki?"

Saeki flushed more deeply this time. "I don't know, sir. Who is the person the boy says he saw?"

The lieutenant looked at Tora and Tora supplied, "He's called Yasumasa. He's the son of a woman who owns a brothel in the quarter. Tanizaki used to be her lover."

The lieutenant said, "You'll go immediately and arrest him, Saeki."

Kobe cleared his throat. "I think perhaps we should all hear what this Yasumasa has to say for himself. Yes, arrest him, Sergeant. We'll wait here."

Tora offered helpfully, "He's either at his mother's house or at the *hananoya,* Saeki."

They waited in the lieutenant's office, talking about the missing Akitada and about the Tanizaki case. Yoichi arrived and was told to wait in another room. When the constables returned with Yasumasa, a tense scene ensued. Not only had Yasumasa been brought in, but his mother had accompanied him and was vociferous in defending her son against unspecified suspicions.

When she saw Tora and Saburo, she cried, "Oh, it's you again! You went and told your lies to the police. The gods will punish you for this."

Saeki snapped, "Shut up, old woman!" He told the lieutenant, "They haven't been informed of the charges, but I think they know there's a witness of sorts. I thought I'd leave it to you to explain."

Before they could do so, more agitated voices could be heard, the door flew open, and Tanizaki rushed in. A constable followed him. The constable said, "He wouldn't stop, sir."

Yasumasa's mother threw herself at Tanizaki, sobbing. "They've arrested Yasumasa. Do something!"

Tanizaki pushed her away. "What's this?" he demanded. He looked at Tora and Saburo and flushed with anger. "Is this more of the persecution I've suffered? Are you now threatening my friends? I'm charging you both with making false accusations. I'll take this all the way to the emperor if need be. We have ancient laws that protect us against false accusations."

Kobe said, "Sit down!"

Tanizaki noticed him. "Who is that? What is he doing here?"

The lieutenant said, "This is Superintendant Kobe." He did not explain that Kobe was no longer active.

Tanizaki sat. A constable took his place behind him.

"Now then," Kobe said, "let's get to the bottom of this, Lieutenant."

The lieutenant nodded. "This investigation concerns the murder of Tomoko, wife of the schoolmaster Tanizaki. It is alleged that the schoolmaster wished to be rid of his wife and that a certain Yasumasa, the son of the woman Miyagi, who owns the *hananoya* brothel, was seen inside the Tanizaki house near the time of the murder."

Loud protests erupted instantly.

Tanizaki insisted that he was innocent and had been cleared; Yasumasa shouted it was all a bunch of lies; and his mother insisted that the *hananoya* was a house of assignation, not a low brothel.

The lieutenant waited until the shouting died down, then said, "We'll hear from the witness who saw Yasumasa." He nodded to the constable behind Tanizaki. He left and brought in Yoichi.

The boy looked nervous, but when his eyes fell on Tora and Saburo, he straightened his back and managed a grin.

Tanizaki sneered, "He is one of the scum who live near my house. They beg and steal for a living. Surely you don't think he's capable of telling the truth."

The lieutenant said, "Let's hear first what he has to say. Go ahead, Yoichi."

Yoichi gulped. He looked around the room and pointed at Yasumasa. "I seen him. He was up there. At the window of the schoolmaster's house. He was lookin' down, but he didn't see me."

Yasumasa cried, "He lies. I've never been in my father's house."

Everybody stared at him in surprise. After a moment, the lieutenant asked, "What did you say? Your father's house?"

Yasumasa flushed and looked at his mother, who clamped a hand over her mouth in shock, then at Tanizaki. The schoolmaster opened and closed his

342

mouth as if snapping for air. He found his voice. "What is he talking about? That's utter nonsense. I don't know this person."

Yasumasa cried, "My mother said you're my father. You've known us all my life."

His mother shook her head and moaned.

Tanizaki looked at him coldly. "I know Miyagi-san distantly. She owns a house of assignation I've visited. I did not know you are her son."

Tora said angrily, "Come on, Tanizaki. You're a regular in the *hananoya*. Of course you know its owner. Your wife used to work there. And Yasumasa still works there. They all knew each other and they knew you. Besides you were seen together, you and Yasumasa."

Tanizaki flushed. "A respectable man may occasionally visit one of these establishments, but that does not mean he acknowledges the staff. It is true my second wife was once briefly employed there, but I took her away from that place quickly enough. I married her, perhaps foolishly . . . I tend to think now it was a great mistake to marry that sort of woman . . . but she was young and healthy and I needed someone to keep my house while I was at work."

Tora laughed. "You were a regular there for years before you fell for Tomoko and married her."

Miyagi cried, "You were my lover long before you met that stupid bitch Tomoko. And Yasumasa *is* your son. You know he is. You've admitted it. You bought me my house when I told you I was pregnant." She burst into tears. "How can you treat me like this, Tanizaki? After all we've been to each other."

Tanizaki shouted, "Shut up, you stupid woman."

343

Yasumasa went to stand beside his mother and glared. "Don't speak to her like that. Not after all she's done for you. And don't deny that I'm your son. Not after what I did for you."

Tanizaki put his head in his hands and moaned.

"So," said the lieutenant, smiling like a cat, "what is it that you did for your father, Yasumasa?"

The handsome young man looked startled. "Er, n-nothing much," he stammered. "I, er, ran errands for him sometimes."

Tora asked, "Really? Was one of those to go kill Tomoko? And did you do as he asked?"

Yasumasa and Tanizaki both cried, "No!"

Tanizaki bowed his head. "He may have misunderstood. I knew nothing about it until it was over. I swear by all the gods, I did not know what he was going to do. It was an awful mistake!" He collapsed into weeping.

Kobe cleared his throat. "I think," he said, "it's time we clarified relationships."

"Yes," said the lieutenant. "I gather that you, Tanizaki, now admit to having had an affair with Miyagi here, and that Yasumasa is your son?"

Tanizaki did not look up. "He may be my son."

Miyagi cried, "Oh, for shame, Tanizaki!"

Tanizaki gave her a sad look. "Yes, he is my son. I wish he had never been born. I wish you had not told them. He killed Tomoko."

Miyagi screamed, "Never!" She flew across the room to hit Tanizaki with both fists. "You lie. He'd never . . ."

344

The constable separated them and pushed Miyagi to the floor, where she cowered, weeping. Yasumasa made a dash for the door.

The constable and Saburo caught him easily. Another constable came and they put chains on Yasumasa and stood over him as he knelt on the floor. His parents huddled in opposite corners weeping.

"Well," the lieutenant said when order had been established. "You, Yasumasa, stand accused of murdering Tomoko, the wife of the schoolmaster Tanizaki, on the seventh day of this month. And you, Tanizaki are accused of having ordered the murder. What do you say?"

Tanizaki said, "I'm innocent. He did it without my knowledge. Or approval."

Yasumasa cried, "You lie! Mother heard you."

Miyagi said nothing.

"Take them away, Constable," the lieutenant ordered. "A judge will work out who is guilty."

Saburo whispered to Tora, "You did it! It's over."

41

A Deadly Game

It was late before Akitada got to bed. Tora and Saburo were full of their own exploits and they also wanted to know what had happened to Akitada. And there was Kobe to be considered. Akitada did his best to satisfy them all and insisted that Kobe spend the night. His own experience coming back from Kobe's house made him very uneasy, though Kobe laughed at his concern. "Probably someone shooting a rabbit for his pot of soup," he said. "We still follow ancient customs in the country." Akitada felt a little foolish and let it go, but Kobe stayed.

The next morning, Akitada overslept and nobody had the heart to wake him. It was nearly mid-morning before he finally went to see Akiko. At his sister's house he found only Toshikage at home. His

I. J. Parker

brother-in-law had heard of his return and expressed his joy.

"Akiko's left on a little trip," he told Akitada. "She got restless. You know how she is. I've never been able to keep her home." He laughed.

Akitada's heart sank. "Yes, I know. But I think she's meddling in the Shirakawa affair. That could be dangerous. Just where has she gone?"

Toshikage's plain face showed some concern. "I hope you're wrong. I couldn't bear it if something happened to her." He brightened. "But this is just a harmless visit to an old friend."

Akitada knew Toshikage well enough not to expect much help. He was fond of his brother-in-law, who was quite wealthy but also incredibly generous and still very much in love with his self-willed wife. He asked again, "Where exactly has she gone?"

Toshikage looked vague. "Let me see. Some temple, I think. Someone else has been asking. She took her maid, but they didn't put on nuns' robes. When she becomes really devout, she dresses for it. I seem to recall something about visiting a counselor's widow."

"Toshikage, didn't you ask her where she was going?"

"No. I trust Akiko. Wonderful woman."

"Who else asked about her?"

"Don't know. One of the servants mentioned someone at the gate."

"When did she leave?"

"This morning."

Akitada bit his lip. He wondered if he could catch up with her if he hurried home for a horse. "Did she say when she'd be back?"

348

"No. But I think soon. Later today."

Not far then.

"Toshikage, think! What did she say? She may be in danger."

Toshikage chuckled at this. "Don't be silly. Akiko's very capable. And she's a good horsewoman. How can a short trip to a temple be dangerous? That road's very safe in the daytime."

"What road? What temple, Toshikage?"

"Some little place in the eastern hills. Not far from Kiyomizu-dera. She went to see this old lady who's a nun. Couldn't be safer. Why are you so nervous?"

"Because she's meddling again. Did she say anything else?"

Toshikage was becoming uneasy. "No. Only that the nun was an old friend. No point in asking me for a name. I don't know." Toshikage paused. "I wish you wouldn't involve her in your cases, Akitada. You know how she is. Is this one of your murders?"

In his frustration with Toshikage and his sister, Akitada snapped, "It's the Shirakawa affair." He turned to leave. "I'm going after her."

His brother-in-law had turned pale.

He returned to the house to find Genba, Tora, and Saburo waiting for him outside. He said, "I cannot stay. My sister may be in danger. She seems to have gone to find a killer."

"We're coming!" Tora and Saburo said together.

"No. I thank you. You would slow me down. Genba, get a horse ready." He ran into the house where he met his wife, looking anxious. "Sadako, help me

349

change. I have to go after Akiko. There's no time to be lost."

In their private apartments, he told her what he had learned from Toshikage as he changed into a hunting jacket and narrow trousers and switched his slippers for boots.

Tears filled Sadako's eyes. "I'm afraid, Akitada."

He held her for a moment. "I'll be back in a few hours. Don't worry."

"You only just came back," she whispered as he headed out the door.

The road was excellent and heavily traveled. Toshikage had been right about that. But it had not been the journey that was dangerous; it was what Akiko might encounter at its end that worried Akitada. And had not Toshikage said someone had asked about Akiko's errand? The fact troubled him. Akitada urged his horse to greater speed.

At Kiyomizu-dera, he asked about a nunnery near the great temple and was directed to a place called Chorakuji. The monk he spoke to said the place was a retreat for noble ladies. It made sense that Akiko's friend should live there, and Akitada rode on into the eastern mountains, among pines and maples that had not yet started turning. It must be beautiful here in the fall, he thought. Beautiful and peaceful. Life at court was a hectic business, not only for the men, struggling daily to gain power, wealth, and influence, but also for the women who shared their lives with them. By early middle age, many of them gave up the struggle and entered a monastery or nunnery.

There was no guarantee that Akiko would have gone there, but Akitada had nothing to rely on except her husband's information. He felt irritated again by his brother-in-law.

Chorakuji turned out to be a very small temple. It had no large halls. It did not even have a modest pagoda. Essentially, the compound consisted of small houses built here and there across the mountainside and in mostly dense woods.

One of the small houses turned out to be the gatekeeper's house, though this nunnery had neither gates nor walls.

A small nun greeted him, still young and eager to carry out her duties. She eyed him sharply and said, "You cannot come in."

Akitada asked if they had had any lady visitors lately and she nodded. "A lady and her maid came earlier. They wanted to see old Lady Gon-dainagon."

His relief was enormous. It must have been Akiko. The lady's name signified that she was the widow of a major counselor, a woman of rank, now living retired in religious seclusion. It was likely that such a woman had some knowledge of events that happened twenty years ago in a noble Taira household.

Akitada said, "The visitor was my sister. She is urgently needed at home."

The young nun frowned. "You are a man. And armed. It is not permitted that you enter Chorakuji."

Akitada resorted to a lie. "Please. I must bring my sister home. One of her children is ill." He added, "I can leave my sword. And my horse."

She thought about it, then nodded. "Go quickly then."

Akitada dismounted, leaving his sword tied to the saddle.

Satisfied that he was no longer a threat, the nun said, "Take the steep path. Lady Gon-dainagon lives in the last house. It's nearly at the mountain top."

The houses were simple but well maintained and had tile roofs. Their occupants no doubt had made substantial gifts to the temple in order to assure themselves some comforts in their isolation. Akitada saw a few lay workers sweeping the paths, and a maidservant carried a basket of laundry.

It was a long walk, or rather climb. The path ascended, sometimes via wooden or stone steps, while winding among dense trees. Here and there he passed other small houses, peaceful and silent in their forest setting. Akitada hurried and was soon out of breath.

He wished he had kept his sword, but the place was peaceful and quiet. If the killer did indeed come here, most likely he would be disarmed by the little nun.

If he bothered to stop there.

Finding Akiko in time was the most important thing. He would bring the women back with him and they would all return to the capital.

He reached the last house and called out at the door. His voice sounded loud and harsh in the still forest air.

There was no answer.

Akitada opened the door to a single plain room, its floor polished wood and its walls unadorned. A plain reed cushion rested in the middle, and beside it he saw a small brazier and a tall candlestick. A second reed cushion lay at a distance. Against one wall stood a single clothes trunk and a small bamboo rack with books and papers.

The room was empty.

Something about it troubled Akitada and he went in. Near the cushion in the center, three small earthenware cups lay scattered, having spilled their content. A tea pot rested beside the large candlestick. It had overturned and the water had leaked out.

Then he noticed a dark stain on the cushion. He bent to look more closely, then lifted the cushion and turned it over. Its back was soaked with the same brownish red color. The smell was unmistakable. His eye went to the heavy candlestick. Its carved foot was stained with more blood. The sight and smell made his stomach clench. Something violent had happened here not long ago.

Sick with fear, Akitada went back outside. The woods were dense. They could be anywhere. And the killer was probably gone. He must find the women. At least one of them had been attacked.

He found the nun quickly.

Her small crumpled body in its brown robe lay behind the house at the edge of the woods. Her white headdress was no longer white but deeply stained with blood. The blood was nearly dry.

The aged face was still aristocratic even in death. Her lips were slightly open as if she were trying to speak, but the powerful blow from the candlestick had crushed her skull. She must have died instantly.

It seemed pointless to kill someone so old, weak, and unworldly. But of course she had known the killer's secret and had become a threat to him.

Why had he dragged her body out here? The traces were clearly visible in the soft moss. There had been no further attempt at hiding her. Perhaps he had just wanted to gain some time.

For what?

Akitada searched among the shrubs and young trees. He found the footprints in the moist moss quickly. Several people had passed this way recently. Some prints were smaller than a man's.

Akiko and her maid! Had they escaped?

He hoped so, but the evidence spoke against it. Whatever had happened had happened hours ago, and if they had escaped after witnessing the attack on the nun, they would surely have raised an alarm.

As he should do now.

Every fiber in Akitada's body rebelled against delay. The path taken by the killer was before him. Akitada told himself that a lot of time had passed already and he had been unable to prevent what must have happened. It was too late. Fear and grief washed over him.

Akiko, the sister who had never been his favorite was most likely dead by now. Too late he realized how much he loved her. Too late he recognized the bond between them. Too late he regretted what might have been.

He turned away from the killer's tracks and returned to the body of the nun. In pity for the slight, frail figure, he bent to arrange her gown in a more seemly manner, to straighten the bloody headdress that had slipped, revealing the shaved and gory head. Lady Gondainagon. A major counselor's widow. No doubt she had been high-born. Probably she had been a mother of high-born children. The killer had murdered her because she had known him, or at least had known of him. It had been Akiko's bad luck that he had found the nun when she did.

Karma is the fate we earn by deeds in our prior lives. Even killers are destined to kill, to carry out someone's destiny and their own. It was what most people believed and there was justice in it, but Akitada knew that human actions could cause other human actions, both good and bad. This poor lady had died because twenty years ago someone had been killed and someone else had sworn revenge.

Revenge is second nature to a soldier. If your friends are killed by the enemy, you hate your enemy enough to kill him also. And you kill your enemies' friends: a sequence of events that continues until it is stopped.

Taking a deep breath, Akitada left the dead woman and plunged into the woods on the killer's trail.

Almost immediately he found the scrap of silk. It had attached itself to a broken branch where someone had passed through the dense growth, and it was new. It was also of a quality that could only come from some high-born woman's gown.

Akiko had come this way.

He hurried on. Within moments he found himself on a rough track leading down the mountain to a few small wooden shacks. Fearful of what he would find, he went to check them.

They were in the largest shed.

When he drew the wooden door back, he came face-to-face with his sister. She was seated on the floor and looked back at him calmly.

He gasped, "Akiko?" and then saw the bloody scratches on her face, the compressed lips, the glaring eyes.

She blinked against the light and asked unsteadily, "Akitada?"

He went to her and knelt. "Are you all right, Akiko?" He saw now that her arms were tied behind her back, and her ankles were lashed together. Somewhere someone whimpered.

She ignored his question. "So you're back then?"

Akitada reached to untie her wrists, "What happened?"

"That stinking piece of shit killed Lady Gondainagon."

Akitada had never heard his sister use such language before. "Where is he?" His eyes had adjusted to the dim interior. He saw his sister's maidservant, also tied, slumped in a corner, but no one else. He struggled with the knots of the rope around Akiko's wrists and freed her arms.

At that moment, the door slammed behind him.

Akitada jumped up and whirled around.

In the sudden darkness a voice said, "We meet again, my lord. I've been waiting for you. A pleasure. For me at least."

A tall shape loomed in the darkness. The shape raised a sword.

"Stay where you are. You've been a major problem. It's time to make an end. Just you and the women and I'm done."

It was nearly completely dark in the shed. Only small slivers of light crept through the chinks of the boards that made up the walls. They did little more than outline the shape of a large man holding a long sword. The maid whimpered again.

Akitada said, "We've met, I think."

The large man chuckled. "So we did. What gave me away? I suppose my voice."

In this dark and confined space, he had no chance against this killer. If he tried to grab for the man's sword and a struggle ensued, the women would get in their way and get hurt. He had missed his chance when the killer had first come in. By now the man's eyes had adjusted to the darkness and he knew exactly where they were.

To gain time, Akitada asked, "Is your name really Hiraga?"

"No. My name is Yamada. For an official, you're a clever bastard, I'll give you that. I went back to Shikino after Kanemori's death to make sure I was free and clear. I was, until you started to meddle."

"Let the women go! This is between us."

A snort and a threatening move with the sword. "Don't be stupid. Your sister knows who I am."

Akiko said, "Oh, yes. Lady Gon-Dainagon told me all about him. He's the depraved half-brother of Yamada Yoshiko. He seduced her, the animal."

The dark shape grunted. "The old nun was my father's sister. She knew about me and she hated me. And you're like your brother. Meddlesome and sanctimonious. You'll die together." He took a step forward.

The maid wailed and started praying to the saints.

The killer raised his sword and roared, "Shut up, bitch, or you'll be first."

She gulped and fell silent.

There was no sound now, except their breathing.

The killer said, "Yoshiko was mine. We loved each other. But our father meant her for the emperor and sent me away into the army. I submitted because I wanted her to become empress and I wanted to be a warrior. I dreamed of winning glory and returning to bow before her and see the pride in her eyes. So I trained and I fought. I was in the battle against Taira Tadatsune. I was fearless. The best. But while I was fighting in the north, she died in the capital." He made a choking sound that could have been grief or fury.

Nobody spoke. The maid sniffled now and then.

Akitada tried to visualize the little he had seen of the shed before the door had closed on all of them. Supplies had been stacked against the walls, boards, tools, bags of things, unidentifiable objects. Was there something he could use for a weapon? Could he reach it? That sword was long and so were the killer's arms. Akitada shifted his feet and moved toward the side with the tools.

The killer reacted by raising his sword. "Stop! You won't escape this time. I've watched your house and waited for you to come back. When you did, I knew you'd talk to the old nun."

A little desperately, Akitada asked, "What happened to you happened twenty years ago. What brought you back now?"

"Stay where you are or I'll take your head off. Your sister can catch it."

Akitada said nothing.

The maid retched.

After a short pause, the killer said, "I didn't know how or why Yoshiko died, so I stayed in the north. I took a wife, had children. When I lost them to the sickness, I decided to come home to my father's house. But I found that was gone, too. And then I heard what had happened to Yoshiko. Yorimune raped her and the Taira family murdered her."

Akitada inched again toward the tools. "You've already killed Yorimune and his family. Why continue the killing? Why kill the innocent? Why kill Kanemori who had done nothing to you? "

"Because I refuse to die for what others did. And Kanemori was disrespectful of my fighting skills. You got in my way next. I hadn't planned on this much trouble, but I don't mind a bit more killing. All you court nobles are worthless. You care nothing for anyone when it's a matter of keeping your power, your wealth, or your women. And your women are the same." He waved the sword toward Akiko. "I'm a warrior. Killing in war is clean. And this is my war."

Akitada moved another step. He could almost touch the nearest tool, some long-handled fork. "Yet you killed Kanemori, a fellow warrior who fought in the same war as you."

The killer grunted. "He fought for my enemies."

"What? You joined the northern rebels? You fought against the emperor's troops?"

"Why not? I found they were better people than the ones I grew up with. I married one of them."

Akitada made a grab for the fork, ducked his head and shoulders, and charged.

The killer lashed out instantly with his long blade.

Akitada felt the rush of air above his neck, as he crouched and struck out with the fork. It missed the killer. The sword came again and this time he managed to catch the blade in the fork. It acted much like a *jitte*, carried by constables to disarm knife-wielding crooks. But Akitada's fork was wood. It splintered and the sword bit into his arm. The killer laughed.

He attacked again, fast and furious this time. Akitada jumped aside, trying to draw him away from the women, but the shed was small and he backed into some of the stored objects. Something fell, and he stumbled. Blood trickled along his arm. The branch in his hand was a good deal shorter and had gained a jagged point, but it was a puny weapon against a sword.

The other man raised his sword again, the same motion at the same height as before, and Akitada ducked again. He stabbed with the branch at the man's chest, failed to hit his mark, but made his enemy move sideways where he could see him better. Twisting down and under the sword, he rammed his branch upward into the other man's throat.

With a choking cry, the killer fell back a few steps. Akitada decided that his adversary had been a better archer than swordsman and advanced with more determination. To his shocked surprise, another shadow rose behind the killer. He sensed a sudden movement and then the sword clattered onto the floorboards.

Akitada dove for it, felt the grip in his hand, and rose to push the weapon with all his force into the killer's belly.

With a scream, the large figure toppled and crashed to the floor.

Before him stood Akiko with a cudgel in both hands. "Good," she said with satisfaction. "You almost left it too long. And you could have picked something a little more lethal than that flimsy branch."

Akitada gaped at her, then started to laugh. It was a weak and shaky laugh, but he was suddenly filled with a great joy. They were safe, life was good, and Akiko was still Akiko.

After a moment, she laughed also. "I'm glad you came, Brother."

The man on the floor convulsed.

Akiko stepped away from him and opened the door. "Ugh!" she said. "You stabbed him in the belly."

"It seemed the right thing to do at the time. Pay no attention. It's a painful way to die, but it was what he did to Kanemori."

"Why didn't you bring your sword?"

"The little nun made me leave it."

"Well," she started, but they heard shouting outside the shed. "Stupid nuns," Akiko said and went out. Akitada followed.

Several nuns and some male lay workers stood in front of the shed. They looked distraught.

"Oh," he said to them, "good. I take it you found Lady Gon-Dainagon. The man who killed her is inside."

Epilogue

It was a messy affair. The local authorities, both constabulary and Buddhist clergy, were called to the scene and demanded explanations for the bloodshed on sacred temple grounds.

It took time. Akitada urged his sister to return home, but she insisted on staying. Brother and sister sat close together. She had bandaged the cut to his shoulder with a piece of silk ripped from her undergown. Akitada touched her hand once and smiled at her. Akiko tossed her head, but she squeezed his hand. He was filled with affection and admiration for his strong-willed and clever sister. Besides, more than likely she had just saved his life.

When the official business was done, they rode back together, followed by Akiko's maid on her pony. For a while neither spoke. They had already answered too many questions.

Finally, Akiko said, "That could have gone wrong."

Akitada glanced at her. Akiko was tall for a woman and rode well, but he had become aware that she was no longer young. Now, with most of her careful make-up gone, along with her straight back and high chin, she looked what she was: a tired, middle-aged woman who had borne five children and spent a harrowing day.

He said, "Yes."

"How did you know to come after me?"

Akitada told again how the bits and pieces had come together almost by accident. He did not comment on her husband's poor memory.

"Not one of your most efficient investigations," she said dryly.

"No." He felt glum. It was over, but at what cost.

She glanced at him. "Oh, well, you got there eventually. Mind you, I got the whole story from poor Lady Gon-Dainagon. Unfortunately, the monster had been lying in wait."

"Yes."

She glanced at him again. "Not only for her. For you also. He wanted you."

"I know. I think he was watching and following me since we met."

"Well, I suppose he wanted both of us." She chuckled. "It felt good, working together. Cheer up, Brother! There will be rewards."

"Rewards? I'll be lucky if I keep my post at the ministry."

"Stop always thinking the worst, Akitada! You can be so depressing."

Akitada was stung by the justice of this. He must be a trial to those around him. He fell silent and hung his head.

Akiko said, "Well, don't you want to know what I learned from poor Lady Gon-Dainagon?"

"Yes."

The man whom you called Hiraga called himself Yamada Yutaka. He claimed to be a son of Yamada Tokihira by his concubine and that his father intended him to be his heir. Lady Gon-Dainagon said he was fathered on a servant by Tokihira. Tokihira spoiled him, being without male offspring from his marriage. The boy was raised with Yoshiko, and when they were old enough, he seduced her. Her father discovered the affair and threw the boy out. Afraid of the scandal, he sent him to the North as a soldier and her to the Taira family. That appears to be the true story."

Akitada said only, "A poorly managed household."

"Yes. Those provincial families live like savages."

Akitada recalled the killer's anger at the court nobility. He had had a point. On the other hand, he had proved them right." He sighed.

At home they were met with relief and satisfaction. Toshikage received his wayward wife with cries of joy and an embrace she found irritating. By contrast, Sadako flew into Akitada's arms before the eyes of his retainers. Tora and Saburo claimed his attention for their own case as soon as he had reported on the outcome of his and Lady Akiko's quest. He was able to smile now at the way Akiko had dealt with the killer.

His sister had a positively mannish courage. And he was fulsome in his praise for Tora and Saburo.

Then, late in the evening, the prime minister summoned him.

This summons was far different from his last. A gentleman who served in the prime minister's office arrived and delivered the message politely. Akitada tried to read his expression and failed. Still, things might have been worse, and the next morning, finding the cut in his shoulder less painful, he dressed in court robes in a reasonably calm mood.

He walked to the *Daidairi* and was pleasantly surprised at the friendly smiles and waves on the way. His mood lifted a little more.

He was admitted immediately, even though a lot of men were waiting. The prime minister rose when he walked in and came toward him with a smile and outstretched arms.

Completely disconcerted, Akitada immediately bowed deeply, and the prime minister was forced to raise him. They were both embarrassed. The prime minister decided that a pat on the shoulder would suffice and invited Akitada to sit. Akitada suppressed a cry of pain. Past meetings had always involved kneeling or standing. This new friendliness was disconcerting.

The prime minister said, "Well, you've done it. Excellent. I thought you might."

Done what? Was this about the land in Sanuki Province? Surely not. The news could not have arrived yet and Akitada had delayed his report. He decided to wait.

The prime minister regarded him expectantly. "Go on! Tell me all about it. How did you work it out?"

Akitada took a breath. "The provincial archives were well kept, your Excellency, and the governor made his staff available to me and advised me." He was happy to give credit to Munesuke. His conscience still pained him about his sudden flight.

The prime minister frowned. "No, no. Never mind that old land case. That's not really why I sent you. Did you speak to the people who knew the story?"

So he knew about the killer. Not only that. He had apparently orchestrated the entire trip to Sanuki Province to point Akitada toward a motive for massacre. Akitada gaped speechlessly at the man who could destroy him and his family for the flagrant disobedience with which Akitada had acted. Gradually resentment also rose. Why this subterfuge? Why put him and his friends and family through this much misery and fear?

He closed his mouth and said stiffly, "I take it your Excellency has been much better informed than I."

"Not at all. Well, perhaps a little since it involved family members, but there could be no certainty. And this was not the only incident that I considered." He paused and sighed. "I am very glad you followed up on that suicide of the Yamada daughter. What a story! Shocking!"

More resentment welled up. "I was under the impression that you ordered me to leave things alone."

The prime minister frowned. "Yes. And you disobeyed. Really, Sugawara, you do ask a great deal sometimes. Some people in the government were outraged. They wanted you dismissed. Exiled even."

Akitada nodded. "I have enemies."

"You don't bother to make friends." The prime minister made it sound like an accusation.

Akitada knew this was true. He said nothing.

"As for Shirakawa, you had no business there. I recall warning you away. You ignored my order."

This also was true. Akitada murmured, "I was asked by my best friend's family to find out what happened to him."

"Yes, Kosehira. But he survived. As did his first lady and his son. But you continued your meddling in my family's affairs."

Akitada bit his lip. "And you had me abducted like a criminal and sent to a distant province."

For a moment, he thought his Excellency would lose his temper, but to his surprise, he laughed softly. "Yes. I enjoyed that. You deserved it. And I sent you where you might find answers. You seemed to be at a loss at the time."

Akitada felt his chin sagging again and controlled his surprise with an effort. "You knew what I would find?"

"Not precisely, but I had asked some questions myself. My brother had also made enemies in his youth. The Yamada case suggested itself as a possible motive."

"The killer is dead."

"Yes, so I heard. Also poor Lady Gon-Dainagon. I'm waiting to hear the details. Did I understand that Lady Akiko was involved?"

Akitada smiled for the first time. "My sister," he said, "is a remarkable woman. She saved my life." And he told the prime minister the whole story.

Later, he walked home in a daze. He thought perhaps he had made a friend after all. And perhaps there might be an award in the future, but for the moment he was happy to return to his family, secure in the knowledge that all were well, and hope to forget that in the fading light of that summer's day of the Tanabata festival, the celebration of the union of the celestial lovers, the field outside Yorimune's country villa had been covered with corpses.

Historical Note

In eleventh century Japan, the country was ruled by an emperor and a court aristocracy. The system was originally Chinese but had taken on Japanese characteristics. The Chinese meritocracy of government by the most learned officials had become hereditary government by the ruling noble family. In the eleventh century, it was a branch of the Fujiwara family.

The Heian era was essentially a peaceful period when the arts prospered and the powerful led charmed lives in the capital Heian-kyo, the modern Kyoto. But all was not well in other parts of Japan. Wars were being fought to suppress rebellions in distant provinces, and there was always frontier duty in the far North or Kyushu. The court nobles were not soldiers. Military duties were carried out by the provincial nobility and, especially in the eleventh and twelfth centuries, by the Minamoto and the Taira, two powerful clans descended from emperors. In the provinces, a separate military culture developed. These clans prized military prowess, and their knights fought on horseback with bow and arrow and the sword. Military crafts prospered for sword smiths and armor makers, and skill with bow and arrow frequently became legendary. In this novel, Jocho, a famous and well-to-do sword smith in the capital, has gathered a group of retired warriors around him. Their mindset and values differ greatly from those of the court aristocracy.

The central administration in Heian-kyo governed the provinces through appointed officials. These governors as a rule belonged to the court aristocracy and were trained for the bureaucracy they served. Akitada, the main character in this novel, works in the Ministry of Justice, but like others of his background he has served as governor. Provincial governors were responsible for law and order, for the upkeep of public roads, and for the collection and transport of annual taxes, mostly rice, though it could also involve horses, silk, or woven goods. By the eleventh century far too many governors enriched themselves and looked to such appointments as lucrative rewards. The provincial aristocracy, made up of descendants of imperial princes who had lost their royal status and by local wealthy landowners, maintained private armies. Eventually, by the end of the twelfth century, these military families will usurp the real power in Japan and begin the samurai era.

The capital Heian-kyo, a city originally laid out like Chinese capitals, had by this time shifted from its rigid rectangle embraced by rivers and mountains. It had spread both to the east and to the north. Originally no temples were permitted in the capital because the emperors had come to fear the power of the Buddhist establishment. Most of the temples in Heian-kyo therefore were outside the city in the foothills. Gradually, devout emperors and aristocrats retired there and built elaborate villas. The villa of Fujiwara Yorimune in the novel represents one of these.

The novel begins on the seventh day of the seventh month in the year 1035. It is the day of the Tanabata festival when, according to an ancient legend, the herdsman god (represented by the star Altair) and the weaver maid goddess (represented by the star Vega) are allowed to meet briefly by crossing the Milky Way on a bridge of magpies. The festival became a popular court celebration. People would gather in their gardens in anticipation of the night when they would watch the heavens and compose poems, play music, and perform magpie dances. In this story the day has been chosen to celebrate the betrothal of Arihito and Hireko.

A word about Japanese education may be necessary. Japan imported also the Chinese university system. Heian-kyo had one imperial university attended by the sons of the court nobility and several family-sponsored academies funded by some of the noble clans for their retainers. In addition, male children in the noble families would have had tutors in their early years. The university taught Chinese, the language of official documents and procedures, the Chinese classics, law, medicine, mathematics, and composition. But by this time, the emphasis on academic subjects was declining. Japanese taste had turned to poetry and the other arts, and all noble children were expected to be well versed in these. Boys would also have had some training in archery and sword fighting. The lower classes remained relatively uneducated, though Buddhist monasteries set up some schools and provincial schools also existed. The schoolmaster in the novel was at one time tutor to Akitada's son and now teaches at one of the academies in the city.

And finally, the inclusion of a "willow quarter" in eleventh century Heian-kyo is poetic license. There is no historical evidence for it, though such an area certainly existed in later centuries. But there was certainly prostitution from the earliest times. The evidence comes from the writings of noblemen, and the practices would have been the ones they were familiar with. Apparently traveling women performers (*kugutsu*) were available to attend parties, and permanently settled companions (*asobi*) existed in the villages on the Yodo River where they catered to river traffic of both noblemen and commoners.

About the Author

I. J. Parker was born and educated in Europe and turned to mystery writing after an academic career in the U.S. She has published her Akitada stories in *Alfred Hitchcock's Mystery Magazine,* winning the Shamus award in 2000. Several stories have also appeared in collections, such as *Fifty Years of Crime and Suspense* and *Shaken.* The award-winning "Akitada's First Case" is available as a podcast.

Many of the stories have been collected in *Akitada and the Way of Justice.*

The Akitada series of crime novels features the same protagonist, an eleventh century Japanese nobleman/detective. *Massacre at Shirakawa* is number twenty. The books are available as e-books, in print, and in audio format, and have been translated into twelve languages. The early novels are published by Penguin.

Books by I. J. Parker

The Akitada series in chronological order

The Dragon Scroll
Rashomon Gate
Black Arrow
Island of Exiles
The Hell Screen
The Convict's Sword
The Masuda Affair
The Fires of the Gods
Death on an Autumn River
The Emperor's Woman
Death of a Doll Maker
The Crane Pavilion
The Old Men of Omi
The Shrine Virgin
The Assassin's Daughter
The Island of the Gods
Ikiryo: Revenge and Justice
The Kindness of Dragons
The Nuns of Nara
Massacre at Shirakawa
The collection of stories
Akitada and the Way of Justice

Other Historical Novels

The HOLLOW REED saga:

Dream of a Spring Night

Dust before the Wind

The Sword Master

The Left-Handed God

Contact Information

Please visit I.J.Parker's web site at www.ijparker.com. You may contact her via e-mail from there. (This way you will be informed when new books come out.)

Trade paperbacks of the novels may be ordered from Amazon. There are electronic versions of all the works. Please do post reviews. They help sell books and keep Akitada novels coming.

Thank you for your support.

Made in the USA
Monee, IL
28 May 2022